JENNA STEPPED BACK, [obscured by barcode] onto the bench.

"Let me see." Ad[obscured] shined it on her foot.

Jenna contemplated the rugged profile of the doctor's face as he removed the splinter. Adam DeSanto might have the temperament of a jaguar, but beneath that was incredible tenderness. She saw it when he was with patients, especially the children.

And now. With her.

"You continue to amaze me, Jenna Marsten."

"Is that an apology for trying to scare me away with that kiss?"

Adam tilted his head. "I am *not* sorry I kissed you. In fact, I am so *unsorry*, that I will do it again!"

Jenna caught her breath as Adam's skilled fingers moved her head back to receive his kiss. Its completeness spread through her veins with a jalapeño effect, warm, elusive at first, then demanding recognition of all her senses.

Suddenly, Adam tore away, staring at her as if she'd grown two heads. "And for the love of Pete's sake, put some dry clothes on!"

Jenna almost corrected Adam's English, but considering the way his kiss still ravaged her senses, proper speech was the *least* of her problems.

Hi Honey, I'm Home

"Not only is Linda Windsor uproariously wicked with her humor, but she creates a heart-touching situation that will capture the imagination of her readers and have them falling in love with her writing style and her characters."

ROMANTIC TIMES MAGAZINE

"Linda Windsor has written a divine love story. Don't miss this one!"

AFFAIRE DE CŒUR MAGAZINE

"This fascinating and in-depth plot takes many interesting turns, helped along by well-drawn supporting characters. God works in mysterious ways, and this beautiful story of love rekindled proves it. Welcome Ms. Windsor to inspirational fiction. Outstanding job and anticipating more."

RENDEZVOUS

"Mix two hurting people with mischievous boys hoping their parents will reunite, and the result is a lively romantic story. Windsor lightly weaves in a spiritual message of forgiveness…fiction fans will have fun en route."

CBA MARKETPLACE

"*Hi Honey I'm Home* is a sweet, and at times, humorous love story that also sends a powerful spiritual message…. Linda Windsor has a wonderful gift for storytelling and she uses it well in *Hi Honey I'm Home*."

BOOKBUG ON THE WEB

"*Hi Honey I'm Home* is a fun book that explores God's place in the 'real' world of dual income families and children. Linda Windsor has written a story that celebrates God's role in life while keeping a light and down to earth tone."

ROMANCE REVIEWS

"This is a delightful book and the message is one of hope, love, and trust. What more could one want in a romance book?"

UNDER THE COVERS BOOK REVIEWS

"A heartwarming story, with a dash of humor and a cup of faith. Readers will be brought to tears of happiness and then be laughing with joy. A special tale not to be missed!"

HUNTRESS BOOK REVIEWS

♛ *Palisades Pure Romance*

Not Exactly
E D E N

Linda Windsor

Palisades is a division of Multnomah Publishers, Inc.

This is a work of fiction. The characters, incidents, and dialogues are products of the author's imagination and are not to be construed as real. Any resemblance to actual events or persons, living or dead, is entirely coincidental.

NOT EXACTLY EDEN

published by Palisades

a division of Multnomah Publishers, Inc.

© 2000 by Linda Windsor

International Standard Book Number: 1-57673-445-5

Published in association with the literary agency of Ethan Ellenberg Agency

Design by Christopher Gilbert

Background cover photo by David Muench/Tony Stone Images

Cover illustration by Aleta Jenks

Scripture quotations are from *The Holy Bible,* King James Version

Palisades is a trademark of Multnomah Publishers, Inc., and is registered in the U.S. Patent and Trademark Office.

Printed in the United States of America

For information:

MULTNOMAH PUBLISHERS, INC.•P.O. BOX 1720•SISTERS, OREGON 97759

Library of Congress Cataloging–in–Publication Data

Windsor, Linda.   Not exactly Eden / by Linda Windsor.

p.cm.–(Palisades pure romance)   ISBN 1-57673-445-5

1. Fathers and daughters—Fiction. 2. Socialites—Fiction. I. Title II. Series.

PS3573.I519 N68 2000 813'.54–dc21 00-008723

00 01 02 03 04 05 06—10 9 8 7 6 5 4 3 2 1

To Jim, my hero, my love, my husband, my friend.

We are troubled on every side, yet not distressed;
we are perplexed, but not in despair.

2 CORINTHIANS 4:8

Prologue

"I KNEW THIS WOULD HAPPEN! IT'S DÉJÀ VU. I FEEL LIKE I'M saying good-bye for the last time."

Jenna Marsten put a comforting arm around her aunt's shoulder and handed her a tissue. Outside the chauffeured limousine, the bypasses and road signs flashed by—a concrete blue interspersed with highway green. With the airport as their destination, this was Violet Winston's last-ditch effort to keep Jenna from making the "mistake of her life," and the woman was giving it all she had.

"Aunt Vi, just because my mother was killed in a jungle plane crash doesn't mean I'll be! Planes and airports have improved over the last few decades in South America, I'm sure."

It wasn't that her aunt was just being her usual dominant self and didn't care. She did. Violet Winston and her late husband, Ben, raised Jenna as their own daughter, giving her the best life one of Boston's blue-blood families had to offer. Her debut into society was one of the most publicized cotillions ever held at the country club. Having gone to all the right schools, here and abroad, Jenna was now assistant director of the Fine Arts Foundation. According to her aunt, she was tossing all away to go into the same tropical wilderness that had killed her parents—or at least *one* of them.

"I wish you'd never seen that ugly little Indian thing. If I'd only been thinking instead of stewing over the cancellations, you never would have…" her aunt fretted, trailing off with a tremulous sigh.

"I'm glad you *were* distracted. I had a right to know my father is alive, even if he didn't want anything to do with me. But let's not go there again," Jenna added, wanting to avoid yet another emotional conflict.

She knew in her heart that Aunt Violet only sought to protect her. From what, remained to be seen. From further rejection? Jenna couldn't…*wouldn't* think about it. She just knew it was something she had to do.

Who'd have guessed that returning gifts from a broken wedding engagement would lead her to discover the truth about the accident, which had left her believing she was an orphan? Her aunt tried to dismiss the crudely wrapped package as coming from one of Jenna's eccentric circle of associates at the art foundation; someone who'd forgotten to include a card. The return address of Ichitas, Peru, and the newspaper in which the carved figure was wrapped told another story.

"Didn't Benjamin and I love you enough?" Violet added the used tissue to the increasing wad she twisted with manicured, jeweled fingers beginning to draw with arthritis. "Why do you have to go look up a father who would rather stay in the jungle than raise his only daughter? He took your mother away from us, and now he's taking you!"

Jenna's heart twinged, nailed once by a spear of guilt and again by angst. It wasn't like she was doing this to hurt the woman. Why couldn't her aunt look beyond her intense dislike of her brother-in-law and see this? If she truly wanted to help, she would not add to the doubt Jenna was trying so desperately to ignore—that her father might not *want* her to find him.

Jenna pushed the lock of honey blond hair she'd been toying with behind her ear before she started to chew on it; a telltale sign of suppressed anxiety since her childhood.

"Aunt Vi, please don't do this. You and Uncle Ben have been the only parents I've ever known. I love you dearly, but I *have* to go. I've always felt there was a part of me that was missing, and now I know why. I want to meet my father."

One of the foundation's experts had identified the figure as an enigma of South American Indian origin. The stone it was fashioned from was quite old, indigenous to the Amazon. An ensuing investigation as to how it came to her at least distracted Jenna from the trauma of Scott Pierson's choosing a lucrative position in a Middle East oil conglomerate and postponing their wedding. At least she knew where she stood in the ambitious engineer's priorities.

"I think Scott actually did me a favor, postponing the wedding." *God, please make the events leading to this no accident. I'm flying blind here. I don't want to look my father up for the wrong reason, running from this recent rejection to another. I just feel like nothing in my life is as I thought, my family, my engagement…*

"I could wring *that* young man's neck, choosing to work halfway around the world when he had a perfectly good job here! It wasn't like he needed the money."

The Piersons were one of Boston's older families. Scott's mother and Violet attended boarding school together, as well as an exclusive women's college. The match was made in heaven as far as they were concerned. Jenna and Scott were the picture perfect couple, both fair and attractive, with promising careers and all the right contacts. Like all of Jenna's life, their future was put together in a neat little package, adorned with approval. Maybe that's what bothered Scott…and in retrospect, Jenna herself.

"Better to find out where I stand now rather than later. Besides, marriage isn't totally out of the question, Aunt Vi. It's just been put off for a while."

Jenna, at least, was over the stage of anger. The sudden decision still hurt, but now that she had found peace and hope with it through her faith and the

Scripture so prevalent in her mother's diaries, she was determined to be relieved. "We are troubled on every side, yet not distressed; we are perplexed, but not in despair."

This *had* happened for a good reason. Neither she nor Scott was as ready for a lifetime commitment to each other as they and everyone else thought. Besides, Jenna consoled herself in the belief that God could take disappointments and turn them into opportunities. The mysterious figurine *had* to be part of His plan.

She leaned back against the plush upholstery of the limo as the driver turned into the airport.

"You just don't know what you're getting into! Lord knows, I've tried to protect you from it. Your mother's journals paint a pretty picture, but she was looking at the world through love-struck eyes."

Jenna had read the yellowed pages over and over through the years in an attempt to get to know Diana Marsten. She knew of her mother's rebellion against the family's wishes as she became a nurse, and worse yet, to marry beneath her station, even if Robert Marsten was a doctor. She felt her mother's excitement as she and the man she loved ventured off into the Amazon to set up a clinic and study jungle medicine. Diana wrote with the heart of a woman who knew where she was going and why—a heart with a purpose.

"And like your mother, you're just as stubborn."

For the first time in her life, Jenna felt like she, too, had a purpose. No longer was she slipping into slot after convenient slot. Long suppressed, her inherited rebellious nature had finally found freedom. Yes, she was going to meet the father she'd never known, the father who had handed her over to the Winstons and never looked back. At least until he'd somehow heard about her wedding plans. This journey, however, was something more than looking up her father. *What* she couldn't say. All she knew was that it was one she had to make.

"But I can tell you right now, dear." Aunt Violet placed her hand over Jenna's and squeezed it with genuine affection. "I've been there, and it's no tropical paradise."

Jenna returned the gesture in earnest. "But I'm not looking for paradise, Aunt Vi. I'm looking for my life."

Not Scott's, not her aunt's nor her uncle's, not her father's nor her mother's—*her* life.

One

ICHITAS WAS HOT IN THE MIDDAY SUN. THE AIR SMACKED Jenna in the face like a heavy, wet blanket as she disembarked from the plane, grateful to be on the ground. She was already eating her words about how air travel had improved in the last twenty-some years and was grateful Aunt Violet was not here to tell her *I told you so*.

The South American flight from Miami had been delayed for service and repairs, and once the plane was airborne, Jenna wasn't at all sure the jumpsuit-clad mechanics had totally fixed the problem. Between turbulence, an engine with an occasional cough, and a teeth-jarring landing, there'd been no chance to catch up on the sleep she'd lost the night before due to excitement. As for the cardboard food served during the flight, if she'd wanted to eat, it would have been a challenge.

The tiny opening in a vast expanse of lush green

landscape was a welcome, if not shocking, sight. The closer the plane came to landing, the smaller she realized Ichitas was. A hint of a mistake in landing and they would be swallowed by the land-devouring rain forest.

"Welcome to the Amazon, Miss Marsten. Have you caught your breath yet?"

Jenna mustered a grin for the pleasant photographer who'd occupied the seat beside her for the flight. If not for his lively conversation, the flight might have been unbearable. Thankfully, he didn't smoke; something that could not be said of most of the passengers.

"The air's almost as thick as that in the plane, but at least it's clean," Jenna replied, unable to shake the Dorothy-like feeling that she wasn't in Kansas anymore.

She couldn't believe it when her companion explained that the spontaneous applause upon arrival had nothing to do with a safe landing, but that they'd landed in Ichitas at all. Evidently, the pilots sometimes decided on their own to ignore the airline schedule and go on to the more populous city four hours away, where most of their families resided. This forced the hapless passengers to make the rest of their journey to Ichitas by bus.

"It is different from your Boston," he admitted with a dazzling smile, "but to me, it is home."

Stefan Murillo was returning to his country to film for a nature channel special. His family ran one of the Amazonian eco-vacation lodges on the river, where nature lovers could bask in the wonders of the river and surrounding rain forest to their hearts' content. His first love, however, was photography, and he was determined to make a go of it, despite his family's pleas for him to take part in the business.

"You say there is someone waiting at the terminal for you?" He arched his brow hopefully. "Because my offer for dinner still stands. I would love to spend the evening entertaining a beautiful señorita on her first night in my country if she will but change her mind!"

What a charmer, ponytail and all. But then, she was always a sucker for an accent. It was almost tempting, but Jenna was expecting Dr. Robert Marsten to meet her at customs.

"Perhaps another time, if our paths cross again."

They entered the terminal, which was allegedly air-conditioned. In reality it was only slightly more bearable than it was outside. In a modest attempt to fan herself, Jenna pulled her sleeveless silk blouse away from where perspiration glued it to her skin. She stood in line waiting to be processed through the gate ahead, where grim uniformed officials scanned carry-on articles and scrutinized the papers of the newly arrived passengers. Problems with Stefan's equipment forced her to take another line, where a portly clerk with an unlit cigar hanging from his mouth took his time with each person's documents.

Travel abroad had bolstered Jenna's Spanish enough to discern from the staccato exchange that Stefan was welcome in the country. He was being treated like a long-lost friend. His equipment, however, was a problem. Jenna didn't envy him the delay.

"*Adiós*, Señorita Marsten. The usual chaos calls, but fortunately I have a large family with positions that are helpful in situations like this. It is my hope that we will meet again. In the meantime, please give my regards to your father and let me know if I can be of any service to you during your stay. You can reach me through the Posada Explorador. The number is on my card."

Jenna waved, somehow reassured that she had made at least one friend in this strange country. She tucked the card in her purse as insurance in case her meeting with Robert Marsten turned out to be a mistake as Aunt Violet had predicted. She watched with a troubled sense of abandonment as Stefan accompanied an official through the crowded terminal toward a side corridor. Over it hung a large sign marked *Aduana* on it. Customs.

She now knew two things: Stefan was justified when he'd expressed some concern about the paperwork coming through for the clearances of his gear in a timely fashion; and she knew that none of the men milling about on the other side of the gates was her father, or Stefan would have pointed him out as he promised. According to him, Ichitas was not so large that those who made their life on the river did not know each other to some degree or another.

She had spied a tall fair-featured gentleman holding a sign, but Stefan told her he was there to gather up the tourists arriving for an eco-vacation at his family's lodge. Besides, he looked nothing like the man in the faded picture Jenna had of her parents at their wedding reception. Since she had been old enough to realize that Violet and Ben Winston were not her real parents, the photo was etched in her memory.

Aside from the tour guide and herself, there were no other fair-haired people in the crowd. Jenna kept her eyes on the terminal doors the entire time she was processed through customs to no avail. Left with no other choice, she proceeded to the baggage claim area, hoping that the officials had not opened either of her cases.

As tightly as she'd packed, they might never get them closed again. After all, she had no idea what sort of day and evening wear she'd need, and from what she'd seen so far, she probably could have left home at least half of what she'd brought. But first impressions were lasting ones, and Jenna wanted to take no chances where Dr. Robert Marsten was concerned.

After tipping a porter generously, she had her bags loaded on a squeaky-wheeled cart and checked them in a holding area. There was still no sign of her father, and anxiety, not to mention the insufferable closeness in the terminal, drove her toward a dingy food bar, where she purchased a fresh fruit salad and bottled water. When all else failed, munch.

She'd no sooner started eating the first meal she'd had since leaving Boston eighteen hours previously than she heard her name come across the static-filled intercom.

"Atención, por favor! Señorita Jenna Marsten…"

Her name came across as Henna Marsten, the "r" practically adding a third syllable to the latter, but it was not the first time Jenna had heard her name pronounced in Spanish. After saying the message in Spanish for her to report to the information desk, the announcer repeated it in stilted English.

Grabbing up her bent Styrofoam cup of fruit and her water bottle, Jenna headed for the tiny cubicle situated by the main entrance of the terminal, where a clerk handed her a hastily scribbled message he'd written. Once again grateful for a month-long art study in Madrid, she quickly deciphered it.

Your escort will be along as soon as possible. There is a problem in acquiring clinic supplies. A. D.

A. D.? Not exactly her father's initials. Jenna fought down the rise of disappointment that Robert Marsten had not come for her himself. Admittedly, their communication prior to her leaving was sketchy at best, considering it had taken place via shortwave radio contact from the clinic. Her mother's journal said there were no phones, but Jenna had thought that, like the air travel, things would have improved in the twenty-three years since. And she *had* sent a letter confirming her travel arrangements via air express.

It was becoming increasingly clear that as well traveled as she was, Jenna's experiences were with population and cultural centers of the world, not the more remote and undeveloped areas. But then, Eden didn't have phones. With that stab at the bright side, she wandered back to the food bar. All the tables were filled. *Okay. I am troubled on every side, and frankly, Lord, I'm starting to get distressed.*

Dr. Adam DeSanto rushed through the doors to the airport terminal, his face a thundercloud of annoyance. In order to save time, he'd arrived the day before by river taxi, but the red tape and paperwork of getting the clinic's new shipment of medical supplies released still tied up all of today. Not that he expected any less.

He had, however, hoped that this time the authorities would not help themselves to a portion. They were particularly fond of antibiotics in this "treat thyself" world, where there was almost no regulation of drugs.

Medicines of any kind, and not necessarily up to any standard, could be purchased over the counter, so the confiscated goods not used by the officials themselves could be used to line their pockets. Much as it grated on him, Adam knew it was a cost of practicing medicine on the Amazon.

And now, to top off an already bad day, he had to pick up a poor little rich girl from Boston and baby-sit her overnight. River traffic this far up stopped at night. As it was, he'd be lucky to pack her off to the Posada Explorador before the power company turned off its electric at midnight. The only decent hotel was booked. So it was either the eco-lodge or stay over at the government hospital, where he was likely to lose more supplies, not from confiscation but because he knew they needed them as much as the clinic.

In the airport, the food bar as well as the offices were closed. In the dim glow of the few fluorescent fixtures that worked, Adam scanned the lounge area, but it was vacant, save for a janitor emptying the trash cans. There was no sign of the young woman whose college graduation picture graced the wall of Dr. Robert Marsten's office.

Adam glanced at his watch and swore beneath his breath. Almost nine o'clock. He should have known better than to expect Jenna Marsten to wait per his message. She'd probably never had to wait a day in her pampered life. He knew the type too well. His late wife came from the same social world. Marina Murillo DeSanto did not know the meaning of the word *wait*. If she had...

Adam's humor did not improve with the sudden backtrack of his thoughts. Scowling, he asked the janitor if he had seen a pretty blond lady, an Americana, who appeared to be expecting someone. After a great deal of chin scratching and a tip, the man's memory improved dramatically.

"*Sí*, I have seen the señorita. How many women with hair like sunshine and eyes like the sky wait alone in such a place as this every day?"

That would be Jenna Marsten. Adam wondered as

he'd studied that picture if those eyes were really that blue or if she wore tinted contacts. He couldn't help himself. Every time he went into Robert's office, his gaze was drawn her. Maybe it was because the doctor's daughter resembled the woman in the other picture the doctor hung beside it—the one of his wedding day.

"She sat right at that table over there all afternoon. She did not look happy."

Adam ignored the twinge of guilt assailing his conscience, compounded by the reproach in the janitor's voice. Ichitas wasn't a large city, but tracking down the Marsten girl would be no easy task, especially since the young woman would have no idea where to go, beyond the hotel, which he knew to be booked already.

"So where is she now?"

"She was very generous, señor."

Mercenary little thief, Adam thought. Biting back his anger at the hint, he gave the man another bill. "So?"

"She is not your wife, is she?"

Exasperated, Adam ran his fingers through the black hair curling at his collar. It needed a cut. Time was relative here. Usually, it made no difference to him. In fact, it was part of this world's charm.

"No, she is a friend."

At that, the little man seemed relieved. His reaction did not instill the same reaction in Adam, who towered over him by a good head. The muscles in Adam's neck tightened even more. Dealing with the world beyond the medical compound had that effect. If he had his way, he'd never leave the compound, where he had been born to an American schoolteacher and Peruvian physician. Schooling was all that took him away, that and Marina. How could Robert ask this task of him, knowing his past?

"When the café closed after the last flight arrived, she made a phone call and Stefan Murillo picked her and all her baggage up in a Posada Explorador vehicle."

"Ah!" With a tight-lipped smile, Adam shook the janitor's hand. *"Gracias, amigo."*

Sometimes the world was small enough to choke a man. Adam should have felt relief that someone with a degree of responsibility was taking care of Robert's daughter, but it came hard. Stefan Murillo was Adam's late wife's cousin, an accomplished photographer and ladies' man by reputation.

Well, at least Señorita Marsten was with her own kind; although Adam could well imagine what the Boston beauty was thinking of the lodge's rustic accommodations. His bride had made fun of them until she saw her new home at Santa Beliza. It was the beginning of the end of their troubled marriage.

Adam swallowed the bitter taste of the past again as he climbed into a jeep he'd borrowed from a friend. At the moment, he had enough to worry about with today's problem. While he understood Robert's having to remain at the clinic at the last minute because of a medical emergency, it didn't make the task any easier, for reasons the older doctor could not even begin to suspect.

The girl in the picture had long intrigued Adam. She'd invaded his thoughts and dreams, both before and after his marriage. She was a fantasy girl; one he'd never meet, and therefore, one he could allow into his heart without the risk of breaking it as Marina had. But now, Jenna Marsten was real and Adam DeSanto had to deal with something that was relatively foreign to him—fear.

Posada Explorador was as charming as Jenna's host and his family. While hardly a five-star hotel, the cluster of lodges, built upon pilings for when the Amazon overran its banks, possessed its own brand of ambiance. Kerosene lanterns provided the bulk of the lighting; although generators provided for some luxury. Giant overhead tanks made running water and showers possible for the guests. It was just the sort of setting Jenna would expect to find for those seeking Mother Nature au naturel, something like the summer wilderness camp she'd attended before her freshman year of college. Aunt Violet had been mortified at the very idea of leaving civilization, as she knew it, for roughing it pioneer style. And would be now, if she were here, Jenna thought, taking a sip of the Posada Punch.

The delicious combination of natural fruit juices was as refreshing as the shower she'd had earlier. Relieved of travel grime and having changed into a cool knit sundress, Jenna felt human again and welcome, rather than abandoned. Even though Stefan Murillo had saved the day, whoever A. D. was, he was going to get a piece of her mind for leaving her stranded at a closing airport in a strange country.

"You, sir, are literally a godsend!" Jenna told her companion. She had to raise her voice above the welcoming music being played by a local group for newly arrived guests.

She'd said more than one prayer in the darkening terminal as she waited for the operator to put her call through to Posada Explorador. She'd already discovered the only hotel recommended by the information desk was booked full and was afraid to venture away from the airport on her own.

Stefan lifted his glass to hers in acknowledgment. "You must stop comparing me to a saint, Señorita Marsten, for the sight of you in that dress…" He shrugged. "Let us say, it does not inspire saintly feelings."

Jenna laughed, not unaccustomed to compliments. However, spoken with that accent, it made her feel positively girlish inside. It was a shame her companion's expression showed he knew it. Definitely a lady-killer, she decided, but nonetheless a gentleman.

"Alas, I have a weakness for fair-haired ladies with— how do you say—browned bare shoulders?"

"Tanned."

"Ah, *tanned*. And they look so soft."

"They're just sagging from exhaustion." Jenna looked at her watch and made a face. "I have got to get some sleep before I fall face down in my punch."

Stefan rose to his feet to pull out her chair as she gathered up her purse.

"Then allow me just the favor of one dance, and I shall walk you to your lodge." At the skeptical lift of Jenna's brow, he added quickly, "Where I will leave you to your dreams. Even though the pathways are lighted with lanterns, it is possible to come across a snake or even a crocodile this close to the water."

"You're kidding."

Stefan gave her a tolerant smile. "Señorita, this *is* the jungle, no?"

The flashlight each guest had been given suddenly seemed lacking in reassurance. Some good it was if she *did* see something! Jenna slung the strap of her purse over one shoulder and held out her arms with a bright smile. "Put that way, how can I resist?"

It came as no surprise that Stefan was a good dancer. Under other circumstances she might have enjoyed his attentions more, but she was tired, not to mention worried about the delay in meeting her father. It hurt that he'd not come himself, more than it did that his envoy had not shown up at all. One of the most important events in her life had been handed off into the hands of some lackey. No doubt by now he had forgotten her completely and was painting the town. Not that it would take long, she mused, biting the inside of her mouth to keep from grinning.

"You find something amusing?"

Boy, did this guy know his women. Jenna gave him

a sheepish grin. "No, I'm just slaphappy from exhaustion. Silly," she explained upon seeing his puzzled reaction.

"Whew! For a moment, I thought you meant… well…somehow that slapping you would make you happy."

At that, Jenna dissolved into a weary fit of giggles, burying her face against Stefan's shoulder, where she remained after the combo wound up the song.

"That's it. I'm done. I have *got* to say good night before I make a fool of myself."

"Perhaps it is already too late for that, señorita."

Startled by the strange, deeply judgmental voice behind her, Jenna turned to see her self-appointed judge and jury. He was a newcomer because she was certain she'd have noticed him before among the group that had started dancing again at the onset of the band's next tune.

Unlike the other guests, who were dressed in loud prints that shouted tourist, he wore loose-fitting cotton drawstring trousers, which fell inches short of once-white and very worn sneakers. His open shirt of the same cool, serviceable material had the sleeves ripped out. He was either an exceedingly tall peasant or…Jenna couldn't decide.

"Adam!"

Obviously no stranger to the man, Stefan broke the circle of his arms about Jenna to shake his hand.

"The time has been too long since I have seen you

emerge from the jungle."

Emerge from the jungle. How apt a description! The black slash of his eyebrows hovered over darker than dark eyes that had an untamed look to them, almost feral at the moment. He stepped forward and took Stefan's hand in a single fluid motion, with a grace not unlike a ballet dancer...or a jungle cat. Who had rattled *his* cage?

"Señorita, I have the idea that this is the *A. D.* who you have been waiting for. Adam DeSanto, may I present to you Señorita Jenna Marsten. But then, I think you know her name, even if you were remiss in picking her up at the airport in a timely fashion."

Jenna snapped out of the curious spell he seemed to cast without even realizing it. So *this* was the negligent lackey who'd made her day a living nightmare. If anyone's cage was rattled, it should be hers!

"You have my apologies, señorita."

He neither extended his hand to her, nor was there a hint of apology in his voice. If anything, Adam DeSanto was condescending. The hackles rose in Jenna's easygoing nature, already raw from her father's slight.

"And well I should!" She tilted her chin imperiously; although just to meet him eye to eye required that. "Indeed, I shall expect another apology from my father for sending some overgrown lackey with no sense of time or responsibility whatsoever to meet me! I'd have thought he'd at least—"

Stefan's guffaw interrupted her. Jenna looked at her

host as if he'd gone slaphappy too. No, she definitely wasn't in Kansas anymore, and at that moment, she'd have given her kingdom for a pair of ruby slippers!

"Señorita, Adam is not Robert Marsten's lackey, as you call him. I should have introduced him as *Dr.* Adam DeSanto *and* your father's partner."

Her right arm for a pair of ruby slippers! Or at least some semblance of a coherent reply.

"I did send a note," Adam DeSanto pointed out flatly.

Jenna nodded, her tongue lost somewhere between embarrassment and indignation.

"Problems with the aduana?"

Thankfully, his dark, unrelenting gaze swung to her companion.

"The usual. They must get their share."

"Amigo, my father has offered on many occasions to speak to the authorities on behalf of the clinic."

"I'm not *that* desperate yet, Murillo."

Stefan threw his hands up in exaggerated resignation. "That is up to you."

There was definitely some history between these two men, but Jenna was in no mood to find out what it was. She was tired, irritable, and, not the least, chewing on humiliation.

"I think I'll leave you two to discuss the customs dilemma of your country. I, on the other hand, have had a long day and look forward to a good night's sleep. Stefan," she said, hugging her deliverer from the depths of her earlier despair, "Thank you for your gallant rescue and hospitality."

She picked up the flashlight off the table they shared before extending a cool hand to her father's partner.

"Dr. DeSanto, perhaps we might start off on a better foot tomorrow." Without waiting for him to answer, she called over her shoulder as she left the room, "You two finish up without me. I can see myself to my lodge."

Jenna had her doubts, as she retreated hastily from the dining hall, that another day would make a difference in her acquaintance with Adam DeSanto. The moment their gazes met, something ignited instantly between them, and it didn't promise to be cordial. She slowed her pace as she came to the tree-lined path leading to the guest lodges, her bravado faltering.

Snakes and crocodiles. Icy fingers of panic tripped up her spine, raising the hairs on the back of her neck. She turned on the flashlight, and with a deep breath, Jenna entered the tree-canopied path.

Heavenly Father, please. You've brought me safe thus far. I know You'll see me home…at least to my lodge.

In the background the music from the dining hall faded and the song of the jungle rose louder and louder with each step. *Lions and tigers and bears, oh my!* Like walking in a zoo, Jenna told herself sternly. *Birds chirped and monkeys chattered…but jaguars didn't make sounds. But then, neither did the birds or monkeys when big cats were around, so she was safe. Or was it the opposite—that they cried loudly when they saw a big cat?*

She stopped, groaning in silence, lest she make a noise to attract any attention, either that of man or beast. The last thing she needed to do was scream and wake up the few guests who had retired early for crack-of-dawn bird-watching. Why hadn't she paid more attention to those nature films Scott was always watching?

"Did you hear something, señorita?"

Jenna jumped straight up in the air at the unmistakable voice of Adam DeSanto directly behind her. Her flashlight fell to the ground as her hands tried to decide whether to smother her scream or hold her heart in her chest. As it was, someone else's clamped in her scream. It escaped, nonetheless, from her nose in a high-pitched but whole-hearted shriek, which ended only when she had no breath left to fuel it.

"Shush, señorita." Jenna couldn't decide if he'd growled or hissed. "You will wake the guests."

Relieved that at least it was a walking, talking animal, Jenna collapsed against the lean-muscled frame of her father's partner. She couldn't move now, even if a real jaguar flew in her face. Instead, she was at the mercy of the human one who kept her from collapsing in a heap at his feet.

"I am sorry," he whispered in her ear. "I did not intend to startle you." When she failed to answer—it was hard to speak with a hand over one's mouth and a heart lodged in one's throat—he stiffened in alarm and leaned ever closer to her ear. "Jenna? You are all right, no?"

If she had it left in her, she'd have laughed hysterically at the absurdity of his question…*and* if her attention hadn't been caught by the soft *J* sound he made when he whispered her name so familiarly.

What he lacked in brains, he made up for in brass. First he showed no remorse for leaving her stranded in Ichitas's dinky little airport. Then he scared the life out of her. And now he wanted to know if she was all right!

Two

─────❈─────

"*Buenos días*, Señorita Marsten."

Jenna bolted upright on the bunk in her cabin, her rumpled hair falling into her face. She knew that voice in her sleep now.

"What are *you* doing in here?" she grumbled, knocking the mosquito netting canopy aside and squinting at Adam DeSanto's tall, dark figure.

"I knocked before breakfast, but you did not stir. We have to get to the river early to get the supplies on the boat, and the door had no lock, so..." A broad-shouldered shrug made the rest of his point.

"But it isn't even full light yet!"

"Here we take advantage of *any* light." He turned toward the door. "I have already loaded your baggage and had some Danish wrapped for you, so I will be waiting in the jeep as soon as you get your female fix-me-ups

35

and such out of the way."

Jenna lifted one corner of her lip in snarl but held her tongue. As smooth and charming as Stefan was, this guy was the total opposite. A gentleman would have at least pretended she didn't look like something the cat dragged in, almost literally.

"Yeah, yeah, I get it."

After her scare the night before, it was hours before she finally closed her eyes. She had no idea the jungle was as noisy as downtown Boston! There *had* been the small comfort of knowing Adam's lodge was next to hers, but as he'd just proven, any animal could get through the flimsy bamboo door.

With a grudging sling of the covers, she climbed out of bed. Her nightshirt fell just above her knees, appropriately emblazoned with an indignant kitten declaring, "I don't do mornings!" It was easier to let the long T-shirt do the talking while she glared at her uncommonly bright companion.

"Ah," he said, backing through the door. "I get it, but this is not Boston, little girl. Welcome to the jungle." As he started to close it behind him, he poked his head back in with a wiseacre grin. "Oh, and there are no lions, tigers, *or* bears, either."

"Wanna bet?" She didn't realize she'd given voice to her fear last night. "Well, I've already seen a homo sapien *bearus!*" Jenna put her hands on her hips, staring down the cranky creature with as much indignation as she could muster.

The crook of one dark brow above the other as he considered her words told her the wry jibe was lost somewhere in the translation. He finally shook his head in dismissal.

"It must have been your imagination."

As the doctor's footsteps faded down the corduroy walk outside the lodge, Jenna grabbed her pillow and slung it at the door. If she were a centipede, she couldn't get off on the right foot with this one.

A half hour later, she dragged her wheeled designer carry-on behind her down to the parking lot. Adam met her halfway at the steps and took it, not so much the gentleman as he was impatient. Jaw tight, he tossed it into the back of the jeep without a second look as to where it fell and hopped into the driver's seat, leaving Jenna standing by the passenger door.

"Well, was I worth waiting for?" she remarked dourly, helping herself into the vehicle.

"I do not think it would be polite to answer that question truthfully. Your Danish and coffee are in that bag there. Don't open it until we are underway."

Her companion jammed the keys into the vehicle and twisted them. The motor fired as though it were intimidated by his dark humor, but Jenna refused to be.

Before he shoved the gearshift into reverse, he afforded Jenna a quick once-over, from stylish khaki romper to beaded sandals. "Not very practical."

"Guess you'll have to give me the name of *your* designer."

She grasped the dash to brace herself as DeSanto accelerated away from the eco-lodge. A grunt was her only answer. Like she said, homo sapien bearus!

Except that there was nothing clumsy or awkward about Dr. Adam DeSanto. He was long limbed and graceful, like the cat she thought had had her for sure last night. Her shadow made more noise than he had!

As winding as the road was, he maneuvered the jeep with a practiced ease once they were underway, and his impatience was assuaged by the wind blowing his thick raven hair away from an aristocratic face. No jerking from gear to gear, this one. The drive was as smooth as the interplay of muscles on the darkly tanned arms exposed by his loose, sleeveless shirt.

Jenna, on the other hand, fought to gather her silky fine windblown locks into a twist, lest it give her the devil with tangles later on. She secured it with a spring-loaded clip.

"After Ichitas, I was astonished to see how good the roads were. I thought we had to reach Santa Beliza by boat."

"Do not be misled, señorita. If you have relatives in the government, then you get a decent road built to your business. This is the only good road within a hundred miles. But today, I am grateful for it." He glanced over at her. "You can eat your breakfast now."

Leetle girl. While he didn't actually say it, his tone did. The man had a bottomless supply of condescension and arrogance. When she was more herself, she'd set him straight. For now, she had to wake up…and she *was* hungry.

The airport at Ichitas was amenity heaven compared to the riverfront where her companion threaded their vehicle through makeshift stalls of vendors and ramshackle concrete buildings with tiled roofs. The paved road ran out the moment they turned away from the sign pointing to the airport, leaving Jenna to think the eco-lodge had no need of the riverside port. She was glad she'd finished her coffee because she would have been wearing it by now, the way the hard, dried ruts in the earthen thoroughfare beneath them tossed the vehicle about.

As if sensing new blood, the hawkers swarmed to her side of the jeep, shoving fruit and homemade jewelry at her. None approached Adam, who kept his determined gaze fixed on his destination, as if his surroundings and those in it did not exist. Not that Jenna could blame them. His demeanor didn't exactly invite approach from her either, so she marveled at the natural wonders along the way in a one-sided conversation.

She felt like a record stuck on "No, gracias" by the time they reached the pier, if one could call a floating barge with a hut in its middle a pier. Dozens of small craft were tied to it like a nursing litter to its mother, from incredibly flimsy-looking dugouts to battered aluminum crafts with outboard engines. Few looked big enough to carry her luggage, much less the medical supplies her companion pointed out, waiting in a truck nearby.

"I don't see a cargo boat," Jenna murmured. The idea of traveling up the Amazon had filled her with excitement until now.

"Precisely."

Jenna was taken back by the look of condemnation Adam gave her. "And this is *my* fault?"

"It was not I who played the part of the sleeping princess."

"Hey," she shouted after him as he plowed a path through the gathered throng toward the supply truck. "The door had no lock, so…" She waved her arms in an exaggerated shrug, mimicking his earlier gesture as well as his accent. After all, he *could* have called her earlier, if he was in such an all-fired rush.

Before his wake closed in his path and she was completely surrounded by natives, both curious and eager to hawk their goods, Jenna hurried after him. Either his stormy face parted the throngs or they knew him and knew he was not a prospective customer. He looked more like Dr. Doom than someone who healed people. His bedside manner must be chilling!

DeSanto was engaged in discussion with the driver of the truck when Jenna reached him. The driver pointed down river and gave Adam one of those sentence-finishing shrugs. From the doctor's angry grimace, he was better at doling them out than accepting them. With no apparent alternative, he nodded and the driver took off in a jog further up the riverfront, disappearing into the clutter of humanity.

"What?" she exclaimed, when DeSanto turned and nailed her with another accusing look. "Have I sunk a boat, too?"

For just a whiff of a second, one corner of Adam's mouth twitched. He *almost* smiled. Considering the rarity of that reaction, Jenna felt rather pleased with herself.

"We have missed the boat I usually use. Joaquin has gone upriver to seek another. I need to get those supplies to Santa Beliza as soon as possible. We gave out the last of our antibiotics last week." The doctor's face softened as he swept an arm out encompassing the area. "These are a hearty people and the human body is resilient, but infections are a matter of course here in the jungle."

So there *was* something he cared about. Warm mammalian blood ran through his veins after all.

"It is not like you and the people who come to Posada Explorador think."

And it certainly wasn't her or her *people*. Jenna echoed her aunt's estimation of the place. "No picnic, huh?"

Again there was almost a quiver of a smile on a mouth that was intriguing, even when thinned and angry. By golly, there might even be a sense of humor behind those incredible eyes of his.

"Precisely."

Never one to back away from a challenge, Jenna linked his arm with hers as they worked their way back to the jeep. "Well, don't worry, Adam. I'm not looking for Eden. I'm looking for my father—and my name isn't even Eve," she added with a grin.

He glanced at her, for a moment puzzled. Suddenly, he threw back his head with an "Ah!" It wasn't exactly a laugh, but it was progress. "No, it is not. It is Jenna."

There it was again. That accent made her name sound like a caress.

"And your mother was Diana, no?"

So, he'd done some homework.

"Yes, I—" Jenna broke off as she spotted a commotion around the jeep.

Whether curious or just thieves, the natives had taken her luggage out and opened one of the largest cases. To her horror, her most intimate apparel was being passed around and held up to the oohs and aahs of the crowd.

"Oh no!"

Beside her, Adam let go with a roar of warning in Spanish and charged the jeep like an angry bull. The natives hastily dropped the silken curiosities and scattered, leaving Jenna's clothing strewn on the earthen road. One man, however, was quite taken with one of the lacy articles and made a dash for it through the carts and vendor shacks.

In an instant, the outraged doctor was on the heels of the thief. Torn between following or salvaging the clothing left spewing out of the open case, Jenna chose the latter. Obviously the designer tapestry of her bags had been too much to ignore, she thought, picking up her lingerie and shaking as much of the dust off as she could before putting them back in the case.

She was wrestling with the zipper when Adam reappeared, soaking with sweat and looking as if he'd skidded on his knees in the reddish tinted dirt. Winded, he leaned against the side of the jeep and briefly examined the tangle of the flimsy garment he'd successfully recovered.

"This contraption has more strings than a hammock."

"They are *not* strings, Dr. DeSanto!" Heat climbed to Jenna's cheeks, despite her unaffected demeanor.

With a shrug, he tossed the item to her and proceeded to take off his damp and dusty shirt, a duplicate of the previous day's wear. Using it as a towel, he mopped his forehead and an admirable expanse of his damp, bronzed chest. The dawning that he'd evidently wrestled someone over her every-which-way-but-loose "contraption" only added to Jenna's embarrassment.

"Señorita," he said, tossing the wadded shirt into the back of the vehicle. "Never, and I mean *never,* leave anything you wish to keep to yourself unsecured and unattended!"

"Ah. So there *are* some things our countries have in common." She should have known better, but it didn't make the belated warning any easier to take.

Oblivious to her innuendo, the doctor reached behind his seat and dug another shirt out of a faded green canvas bag, replacing it in the bag with the sweaty, soiled one.

Since she was obviously going to get no help, Jenna dropped the delicate apparel on top of her other things and closed the lid. But in order to zip it shut, she had to climb atop the oversized Pullman. Even then she had to stop a few times to tuck in the this and thats which insisted on slipping out before rising and brushing the dust off her hands.

With the sun climbing higher in the sky by the minute, her companion again delved into the back of the jeep and pulled out a wide-brimmed straw hat, which he slapped on his head without much fanfare.

"If you have a hat, I'd suggest you put it on. The sun is not kind to pretty blond in this collar of the woods."

Jenna grinned. "You mean *neck,* Dr. DeSanto."

"Neck of the woods," he repeated to himself, intent on making a mental note. "Ah, for all the time I spent in the States, Spanish is still my native language. One forgets so much when English isn't used a lot down here. Those English idioms drive me loco." He made a small circle with his finger over his head and grimaced. "And there is little need for such formalities here in the jungle. You may call me Adam."

"I'm honored, Adam!"

Ignoring her cynicism, he grinned. The effect nearly turned Jenna's knees to water. This man was entirely too handsome for his own good, like a bloomin' Tarzan the jungle man in pajamas.

"Well, after all, Jenna," he replied, a spark of mischief kindling in his philosophical expression. "I *did* rescue your…um…" His seldom-used vocabulary was obviously giving him another challenge. Then his face brightened. "Ah, *necessities!*"

"Doctor! Dr. Adam!"

Thankfully, her companion's attention was drawn to where a small man worked his way through the market chaos and Jenna was spared the effort of finding a ready reply. The frantic stranger wore a ratty T-shirt over a pair of faded and extensively patched denims and babbled in a dialect of Spanish that plagued Jenna's translation. All she could make out was that it was some sort of medical emergency.

Giving up, she turned to her luggage and opened an outside compartment where she'd packed a sun hat, which unfolded with an umbrella-like snap. She put it on and adjusted it to a fashionable tilt in a side view mirror; although she had the feeling the effort was already too late.

Thankfully, the jungle doc was too involved with the excited stranger to notice her discomfiture. She was supposed to be reeling from a broken engagement and instead, her insides were aflutter over some jungle doc with an attitude.

Jenna touched up her sunscreen lip gloss with a vengeance, haunted by an old prep school taunt. *Twitter, twitter, brain's a fritter!*

She waited in the shade of a giant ficus tree while Adam, the truck driver, and the man with the medical emergency proceeded to move the supplies from the truck onto what looked like a reject from the *African Queen*. The boat was in sad need of paint. Its planked sides looked cracked and swollen, with dubious raw plywood patches. The hiss and cough of its idling engine did little to assuage Jenna's fear of being stranded in the infamous current of the café au lait colored river, if it didn't sink before it left the dock under the weight of its load.

When her suitcases were strapped atop a stack of boxes covered with a red cross and more government stamps and stickers than there was space for, Adam paid the driver and came ashore behind him.

"*Bueno,* we are ready. You will go with Joaquin's cousin upriver to Santa Beliza on the boat."

"*I* will? Like in me, by myself?"

"Yamo has a sick child," Adam nodded toward the barefoot Indian shadowing him. "He cut himself with a machete last week and it is not healing properly. They can not get his fever down with the antibiotics they have."

"You mean he's already seen a doctor?"

"No, he treated the boy himself. With the shortage of medical personnel and facilities, it is a necessity."

Jenna couldn't help but notice the anxious native was missing two toes on his right foot. It looked as if they'd rotted off, from the ragged, discolored scar tissue left. She wondered if the same thing had happened to him and they'd had to be amputated.

"But back to me. Why can't I just wait for you at

Posada Explorador, or go with you for that matter?"

The idea of riding upriver alone with a toothless captain who smelled of fermented liquor of some kind and didn't speak English did not sit well with Jenna at all. Neither did traipsing through the jungle with Doc Tarzan, either, but it *was* the lesser of the two evils.

"There are no roads to the village. We will be afoot. We will make better time to the village without you, and I will not be coming back this way once I've seen the boy. I'll be taking the land route to Santa Beliza, the village being on the way," Adam explained matter-of-factly. "It is common sense, no?"

"No! I'm not taking off alone with a total stranger who speaks no English and is drinking jungle booze to boot. I am dumbfounded that you think I will!"

"But señorita…"

"Don't señorita me!" Jenna warned with a stubborn set of her jaw. She tugged up the handle of her wheeled carry-on till it snapped into a locked position. "I'm going with you. I've set records speeding through the busiest airport jungles in the world with this baby. I'm sure I can keep up."

Adam gave the bag a skeptical glance. "It's not the same jungle, Jenna."

"And I went to wilderness camp, so I'm not exactly a novice."

"And we don't give medals for surviving. Life itself is the reward here."

"No."

"We may have to stay over. Believe me, you'll barely reach Santa Beliza by dark in the boat as it is. And Joaquin says his cousin has a high tolerance for *cachaça*. Distilled sugar cane is like the wine of Italy or France and is consumed from a very young age."

"No, no, *no!*"

Clearly perturbed, the doctor switched tactics. "It wasn't I who caused us to miss our regular delivery boat."

"So because of some guilt charge conjured up on your part, I should go upriver with Captain Cane-Breath, who will run us into some floating log or worse and get us dragged off by a crocodile for dinner?"

Jenna was starting to panic now. Dr. DeSanto could go where he pleased, but she was not letting him out of her sight until he'd done what her father had sent him to do—deliver her safely to Santa Beliza.

"I don't think so, Doc. You just lead the way, 'cause I'm gonna stick to you like glue till I see my father. Is that clear?" She hated the way her voice quivered when she was upset, but it made her resolve no less determined.

"Just remember, señorita, this is your choice, not mine."

After another long, penetrating look, which Jenna returned with equal determination, her companion reached down and picked up the case. The ligaments in his strong back and arms rippled with impressive precision as he tossed it into the back of the jeep.

"Thought you said we were walking." Jenna climbed

into the passenger seat and strapped on her seat belt.

"We are. But first, I will return the jeep to my friend's workplace, since it is on the way."

Adam motioned to the native to hop into the back, which the man did without the use of a door. As nimble as Jack be quick, he settled and parked his feet on the console between the two front seats. A closer look at the dirt-caked, scarred foot made Jenna draw instinctively closer to the door, as though whatever malady had befallen it might be catching. Oblivious, Adam started the jeep and shoved it into gear. With a quick three-point turn, which scattered a cluster of chickens doomed for a cook pot, they were headed back into the city on its one main street.

The wind played havoc with the wisps of hair that escaped from Jenna's hastily clamped-up do, while questions of self-doubt and insecurities did the same to her mind.

Lord, what have I gotten myself into? What if I've made a mistake in thinking the wedding present was Father's subtle request to meet me at last? Had he shouted on the shortwave radio contact because of the static or because of a genuine excitement to hear from me? And why do I get the distinct feeling I've leapt from the proverbial pan into the fire? Lord, please help me not to despair!

Three

"EVERYTHING OKAY BACK THERE?"

"Oh, peachy!" Jenna answered Adam DeSanto, who was well ahead of her on the jungle trail with their anxious guide.

I will NOT despair!

She winced as she tugged away a thorny vine that wrapped around her ankle, nearly tripping her on the jungle path. She'd been through worse walking her horse through the club's riding trails at the onset of spring, when the groundskeepers were suddenly overwhelmed by Mother Nature's jumpstart of warm weather. However, considering the air was so thick in the midday that walking through it was like passing through a mist, *this* felt like her worst day in wilderness camp magnified a thousand times over.

At least then she had a backpack, not a wheeled

carry-on, which had its own problems with the terrain and wild creeping vines. Jenna tore more of nature's spiny crazy string away from the wheels with a glance over her shoulder to where Adam and the native were making annoyingly good time ahead of her. After rubbing the latest assault wave of insects off her legs, she righted her case and charged off after them.

She'd rather abandon the bag than ask them to hold back on her account, especially after she insisted to Adam she was more than up to the trek. Her fingers tightened on the green molded handle of her case as if in protest of the thought of letting it go. It was the last shred of civilization to comfort her. Heaven knew she'd get no sympathy from Doc Tarzan!

Okay. So you can look at the glass as half empty or half full. Take your pick.

"Full!" Jenna ground out through her teeth. Renewed with stubborn resolve, she rushed after her companions before they disappeared in the thick mass of trees, vines, and shrub ahead.

If they hadn't been in such a blooming hurry and she had a backpack for her civilized necessities, it would actually be beautiful. Oh, and if she ditched the expensive beaded sandals for good walking shoes and the short romper for long pants. Since her insect repellent was now making its way up the Amazon in one of her other bags, her legs and arms were a mass of welts.

And a potty stop was an adventure in itself, especially when she had to undress for the occasion and count on the discretion of her companions. Of course, the way she was sweating, thank goodness, frequency wouldn't be much of an issue. Jenna smiled to herself, pleased with the stab at optimism. *Half full!*

The fact was, the scenery was breathtaking. There were trees, the likes of which she'd never seen, and the wild orchids and flowers splashed color here and there against the lush green as if they'd been arranged by a master florist. But then they *had,* she supposed.

Her quiet reverie erupted in an exclamation of surprise when the tip of her sandal caught on a root and sent her sprawling on to the damp, decaying carpet of leaf litter. As she landed, her head struck a gnarled tree tentacle. For a few seconds she lay there, winded from the unexpected plunge, her carry-on lying atop her. She could hardly see the sky through the canopy of ancient trees, some well over a hundred feet tall, if an inch.

"Jenna! Are you all right?"

Adam materialized at her side and lifted her head, his fingers probing an incredibly sore spot.

She winced and smiled at him. "No wonder it looks like a carpet from the air."

Adam pried her fingers away from the luggage and tossed it aside. Then cradling her with one arm, he thumbed open the water canteen hanging from a cord about his neck and put it to her lips.

"Are you feeling any cramping?"

Jenna took a swallow of water, shaking her head at the same time. What a picture this must be. One adult feeding another from a water bottle like a mama with its baby.

She laughed at the mental image.

"I'm just part cat—the part that loves to wallow in the dirt, not the graceful one." Upon seeing her humor fall short at the doctor's concerned demeanor, she reassured him. "I'm fine, Adam. I'm just a klutz in the jungle."

She sat up on her own and scrambled to her feet, brushing away the forest debris clinging to her sweat-dampened clothing.

"A fashionable klutz, but a klutz, just the same." Jenna checked the tender spot on her head with her fingers. They came away blood free. She tried again to cover her embarrassment with humor. "Whattaya think, Doc, one lump or two?"

Adam's lips thinned as he reached over to pick up the carry-on. It was almost a smile. "I think that I should carry this before you hurt yourself with it."

"No!" Jenna snatched the handle out of his grasp, startling him. "I said I didn't need help and I meant it."

"Señorita, do not be foolish as well as stubborn."

"I can do it!"

As if to prove it, she set off on the path ahead of them like she was about to miss a flight. Behind her, the case bounced over roots that grew across the path. When she'd gone several yards, it dawned on Jenna that she was alone. Glancing back, she saw Adam DeSanto standing, arms crossed and legs braced next to an offshoot of the trail she'd not seen in passing. Next to him was their native companion, his face a mirror of confusion. With a grating smile, Adam pointed in the right direction.

Color climbing to her face to rival the red of the strange flower growing along the trail, her head held high Jenna backtracked and wheeled past the man with the condescending dark gaze.

"So I don't have a cat's sense of direction, either!"

A short time later, they stopped alongside a jungle creek, where Adam produced the *empanadas* he'd purchased from a street vendor before leaving. Soaking her feet in the water to cool off, Jenna nibbled cautiously at the fritters, not wholly confident that the meat in the center of the mashed, boiled yucca root was indeed the chicken it was professed to be. After all, she'd seen caiman, turtle, and monkey being touted as fresh and delicious at the riverside market.

Regardless, she was hungry and it tasted like chicken. But then, what weird meat concoction didn't?

At least her companions showed no reluctance in devouring their share. There was a minimal exchange of conversation regarding Yamo's treatment of his son's wound, some of which Jenna was able to discern. The Indian spoke his own dialect of Spanish and did so too quickly to translate with any certainty. She watched Adam's face for some sign of the degree of seriousness, but to little avail. He was perpetually grim, as though the weight of the entire world lay upon his shoulders, including one clumsy *turista* with a warped sense of humor.

She spent the remainder of the journey wondering what robbed the handsome doctor of his love for the life he pledged to preserve in others, yet not in himself. What made him tick?

Call it curiosity. Call it some kind of jungle delirium. Or maybe it was the infamous genetic defect Aunt Violet blamed on Robert Marsten when Jenna got some outlandish notion in her mind. Whatever the reason, she was determined to find out.

A gentle rain started just before they reached Yamo's village, its patter on the leaves above them a balm to her nerves. As it dripped through, Jenna welcomed the relief from the heat not to mention the impromptu shower. From the looks of the creekside community, it was likely the closest to one she was going to get.

Some village women found shelter from both rain and sunshine while going about daily chores under open structures roofed with thatch and tied together with vines. Instead of seeking refuge from the sprinkle, Jenna removed her hat and let the fresh water rinse her face of the grime from their journey.

Immediately she was surrounded by the bolder of the half-naked children playing here and there. Two or three dared to touch her and then withdrew their hands as if they been shocked into a fit of giggles.

Adam turned from the entrance of the casa that Yamo disappeared into and glanced over his shoulder at her.

"You are all right, no?"

"I'm fine. They're just curious."

She squatted down to the children's level and extended her hand. *"Me llamo Jenna,"* she said to one of the boys standing closest. *"Comó te llamas?"*

Another wave of giggles swept through the crowd. In the periphery of her vision, Jenna saw Adam duck inside the bamboo-walled hut. She waited for the boy to answer, smiling broadly in an attempt to reassure him. Eventually he summoned enough nerve to answer. His name was Jorge.

About ten or so, with bright brown eyes, the young boy appointed himself Jenna's host and began introducing his companions. Evidently thinking that she was also a *médico* or doctor, the children proceeded to show her every bug bite and boo-boo on their swarthy brown bodies. After a while, she gave up trying to explain in her textbook Spanish that she was only a friend of the doctor's for her meaning fell through the dialect window.

Instead, she proceeded to look at each one with an appropriate ooh or ah of concern and handed out a breath mint from the box she kept in her purse. Its colorful tapestry drew as much attention as her blond hair, especially from the women of the village. They watched Jenna rummage through the bag as though expecting her to pull out something exotic and strange.

Later, Adam emerged from the native hut with Yamo and a woman, whom Jenna took to be the mother of the sick child. Jenna had a line of patients by now, each waiting their turn to be seen. Upon seeing the attention centered around Jenna, Adam broke away from his deep conversation with the boy's parents and strode toward her with an incredulous look on his face.

"What *are* you doing?"

"Looking at boo-boos and passing out mints." At the reprimanding lift of Adam's brow, she added, "Hey, I tried to explain I wasn't a doctor."

With a spat of the half Indian, half Spanish language, Adam exposed her, but the villagers were still interested in getting their dose of candy "medicine" and refused to lose their place in line. When he began to repeat his disclaimer, Jenna put a hand on his arm.

"Wait, I can fix this. *You* watch my bag." The last thing she needed was a handful of nosey Indians going through her things again!

"But—"

She cut him off with his own favorite expression. "Ah!"

Jenna walked down the waiting line, stopping only long enough to dole out one of the tiny mints per customer. Some wanted an examination, but she just shook her head and pointed to the bemused and brooding médico watching her.

"So, how is the boy?" she called over her shoulder.

"Very ill. Had his father not gotten help, there is no doubt he would have lost his leg, if he survived at all. He may *still* lose it. Fortunately, I was able to restock my bag with ciproflaxin. The antibiotic they had given him was either out of date or not strong enough."

"Is that it, then? You make a house call, give him a shot, and we're on our way?"

"Not exactly."

The last of the mints were gone. Jenna held up the empty container so that all could see. Then she handed it to one of the children for whom there'd been no treat. Judging by the excitement in the little girl's beautiful dark eyes, Jenna had won a friend for life.

"What do you mean, *not exactly?*"

"I will need to watch him overnight. His fever is very high, despite the women's bathing him. Tomorrow, if there is improvement and no necrotic development…"

Jenna shivered at the sound of the word. Having served as a volunteer at the hospital in the children's ward during her junior-senior summer of high school, she'd learned more about medicine than she really wanted to know.

"Is that what happened to the boy's father's foot?"

Adam shook his head. "No, that was snakebite."

Snakebite. That, too, sent a shiver down her spine. "Thank goodness we didn't see any today!"

"None that were poisonous anyway."

Jenna's breath of relief stalled in her chest. "You saw snakes and didn't tell me?"

He shrugged. "I saw no reason to alarm you. They were harmless."

"Oh."

She tried to appear as nonchalant as her companion,

but her insides were jumping up and down with the willies. In her book, a snake was a snake was a snake! How did the saying go about what one didn't know, didn't hurt one?

Before Jenna could pursue the topic further, not that she really wanted to, Adam turned away to introduce her to Yamo's wife, Alma. Jenna could see the worry engraved on a face already showing a lifetime of hard work. The woman had deep circles under her eyes from lack of sleep and practically swayed on her feet.

"Mucho gusto!" Jenna shook her hand firmly. It was rough from the hard work of jungle housekeeping, raising a family, and tending the casa and well-manicured herb and vegetable garden next to it.

"We will be Yamo and Alma's guests this evening."

The natives' house was hardly big enough to accommodate the parents and the children Yamo pointed proudly to as his own, much less two more adults.

"Do you think we should impose? I mean, it looks small to me."

"There is an—how do you say—*awning* of thatch extending from the kitchen in the back. We can sling hammocks there."

"Hammocks?" Now *there* was a challenge.

"You would prefer to sleep on the floor or the ground?"

"Considering the snakes and all manner of creepy crawlies, a hammock sounds divine," Jenna replied, on second thought.

"The smoke from the kitchen fire will help with the insects."

Realizing that neither Yamo nor his wife understood a whit of what was being said, Jenna gave them a big smile. *"Muchas gracias por la hospitalidad.* Is there anything I can do to help you?" she went on in Spanish.

"Qué?" The couple looked at Adam for help in understanding.

Jenna repeated her question more slowly, mentally checking behind herself with each syllable. It worked, although not exactly the way she'd intended. Alma's face contracted in horror at her guest's suggestion.

"Oh, no, no, no!" she exclaimed, adding a rattle of words that Adam needlessly translated into "she would not think of such a thing!"

"Adelante, Señorita Marsten."

The *r* in *Marsten* rolled off the woman's tongue like the exaggeration of *butter* in a television commercial. Before Jenna knew what was happening, she was being ushered around the corner of the native casa, her hostess clucking like a mother hen beside her. Neither language nor sickness was going to stand in the way of hospitality.

Jenna's apprehension over supper, or rather what supper would be, was put to rest when a platter of delicious fried fish was served with an assortment of fruit, tomatoes, and flat loaves of manioc bread. The two older daughters helped their mother and took over the cleaning up completely after dinner. Since they didn't use dishes or eating utensils, save the serving platters themselves, it wasn't all that much work.

Afterward, the men who'd been working on the forest farms or *chacras* farther inland during the day joined
the boys in a game of soccer on a makeshift field at the
end of the little community. The women continued to
work, tending children, getting the home ready for the
coming of night. Relegated as a guest, Jenna sat on a
bench in the open-railed *sala*, the equivalent to family
room, and watched the fierce competition until two of
the youngest family members coaxed her into a game of
jacks on the palm slat floor.

When it became more and more difficult to see,
Alma and her daughters lit kerosene lamps, which had
been made of discarded coffee cans with rags for wicks.
The entire building smacked of the scent. Kerosene,
Adam told her, was the exterminating chemical of choice
against ever-present termites. While Jenna hadn't seen
termites, she'd seen prehistoric-sized *cucarachas*—cockroaches. The idea of sleeping in a hammock was becoming more and more appealing all the time.

Outside, the game was called for the night. Stripped
of his shirt, Adam came in from the playing field with
Yamo and his sons. His loose trousers hung low on his
lean hips, rolled up above the knees. Looking more like
a native than a physician, he checked in on his patient
once more and then relaxed with Yamo and some of the
village men who'd gathered outside the casa with cups
of a sugarcane drink, the nonalcoholic version of *chicha*
with fruit juices added.

If the insects eating Jenna alive bothered the jungle doctor, it certainly didn't show. Gleaming as if it had been oiled for a photography shoot, his back rippled, unblemished by welts in the lamplight, when he lifted his cup or used his hands to participate in the friendly discussion. For the first time since she'd met him, he was relaxed rather than uptight, like an overwound clock. Swapping hunting tales was more to his liking. At least that's what she supposed was happening from the tidbits of conversation she was able to make out.

He was far more at home here than he'd been at the Posada Explorador or in the city—unless he caught her watching him. Then his back grew ramrod straight and he threw himself into his tale even more, until she was once again no more than an insect on the wall. Jenna couldn't tell if he'd been flattered or annoyed. The man was more difficult to read than Nantucket's weather.

When the women started taking down clothing from the open rafters of the thatched-covered home, the social gathering started to break up. At their mother's instruction, Jenna's gaming partners put away the jacks and gave Jenna an enthusiastic good-night hug. Their beds were simply a pile of clothing. Mother and children recited their prayers together before the lamp was turned down in the sala.

"You know, I couldn't help overhearing the prayers back there," Jenna said to Adam later when she accompanied him down to the creek to fetch more bathwater for the patient and for their own use. "By our standards they have nothing, yet they thanked God for their bounty."

"You mean by *your* standards."

"Hey, that was you driving around in a jeep earlier, wasn't it?"

"It was my friend's."

Jenna was unconvinced. "I'll bet you used all the conveniences when you were in the States too."

"Fine, *our* standards. Now, are you happy?"

"No, I just..." What? Something about this guy sparked her annoyance like flint to tinder. *Heavenly Father!* Taking a deep breath, she regrouped and headed for more neutral ground. "I only meant to say that seeing the family praying together was touching."

"It makes them feel better, I suppose."

Well, she *thought* it would be neutral ground. The raw cynicism in the doctor's voice took Jenna back.

"You don't believe in prayer?" Then the utterly incredulous crossed her mind. "Don't tell me you don't believe in God, not when you live here in this tropical paradise!"

"Oh, I do not question that there is a God. I just happen to believe that He is not the all-loving Creator the missionaries and priests would have us believe. This *paradise* as you call it is as harsh and loveless as it is beautiful, señorita."

Uncertain as to how to answer, Jenna laughed nervously. "My aunt already warned me of that when she tried to keep me from coming."

"Perhaps you should have listened."

Adam wished that she had. His impassive look masked a storm of feelings brewing inside. He liked his world the way it was without some prima donna socialite invading it with delusions of paradise and rose-colored faith. The latter was for children, innocents who'd not been stung by the bite of reality. Or for those who'd grown spiritually past their earthly trials, like Robert Marsten. Marina's death left Adam neither.

"Well, I don't always do what I *should* do," Jenna shot back. "So you'll just have to get used to me, I guess."

"Now I am really frightened."

His facetious tone belied his real feelings. There was something about Jenna Marsten that was frightening, something that went beyond his fascination with the picture in her father's office of a fresh-faced college graduate, whose eyes shone bright with naive anticipation of all the wonderful things the future had in store for her. It was like a light in a dark world, untarnished by reality. Despite his resentment of it, Adam did not want to see it dimmed, although with her innocent faith, he feared the inevitability.

"Besides, you know nothing of real life and disappointment."

Jenna's head shot up. "Hah, I beg to differ, Mr. Know-It-All, Done-It-All! Just because you live surrounded by luxuries doesn't guarantee happiness. Not only did my fiancé choose a choice job over me, but I just discovered that I was abandoned as a child by my own father. I always knew there was something missing in my relationship with Scott and my life, and suddenly...*bam!* I'm smacked on the side of the head that I'm not only not wanted now, but was never wanted. And I'll tell you something, *Dr. Adam DeSanto*, it hurts!"

Adam felt miserable at the quiver of her chin. "Okay, you know what hurt is. I had no right to presume."

"No, you didn't!"

"I said I was sorry."

The young woman was only catching her second wind. "But I'll tell you something else."

He was glad he hadn't given in to the compelling urge to hug her. There was no quivering chin now, just a glossy glare hot enough to singe the hair off a pig. When it came to arguing, women were the most resilient creatures he'd ever known. They could turn tears to steam in that one long seemingly fragile breath they always took before blasting a man with the steel of exactly what they thought.

"*I'm* not going to turn into a cynical pig like you."

"A pig, is it?"

Pig. Ach, he was beginning to think along the same lines as her! He should be insulted, at least alarmed, but somehow the notion struck him as humorous. His emotions and thoughts had become one huge scramble where Jenna was concerned. She even confused his body! Here it was jungle hot, and the hair on his arms stood up as if he'd taken a chill—or was it just bracing for a good singeing?

As if someone pulled in on the reins of her outburst, she let it out in sigh. "I'm sorry. I don't know what's wrong with me. I guess I just need a good night's sleep." She slapped at a mosquito on her arm. "And a portable mosquito net!"

"*De nada*, señorita." It was nothing. How could it be when her lower lip ventured out past its mate, infected with such contrition? He was almost tempted again to hug her. Almost.

"No, it isn't. I told you I don't always do as I should. It's not your fault, you're ignorant—of God and prayer, that is," she added hastily. "I'm supposed to be setting an example, not egging you on. I mean, how can I convince you that God can take our trials and turn them into blessings while verbally taking off your head!"

His companion could set the finest example in the world for him and talk till she was blue in the face, but it would make no difference. She was lucky God chose to stick with her and see her through her rejections. He was not so lucky. He'd been abandoned.

The zip of her opening that ridiculous, out-of-place piece of luggage cut through the nocturnal jungle din. Grateful for the distraction, Adam chose to pursue humor rather than sink deeper into the dark abyss of his past. He forced the image of his companion, decked out for a posh safari with designer luggage in tow, into his mind rather than the haunting face of his Marina.

Maybe she was older than her years, spiritually. Maybe that was why God hadn't been there for him, yet carried Jenna through her ups and downs. And she'd had more than a few, just since arriving in Ichitas. Not once did Jenna whine or complain, despite the way the flies and mosquitoes flocked to sample her soft golden skin. Marina would have collapsed in a tantrum of tears at first bite or tumble. Adam found himself smiling.

And the candy clinic. His late wife wouldn't try to communicate with the natives, much less let them touch her. Marina wanted him but no part of his work. He should have seen it, but he didn't. She was so beautiful, so fragile, so pampered. And he'd taken the hothouse rose from her familiar surroundings to his. He'd prayed she would adapt, but she hadn't. Adam's heart grew hard in his chest, drawing the tilt from his lips. So much for God and turning hardship into blessings.

The sight of his unpredictable companion shedding her sandals at the water's edge brought him back to the present again. "What are you doing?"

Jenna stepped into the creek and hesitated. "Keep that light over here, will ya? If an alligator's going to get me, he's going to have a clean meal. I feel like one big, filthy itch!"

"No, Jenna." Adam grabbed her arm, certain she'd taken leave of her senses. "You still have your clothes on."

"Of course I do. They need washing too." She stared up at him with an impish look that made Adam's belly feel as thought he'd just dropped from the roller coaster he'd ridden while in stateside medical school. "I mean, it's not like I'll catch pneumonia from a chill."

The slam of her thinking along the same lines as him again caught him off guard. His pulse staggered and then rushed to make up for it. This was something he'd do, not a cultured rose from the civilized world.

"Besides, Jorge said that nothing bit in the creek." The glow faded from her expression. "Nothing *does*, does it?"

Instead of answering, Adam set down the two buckets he carried and shone his flashlight over the water, scanning first one bank and then the other. It wasn't likely, considering the continuous human activity at the village banks, but then the law of the jungle could be as fickle as it was dangerous. He'd learned from growing up here that there were no absolutes where it was concerned.

Satisfied that there were no suspicious looking "logs" floating or lying about, he swept his hand toward the moonlit water. "Be my guest, señorita, but if you feel so much as a tickle, shout."

"Hah! They'll hear me in Ichitas."

Adam sat down on a nearby rock to keep lookout, no more comfortable than he'd been before he checked out the place for danger. The biggest danger in sight was that of a leggy blond attacking her body and clothing with a vengeance and the bar of soap, which she produced from her precious bag of feminine trappings. The scent drifted Adam's way, clean yet hinting of something fresh, not quite floral not quite…

She went under in the shallow water and shot up like a comic Venus, glancing about her frantically before the water was even out of her eyes. Yet the sight of his colleague's daughter was no less stirring to his masculine nature than if she'd been the goddess of beauty and love herself, arrayed in Mother Nature's own gown rather than disheveled clothes bulging with air and water and oozing soap at the seams.

Jenna Marsten was as tall and fair as Marina had been dark and petite. He swore silently and forced himself to watch the water rather than the haphazard goddess. Like day and night, he thought, confounded by the fact that he could not keep from comparing the living with the dead. Would he ever put his late wife's memory to rest? No matter how many assured him otherwise, Adam blamed himself for Marina's death.

"There! I feel like a new person." Wringing the excess water from the hem of her garment, Jenna traipsed out of the water and daintily slipped her toes into her sandals. "Want me to hold the light while you bathe? I can loan you my soap."

"No!" Adam winced inwardly. He didn't mean to sound so harsh, to loose the anger that would not leave him be. "I...um...I don't want to use anything that would attract the insects."

"So stinky sweat keeps them at bay?"

Jenna was genuinely interested and Adam couldn't blame her. He'd noticed the welts and the way she'd been scratching. New blood, the natives joked among each other. Or perhaps the reason his blood wasn't as appetizing was bitterness. Hers would be sweet.

"That isn't what I meant," she added in a rush, her eyes growing wide with embarrassment. "I haven't smelled you or anything."

Perhaps not, but he had. With a grimace, Adam handed her the flashlight. "Perhaps, señorita, I should take a dip for the sake of mankind, no?"

The fact of the matter was, he had forgotten consideration for feminine sensibilities. His mind was on tending his patient and delivering his charge to her father—his duty. Robert called him obsessive about his work, but it was a way of escaping idle hours when the past came back to plague him.

The water was as refreshing as the young woman on the bank said. Rubbing the grime of the day off his skin with his hands, Adam took a second dip under water. There in the pressing cool quiet, he could hear the strong pulse at his temples magnified. He listened with a medical ear, noting it was faster than it should be. It was one more sign that he had been in the jungle, away from civilization and the fairer sex too long.

When Adam came up, it was in the direct glow of the blinding flashlight. He focused on the stricken woman standing at the water's edge, her free hand plastered against her chest. Combing his dark hair away from his face, he couldn't help but tease. "Do you look for me, señorita, or a caiman?"

"You...both actually. I mean, you were the one who

talked about how harsh the jungle was, and then you up and disappeared underwater like that! I've seen movies where crocodiles snatch men under."

"Jenna, Jenna. I assure you, if a caiman had grabbed me you would have heard *me* in Ichitas as well."

With the slight grin his guarded emotion would allow, he took up the two buckets. He needed to get back to the village to check on the boy's vital signs again, although it would be morning before they knew for certain if the injection Adam gave him was going to work.

"Well, at least I know what makes you smile. At least I *think* that's what I just saw," she added dourly, not at all impressed with his brand of humor. "Scaring the life out of me!" With a jerk of her hand and a twist of her lips, she pulled up on the handle of her bag, and chin aloof, stomped off.

As if it were contagious, Adam tried not to notice the feminine, if decidedly piqued, sway of her hips. Instead, he focused on the clumsy flowered bag bouncing and banging on every rock in the path. Whatever brand of luggage it was, it got his vote for durability.

A barking dog heralded their return to the village. But for the moon and occasional glow of a kerosene lamp, it was totally dark. The people of the jungle rose and went to bed with the sun except on fiesta. Hanging in the rafters over the sick boy's pallet was a brightly colored paper animal with a hole in its belly where birthday candy had poured out—a piñata. His mother thought it would cheer him, but the child slept through the fever engulfing his small frame.

Next to it hung a bag of IV fluids Adam started as soon as he arrived with Yamo. It was the only one he had and, unless the child was awake and able to drink tomorrow, he might have to carry the patient back to the clinic.

Adam took the boy's temperature and blood pressure. The fever had dropped a little, but it was still dangerously high. The boy's eldest sister, a young woman rounding out in her eight month with child, had come over to relieve their mother of the *velorio*. She would continue the vigil, keeping his frail body wrapped in cool wet cloths. Not that it would be easy. As low as she was carrying, perhaps he'd have to deliver a baby before he left; although usually the village midwives took care of those details. Adam was only called in when there was difficulty.

"Call me if he awakens," he said to the expectant mother. "Or if you need more water."

Adam learned early on in his practice that to stay up all night with a patient when there was someone else to do it was to deny that patient or another of a sharp-witted physician the following morning. It was a luxury he seldom could afford.

When he entered the kitchen, a separate dwelling adjoining the main house by a raised walkway, Jenna was struggling into one of the hammocks their humble hosts had slung for their guests. It swung precariously, threatening to flip her out at any moment.

"The object is to rest in it, señorita, not wrestle with it. You look as if you are trying to climb the rope ladder game…eh…Jacob's ladder!"

Jenna Marsten *was* as loveable as a kitten, able to work its way into the hardest of hearts.

"I'll get it," she said with the stubbornness of the creature she reminded Adam of, one about to discover it did not always land on its feet.

Adam leaned over and tried to steady it for her. The elbow upon which she rested, however, slipped through the weave, costing Jenna her balance. In the flash of an eye, she lay sprawled at his feet, her expression as disgruntled as it was surprised. Leaning down, he held out his hand.

"Come, Jenna. There is a trick." He hauled her to her feet.

"Like sleeping on the floor with the kids?"

She'd changed out of her wet clothes, which lay draped over the rail of the open room, into an oversized T-shirt and shorts. Her hair was bound in a pixieish knot atop her head, the strands too short to be caught hanging in golden wisps about her face.

"And the *cockroaches*," she whispered, as if to keep their hosts from hearing. With a wide-eyed shudder, she rubbed her arms, opening a welt she had scratched too hard.

"Among other things." Adam's confirmation did not reassure her. "But first, I will paint you in calamine. Then

I will show you how to master sleep in the hammock."

He retrieved a bottle out of his bag and shook it, all the while taking in his companion's splotched skin. Although his specialty was pediatrics, Adam dealt with female patients regularly. Still, he had to concentrate to keep his hand steady as he removed the bottle cap.

"I can do it!"

Independence recovered, Jenna took the bottle and walked over to a bench before he even felt his relief at being spared that particular contact. Adam told himself that this was just another woman, but his body refused to accept rationalization in any form. Even in sloppy clothes with her hair askew and her skin splotched with pinkish patches of ointment, it was an effort to keep his eyes off Jenna Marsten.

Wholesome came to Adam's mind as he walked away. She needed none of the beauty enhancing tubes and bottles that she dragged behind her all day as though clinging to the last thread of civilization in sight. Leaning against the doorjamb of the hut, he became lost in the stars twinkling overhead and the image of a long-legged sprite with baggage in tow.

"Can you get my back? I can't quite reach all of it."

At the nearness of Jenna's voice behind him, Adam started. Heat warmed his face and neck, as though he'd been caught looking.

"But of course." He cleared his throat of the rasp infecting it, wishing his hands were as dry.

Turning away, Jenna hauled up the back of her shirt,

exposing her welted skin in the light of the moon in the doorway.

"I would suggest you use no perfume," Adam said, smearing the chalky liquid over her shoulders and between the outlines of the scapulas in a brisk fashion. He was eager to be done before his voice betrayed the riot of reaction clamoring in his brain. With a hasty sweep between *latissimus dorsi* of her lower back, he finished and capped the bottle.

"And now watch, señorita. This is how you approach the hammock."

Adam backed against the center of the netting and, once certain it was spread adequately, sat down. The hammock creaked under his weight, and sure of himself, he swung his legs about and laid flat on his back.

"As the French say, *voilà!*"

As if on cue, the rope holding the foot of the makeshift bed to one of the doorposts gave way with an incredibly loud snap. Although Adam grasped the edges of the bed instinctively, he slammed, bottom first, onto the plank floor of the kitchen with an unceremonious grunt of surprise.

To say Jenna Marsten was amused was a gross understatement. The young woman clutched her stomach and cackled like a ticklish baby.

Grinning through clenched teeth, Adam climbed to his feet, certain the heat of his humiliation made him glow in the dark. As he picked up the end of the net bed that had come loose, Jenna caught her breath with a hysterical "voilà!" and launched into another fit of laughter.

"And," he went on matter-of-factly, as though nothing had transpired to interrupt his lecture on mastering the hammock, "never forget to check the ropes, to be certain that your hosts have tied them securely."

He tied and checked his own before making sure Jenna's was safe as well.

"Now it is your turn."

Jenna pulled a straight face with some difficulty and tested the knots holding her own sling. Carefully, she backed into it and laid down exactly as he'd shown her. But when she glanced at him for approval, she couldn't seem to help the giggle in her imitation of him.

"As the French say, voilà!"

Four

"THERE IS DEFINITELY AN ART TO SLEEPING IN A HAMMOCK."
Jenna grimaced as she checked her arm. Aside from
skinning an elbow getting out of the swinging bed that
morning, she'd come through the night unscathed.
Getting up, however, was a lot trickier than lying down.
One wrong move and voilà!

"And what about those wedding hammocks for
two? Hardly conducive to romance, I'd think."

"I would not know."

Adam forged ahead of her on the jungle path, clearing any vines that had encroached since the last human
passage with impatient chops of a machete. If Jenna
hadn't known better, she'd swear Doc Grumpy hadn't
slept. However, considering she'd lain awake half the
night afraid to move, lest she be dumped onto the rough
planked floor, she listened to his peaceful snoring with
outright envy.

"So how will his parents get the boy to the clinic if his fever comes back?"

"A litter, most likely."

She'd seen the young patient for the first time that morning when she accompanied his mother into the tiny bedroom adjacent to the sala to help put the bed clothing back up in the rafters of the thatched roof. He couldn't have been more than nine or ten, yet he'd been working on the forest farm with the men of the village when the machete accident occurred.

Adam removed the IV from the child's slender brown arm, producing a big smile. All the doctor chatted brightly about was the previous night's *futbol* game. He even got the boy to chuckle by brandishing a skinned knee like a banner of courage. Whatever this man put his mind to, he certainly threw himself into it wholeheartedly.

"But you think he'll be all right with the antibiotics you left?"

"If I did not think so, I would not have left him."

The doctor's warmth was obviously reserved for his patients. He was as bristly as the onset of the beard shadowing his face. Sinister charm, Jenna thought dourly, dogged by the fact that there was a certain attraction to it.

There'd been nothing sinister about Scott Pierson. Jenna's thoughts stumbled. Funny, but Scott had not crossed her mind since arriving in the Peruvian Amazon. Did that tell her something or what? She fought a rise of guilt that she'd not been the devastated, jilted bride-to-be her friends and family expected. Instead, she found herself comparing the handsome engineer's fair features, fresh and wholesome as a choirboy's, to those of the man who moved ahead of her with the ease of a jungle cat. Like day and night, she mused.

Not that she and Adam DeSanto were any more alike. Jenna struggled with the grace of an orangutan in heels to keep from turning an ankle and wrestled with her luggage over the red-packed clay edged with coarse grass in order to keep up. Oh, the jungle doc had offered to take it for her, but she wouldn't give him the satisfaction of admitting she was out of her element and needed help. He made it a goal to point that out to her at every opportunity. His message was loud and clear: You don't belong here.

Although why it mattered to him one way or the other puzzled Jenna. She really hadn't held him up or caused him undue trouble. She'd pulled her load, quite literally, even afforded him a few laughs at her expense. At least she *thought* those irregular twitches on either side of the perpetual line of his lips were evidence of humor.

What made Adam DeSanto so grim? Yes, the jungle could be a savage place, but it was also a place of uncommon beauty. Like life, one could concentrate on the blessings or the hardships. *Father, he annoys the daylights out of me, but if You will show me some way to help him escape whatever darkness enshrouds him, I'll give it a try.*

"You know what impressed me most about our

hosts?" she said out of the blue.

"What is that, Jenna?" The doctor didn't glance back at her, but at least he replied.

"How rich they were."

Adam stopped and turned, head cocked. His gaze narrowed as though seeing right through her impulsive attempt to swing the conversation toward a more spiritual plane.

"We could learn a lot from them, I think."

She waited, expecting the opinion swirling behind the doctor's appraisal, but all she received was the all-expressive shrug, so popular in this culture. End of philosophical pursuit. March!

"I am perplexed, but *not* in despair!" she paraphrased aloud, to no one in particular. It was just as well. Her companion refused to acknowledge her.

Jenna gave up and wiped perspiration from her brow with the back of her hand. Regardless of what Adam did or did not think of the subject, Jenna had a new, deeper understanding of her mother. Diana Marsten's journals made the same observations regarding the simple wealth of the natives on several occasions. Jenna warmed, as if her mother had reached out from the past and embraced her.

For all her years and schooling, for all her poise and self-assured manner, part of Jenna was still a little girl, still wondering who she was and from whence she'd come. Her aunt and uncle were everything a child would want in parents, but there was still a void, which Jenna had always felt and kept to herself for fear of hurting them. Although she adapted easily, she felt like the odd puzzle piece that didn't quite fit in the life laid out for her.

Her mother's journals only sharpened Jenna's awareness of it in her later years, yet the alternative eluded her. Her father's mysterious gift had come at just the right time in her life to keep her from making a commitment she was obviously not ready for with a man no more prepared for *till death do us part* than she was. It wasn't a coincidence. Of that, Jenna was certain. God had to have a hand in this. She and Scott both needed more time to think about the commitment. God was surely going to turn that hurt into a blessing.

Diana Marsten's writings about the jungle and its lure were true. So how could her references to the strapping young physician who'd won her heart and fathered her child be otherwise? Dr. Robert Marsten delivered Jenna himself, and her mother's account of the birth never failed to make Jenna cry. He'd really wanted her as much as her mother. He'd built a nursery on to the thatched cottage that had been their home and clinic, painted the bamboo curtains pink.

So how could this be the same man Aunt Violet accused of choosing his work over his daughter? The man who'd given up all rights of guardianship and never bothered to contact the child again until her wedding announcement; and then, it was anonymously.

Jenna blinked away the glaze stemming from her

emotional debate. She was just tired. After all, she hadn't slept a decent night since before she'd left Boston. And when she got tired, she got weepy.

Even if the man hadn't come for her himself, Aunt Vi was wrong about the gift coming as a result of guilt rather than her father's really caring. Robert Marsten couldn't possibly resent her coming more than the stonehearted man he'd sent to fetch her.

Adam stopped abruptly ahead of her. "There."

Taken by surprise, Jenna collided into the blur of his back, her battered bag on wheels rolling up on her ankle.

The doctor caught her before she tumbled over the buttress of a large tropical tree, gathering her to him.

"Jenna?" he asked, showing surprise at the wetness of her cheek against his arm.

Jenna forced a laugh. "I think I'm allergic to the jungle."

Like most of her attempts at humor with the man, it missed the mark.

"No, those are tears." He stepped away, looking down at her in alarm. "What is it? Did something sting you?"

She shook her head. "I'm just tired," she insisted. "My eyes water when I haven't slept for nearly three days."

"Then you must not despair, chica. Remember, you said that you were perplexed, but not in despair—and Jenna, *this* looks like despair to me."

And she thought he hadn't heard her.

He lifted her chin and turned it toward where the

forest thinned. A tall chain-link fence rose, out of place, amidst the greenery. Beyond it were a scatter of thatched cottages in a clearing.

"And all this for nothing," he chided gently, "for *there* is Santa Beliza."

It looked like a village, enclosed for safety's sake— in as much as one could enclose a jungle compound. Since they had come up behind the establishment, Jenna and Adam walked around the perimeter to the main gate, which was manned by day and locked at night.

She felt foolish, crying like a baby. Her innermost fear simply sneaked up on her during an unguarded moment of weariness. Of all the people to see her like this, it had to be the one who'd stated from the beginning that she didn't belong. She pulled herself together as best she could.

"There is the clinic." Adam pointed to a long narrow building, covered with thatching and half walled to allow open air. Hanging up under the eaves and serving as awnings were hinged storm covers that could be closed against the elements.

"And over there," he added with brightness previously unheard in his voice, "is going to be our lab, if we ever get enough funds to equip it."

Instead of the typical jungle structure this one was a Quonset hut, gleaming bright metal beneath a cooling canopy of tall trees, which helped offset the heat.

"It has an air-conditioner to keep the inside as contaminant-free as possible. Behind it is the power plant, where our electricity comes from."

Jenna couldn't tell if the jungle doctor was excited over the new lab or just desperate to keep her from crying again. The look on his face when he saw her tears was nothing short of thunderstruck. She forced an acknowledging smile of approval.

"Of course, all the houses we saw from the back are homes of the staff. We have a big family, a village if you will. Even a school for the children."

She must have either scared the sulkiness out of her companion or he was incredibly glad to be home and almost rid of her—or both. He'd said more to her in the last five minutes than he said in the sum total of three days!

"And there, Señorita Marsten, is our *hacienda,* where I can assure you we have all the amenities of home."

"Doctor Adam! Doctor Adam!"

Crawling out from under the stilted veranda of the sprawling hacienda, a small Indian boy ran toward them, arms outstretched. A small monkey ambled along after him, chattering away in its own greeting.

"Hola, Pepito!"

The youngster wrapped himself around one of Adam's long legs with an enthusiastic hug, but the monkey was more curious about Jenna. To her horror, it vaulted up her body and latched onto Jenna's head, its skinny arms clenching and shoving the wide brim of her hat down over her eyes.

Afraid to push the animal away for fear it might bite,

Jenna ran in place and screamed, "Get it off! Get it off!"

"Rita. Shame on you."

Adam lifted the monkey away, scolding it gently. It climbed up on his shoulder and mocked Jenna's shriek, its tiny hands clamped about its furry head.

"She is just too curious for her own good, señorita, but she would not harm anyone."

Tilting her head up so she could see from under the smashed brim of her hat, Jenna eyed the animal warily. Her heart was plastered against her vocal cords, the screams having taken the last coherent words she was capable of.

"This is Rita, a mischievous marmoset, and this..." Adam went on, oblivious to a dizzy heat wave descending upon them, "is Pepito, her human counterpart."

"She is Dr. Roberto's daughter, no?"

Funny, Jenna could see the boy no more than an arm's length away, yet his question sounded as though it came from a distance.

"Sí, this is Señorita Marsten and she has come a long way from..."

Boston. Yes, it was a long way away, just like Adam DeSanto's voice. Jenna licked her lips. They were rough and dry. She needed more lip balm. Her thoughts became as slow as the scene unfolding before her eyes. And she needed to let go of the brim of her hat because she was falling. Her knees gave way, as if the blood draining from her face had deserted them as well, taking strength with them.

"Jenna!"

She heard Adam's exclamation of surprise, but she no longer saw him, the boy, or the monkey. Instead, she looked at the sun-dappled canopy spinning over their heads and allowed herself to plunge backward on to a floating mattress of oblivion.

Or was it Adam's arms? It wasn't quite as comfortable as she'd thought oblivion to be.

"*Vámanos!* Take Rita and get Dr. Robert!"

And why was DeSanto's voice rattling in her ear, as deep as the panicked shriek of the monkey in the background was high? It disrupted the more comforting sound of the heartbeat of her pillow. Jenna cracked open one eyelid reluctantly. Trees and a trellis of lovely roses passed by before they were wiped out of her vision by a roof of some sort.

"Tilda!"

There was the creak of an opening door, a hasty shuffle of footsteps, and the slam of the door behind them.

"Dr. Adam! *Qué pasa?*"

Adam told the distraught woman something about heat and water. Water, Jenna could use, but the last thing she needed was heat! She tried to collect her thoughts, to separate sensation from the reality that whirred past her.

Suddenly she was drifting down. The coolness of the bed was inviting, yet giving up the warmth of Adam's arms made Jenna shudder. She held on to one, as though it were her last line to reality.

"Shush…you are fine, Jenna. A little too much sun, perhaps."

He pressed his fingers against the side of her throat for a few moments, then pulled away with an unremarkable grunt.

Jenna struggled to keep from slipping into the comfort promised by the bed beneath her.

"It's a *real* bed." she remarked in wonder, scrunching up the sheets with her fingers.

Adam gave her an indulgent nod. "Sí, and you are in a real house. You are home, Jenna."

Home. The word had such a soothing, enveloping effect, just like Adam's rendition of her name. If they could put that in a pill…

Her thoughts broke off as Adam removed her sandals, those hundred dollar slabs of leather, beads, and heels that had made the jaunt through the jungle a test of coordination. Suddenly, horror gripped Jenna.

She bolted upright in protest. "Oh no, Adam! I'm so dirty I'll ruin the sheets!"

The strangely tolerant doctor eased her back against the marvelously soft pillow with a firm hand. "Tilda has more than one set, I am certain."

"But I need a bath. I can't meet father like this!"

"Robert will be delighted to see you, no matter what you look like. That I promise." He reached down and gently wiped away a tear that wandered down her cheek.

Where did *that* come from?

"I'm not crying because the trip was hard."

"Of course not." There it was again. That indulgent nod, the smile. Adam was treating her like a crying baby, which was exactly what she was, for some unearthly reason.

"I didn't hold you up one bit!"

"Of course you didn't. But you did not, I think, drink the water I gave you."

Water. Jenna licked her dry lips, pondering the validity of the gentle accusation. Ah yes, the water bottle. She'd gotten tired of it slamming against her and unslung it from her shoulder to put in one of the outside compartments of her carry-on.

Besides, he'd filled it from a stream when they stopped for cold rice balls at lunch—the same stream she watched fish swimming in!

"I'm sorry, but…well, fish do more than *swim* in that water, you know."

Adam laughed outright. It was a foreign sound coming from the ever-sober doctor.

Jenna made a face. "It was like drinking from Uncle Ben's aquarium…and I've helped cleaned that baby out!"

"Ah, but Jenna."

If they could bottle the effect of Adam's pronunciation of her name, she'd stay high, without inhibition.

"Mother Nature cleans after herself given the chance. Just as she has done for eons."

"You mean God tends the Amazon aquarium." But the water *still* had fish in it. Every travel agent worth his fee warned clients not to drink the water.

"No, *Dr. Robert,*" he chided, "I will not be dragged into the discussion of faith again! You are like your father."

A curtain dropped in Adam's gaze, putting out the lights of mischief dancing there only moments before. Jenna felt pangs of regret and pity, but that she'd been compared to her father was reassuring, in spite of the fact that she'd yet to meet him.

"Is he coming? My father, I mean?"

Jenna started to get up again, but a voice at the doorway stopped her.

"No, señorita. Dr. Robert is upriver, but he will be home this evening."

A short round woman of mixed Spanish and Indian blood hustled in with a tray. On it was a tall glass of juice, tinkling with ice.

"Anything serious?" Adam asked her.

"He goes to deliver the just-arrived antivenin and show the people how to use it." Turning from Adam, the woman brightened for Jenna's sake.

"I am Tilda, Señorita Marsten, and I am so glad to see you! But now, it is for you to rest and recover from your trip, no?"

Adam helped Jenna sit upright as Tilda handed her the glass.

"Thank you, Tilda…gracias."

"The juice will restore the electrolytes you lost in the last couple of days, so drink it all. Tilda will bring more."

The juice was refreshing, like a magic jungle nectar. Jenna felt her mind clearing a bit as her heart sank from the news the housekeeper brought. Her father was not here. Once again the ugly head of doubt reared in her mind, battering her defenses. She forced down more of the pineapple-banana concoction, attempting to rein in her teetering emotions.

"*Pobrecita.* Dr. Adam has dragged you all over the jungle. The boy, he is going to be all right?" Despite the initial chide in her voice, Tilda looked up at Adam DeSanto with nothing short of adoration.

There was definitely a history here, but Jenna was too distracted by her own history to pursue it—a history of life with a father she'd never met, a father whom fate seemed intent on keeping unknown to her.

"I believe he will be fine."

Of course, a doctor's life was ruled by his patients' needs. Jenna had already seen evidence of that in the last seventy-two hours. The best-laid plans changed according to the winds of infection or trauma.

"Bueno. I will fetch some towels, and when Señorita Marsten is ready, she can fresh herself up."

"Tilda, please call me Jenna." It was not just a stab of politeness. Jenna needed to feel a part of this place. She needed…

The woman's face crinkled in delight. "You are so like your mama's picture! She is beautiful, no, Dr. Adam?"

"Very." Adam's tone was less than committed. "I am

going to the clinic. If you need anything, ask Tilda. This is *her* kingdom. She will take good care of you."

Jenna nodded, a blade of dread tearing at her throat. She wasn't a child, yet she felt like one, a lost one—one about to lose the only familiar face in a strange world.

"I will see you this evening at dinner."

She nodded again and strained to hold back the tears threatening her eyes. *Lord, we are perplexed but not in despair.*

"Thanks, Doc."

It was just as well that her father wasn't there. She didn't want to impress him as a babbling crybaby. Where was all this doubt and fear coming from? Jenna didn't have to dwell on the answer very long. She rebelled against them, but she was so tired, so confused, so perplexed. *Lord, help!*

"Now, you just rest!" Tilda slipped through the door to the room. "An' try not to let those awful pink blinds give you nightmares. I use bleach on them, but the jungle rot over twenty-something years is bad. They will scare her away, I tell Dr. Robert, but no, he insists I put them up for you. Who knows?"

The door clicked behind Tilda's retreating form, muffling her commentary on blind cleaning and storage. Jenna stared at the open windows where curtains of an Indian design hung, bright, geometric, and made to match the spread folded at the foot of the bed. But the curtains were drawn back. Beneath them hung the rattiest-looking pink bamboo shades Jenna had ever seen, splotched by mildew and faded by time. The words of her mother's journal came back to her about the absurd pink nursery blinds Robert Marsten had painted for their new baby girl.

Despair dissipated as quickly as it mustered. With a prayer dart of gratitude, Jenna closed her eyes, enveloped in the warmth of God's unexpected and sweet reassurance.

Five

A LOUD WHISTLE PENETRATED THE FOG OF JENNA'S EXHAUSTION, drawing her into wakefulness with a jerk. She bolted upright in bed, staring at her strange surroundings while trying to make sense of the noise. It was more of a horn sound, like that from a steam ship in a black and white film. A glance out the open window revealed no sign of ensuing activity. Instead Jenna saw a tranquil garden setting, beautifully laid out and maintained. A gorgeous trellis of roses marked the entrance to the courtyard from an open space beyond. The ones she'd seen when Adam brought her inside? Before she had the chance to get her bearings, there was a knock on her door.

"Yes?"

The door opened, admitting a grinning Tilda. "Buenas tardes, Señorita Jenna—"

"Just Jenna, please."

"Jenna, it will be then. Did you sleep good, Jenna?"

"Like a log. What time is it?"

Tilda shrugged. "Time to get up! That is your papa's boat coming to the dock on the river."

Jenna's pulse flipped into high gear. She glanced at the mirror on a closet door. She was a sight, painted with calamine and her clothing wrinkled beyond description. As for her hair, its clip dangled uselessly from a disheveled mess.

"I have already unpacked your cases." The housekeeper pulled open the closet door to show Jenna her clothing. They hung like new, freshly pressed on hangers. "I hope you don't mind. Such pretty things for a pretty señorita!"

"Thank you, Tilda. I appreciate your help. I wasn't certain my bags would even arrive intact."

Jenna recalled the canteen-tipping captain with no teeth and breath strong enough to knock one over. She was also glad Adam would have no further reason to blame her for the disruption of life as he knew it; for if her bags had arrived, so had his precious cargo.

"Where is the bathroom? I'd like to take a shower and get the grime from our trip off." She'd have preferred to shower *before* sleeping, but she'd just been too exhausted.

"But of course you do, chica! Sometimes I think our Adam has been in the jungle so long that he forgets those who are not as, how do you say? at *home* here." Tilda gathered up a set of towels from the bench of a mahogany dressing table. "Come, señorita. I will show you to the bathroom. Ours is *inside* the house!" This was clearly a novelty, judging from the housekeeper's uncommon pride. "Dr. Adam had it built inside for his bride, rest her soul."

The woman made a cross and dashed into the hall. For such a round bundle of pleasantness, Tilda could move with the speed of a sprite.

"What happened to her?"

And could stop just as quickly. Jenna checked her step before running into the housekeeper.

"*Aquí!* Here you are! The other houses in the compound share a shower house, but la señora, she is hateful of everything here."

The shrug was definitely an art form with as many interpretations as needed. Tilda's exaggerated toss of her shoulders ended the conversation but also expressed her confusion as to what could have been wrong with Adam DeSanto's late wife.

Left to her own devices in the large tiled room, complete with windows that opened onto the roof, Jenna shed her travel-filthy clothes in short order. There was a Jacuzzi in the center of the room, large enough for two, but she left that and the curious thoughts it provoked regarding the DeSantos alone. She elected to use the separate shower instead.

It was no less elegant and out of place in the primitive surroundings. Glass blocks filled the series of tiled arches that made up the walls. No chance of any elbow bumping here, Jenna thought, taking up a bar of soap from a ceramic shelf built in at eye level. The spicy scent was decidedly masculine. Adam DeSanto, she wondered, or Robert Marsten?

She savored it for a moment and tucked its memory away with the thoughtfulness of the pink shades before returning it unused to its place. Making a mental note to bring her own next time, she made do with the unisex shampoo for both hair and body wash and let the steamy cascade of water beat the tension and weariness out of her body.

It wasn't until she stepped out of the shower, now wide awake and totally renewed, that she realized she'd followed Tilda like an absentminded lamb, leaving her robe and clean underwear behind. As she towel dried off, however, a large French terry bathrobe caught her eye. It hung on the back of a door she'd not noticed at first.

"Just what the doctor ordered!"

Snickering at her own pun, Jenna slipped into the robe, which dragged on the floor as she padded over to the sink to make some semblance of order out of the spiked tangle of her wet hair. It crossed her mind that a body could literally dance in the spaciousness, and she gave into the whimsy, swinging the dragging hem of the robe around her ankles to a flamenco beat. *Dadat, dat, da!*

Knock-knock, knock, knock!

Her hands still together, Jenna spun on the spot.

With the terry wrapping around the full length of her legs, she stared at the door where only moments ago the voluminous robe had hung. Bewildered, she opened it to see a smirking Adam DeSanto.

"I see you are feeling much better, señorita."

"I thought this was a closet!"

Adam stepped back and made a sweeping gesture toward the adjoining room where a king-size bed with a large fan-shaped headboard of intricately woven palm and bamboo dominated the far wall.

"Is *that* yours?" Jenna bit her bottom lip, her blurted words not at all what she intended to say. Heat shot to her face. "I mean, is this house yours? I mean, why am I here? That is to say, I came to visit my father and…"

"Ah, ah, ah!"

This time she seized her tongue between her teeth before it made a total fool of her. She knew what she meant to say. It just wasn't coming out coherently!

"This, señorita, is *our* home. Dr. Marsten and I share it." Adam gave her a head-to-toe sweep with his gaze. "As it seems, you and I are sharing my robe."

"Oh, this!" Jenna clasped it closer to her, as if that might return some semblance of dignity to her situation. "I'm sorry. I didn't see my carry-on, so I made do with what I could find. I'll get it back to you as soon as possible!"

At the curious cock of Adam's head, she turned and gathered up her soiled clothes for a hasty exit. At the main door to the hall she looked over her shoulder and froze to see her companion standing behind her, holding out her discarded lingerie between his forefinger and thumb.

"I believe you forgot *this.*"

Indignation flushed in scarlet contrast to the pure white of Jenna's borrowed garment. With a dignified toss of her head, she snatched it to her.

"It doesn't bite, for heaven's sake!"

"No."

Her companion bit the insides of his cheeks with his teeth, simultaneously sucking them in, but it was hard to say if it was humor or disdain threatening to rob her of her last shred of poise.

"Although," he said, cupping his chin in a philosophical pose, "I have heard that the species who wears them have been known to on occasion."

With a sarcastic lift of her upper lip, Jenna tugged the hem of her robe out of the way of the closing door and sought the familiar haven of the guest room.

Her carryall sat on the woven straps of a hand-carved luggage rack at the foot of her bed. Relieved to have her essentials at hand, Jenna unzipped the bag and finished unpacking her things before choosing a dress for the evening. It was simple, yet classic in design—a white embroidered eyelet, sleeveless and belted, with a full skirt. She'd bought it for a summer dance at the country club.

By the time she'd blown her hair dry and applied a few touches of makeup for accent, she actually felt civilized again and ready to meet the world, or at least one particular doctor. Dutifully, Jenna finished the last of her juice, which had evidently been brought in along with the carryall while she was in the shower. Standing before her in the mirror was the image of a self-possessed young woman—tall, slender, and graceful in picture-perfect form, but inside was an altogether different story.

Closing her eyes, Jenna once again sought God's embrace, His strength to face the moment she'd come all this way for. Three days ago, she'd been prepared. At least, she *thought* she'd been. But, not for the first time in her life, her timing and God's timing were not coinciding. Her well-rehearsed opening speech had somehow been lost somewhere in the jungle between Ichitas and Santa Beliza.

She couldn't even think what to call him! Papa? Father? She would ask him what he preferred. Surely he was as nervous as she was, probably wondering the same silly questions.

A tap on the door gave Jenna a start. She turned and swallowed her heart.

"Yes?"

"Señorita, your papa, he is waiting on the veranda when you are ready."

Jenna forcibly exhaled to relax the constricting muscles in her chest. Ready or not, this was the moment of truth. *Father, help me accept whatever lies head, be it acceptance or rejection. I'm so scared.*

"I'm ready now, Tilda, if you'll show me the way." *You too, Lord.*

The hacienda was built around a garden on three sides. About the inner perimeter was open covered passage that allowed access to all the rooms. It was the same courtyard Jenna had seen from the bathroom window, with luxurious beds of red, orange, pink, and yellow flowers, nested in unparalleled greenery. Across the front rooms on the outside was the veranda she'd seen earlier that day. Tilda motioned for her to walk through the formal dining room, where a table had been set for three, to a screened and louvered door beyond it.

"I will call you for dinner when it is ready," the housekeeper announced, swishing her hand as if to shoo a worrisome child on her way. "You go. You and your papa, you wait long time for this."

It helped to know she wasn't the only one who'd waited. Jenna wanted to hug the friendly housekeeper. Instead, she braced her shoulders and stepped through the door into the bright light of the setting sun. A man rose into her line of vision, not much more than a shadow at first, and adjusted the louvered blinds so that the glare was cast downward on the planking.

No longer having to squint and shade her eyes, Jenna could see now. He was slightly taller than she, with thinning reddish gold hair, heavily salted at the temples.

With charm school composure, Jenna stepped forward and extended her hand. "Hello. I'm Jenna Marsten." Somehow she'd thought her first words to her father would not be so...so formal and polite.

The man, no more at ease than she, clasped Jenna's hand between his own and stood there, squeezing it and staring at her in a mixture of wonder and delight. "So you are! So you are!"

A glaze formed over his eyes. They were blue. The light might be diminished in the room, but Jenna had memorized them from the picture she'd kept in her bedroom for as long as she could remember. Whatever form of speechlessness infected him worked its way with her too, despite the tide of a thousand words, a thousand questions building within.

"I've been practicing—"

"I practiced—"

They spoke and broke off at the same time. And then they laughed. It wasn't one of open amusement, but one of relief.

Suddenly, the invisible barrier that kept them at arm's length dissipated, and they were engulfed in each other's fervent embrace. They held to each other, making up for a lifetime of missed hugs and father-daughter talks. All the words Jenna had wanted to say were expressed so eloquently in the potent heart-to-heart of souls that none were needed.

She felt like a changeling, part little girl, part woman, growing up from one to the other in the span of her father's strong embrace. He was real, warm flesh and blood, not some picture she dreamed about. He lived and breathed, strong as she'd always imagined, yet possessing a tenderness that belied his work-hardened, tanned body.

He smelled of fresh air and the soap she'd found in the shower. Her head nestled on his shoulder, Jenna didn't want to give him up, nor it seemed, did he want to end the poignant exchange of a lifetime of longing.

"God is truly merciful, child," he whispered against her hair. "He's given me a second chance. I can only pray you'll do the same."

Her father heaved a breath, shaken with emotion. Shocked at the depth of his words, Jenna lifted her head and stared up into his face. Emotion amplified the blue of his eyes as well as his feelings. The lines of his face, engraved by time and compassion, relaxed as she traced them with her fingers. They hadn't been on her picture, and she wanted to remember every detail of this meeting. The dashing, aristocratic features her mother wrote of in her journals were still there, just enhanced by time and character.

"It's why I came," she said at last. "God has a way of turning disappointment into opportunity."

Her words sounded good. She believed in them. Yet from out of nowhere, a terrible anguish twisted Jenna, inside and out. It was as if her broken engagement to Scott Pierson finally registered. What she'd glibly put aside as a postponement rather than a rejection slapped her in the face; the raw hurt of it suddenly exposed by an insecurity she'd nearly convinced herself didn't exist.

"I thought you didn't want me, and now Scott—oh, Daddy!"

The endearment came out in a sob, distorted with

pain, yet somehow liberating. Her uncle and aunt brought her up in the center of a world filled with love. Rejection was something Jenna had never faced until the last few weeks. Then suddenly her fiancé, the young man who'd fit perfectly into her carefully arranged world, decided he didn't want it or her.

As if she'd been schooled for that as well, Jenna methodically proceeded to take apart the wedding plans as efficiently as they'd been put together. Calls were made. Condolences were accepted with a photographic smile. She thought she'd been brave, philosophical at the least. Had fear of a second rejection in such a short time pushed her over the edge?

Who was this full-grown woman crying like a baby in a stranger's arms? Jenna didn't know the stranger. She didn't recognize this boiling pot of emotion. It wasn't her, Miss Take-It-All-in-Stride. Or was it?

Confused, Jenna pulled away.

"I...I'm sorry! I don't know what's wrong with me!"

"You're hurt, Jenna. Though it wasn't my intention, I hurt you. And now, the only other man you've allowed into your heart has done the same. If you hadn't become emotional, I would be more concerned."

Dr. Robert Marsten reached into his pocket and withdrew a clean, pressed handkerchief. Gently, he dabbed at Jenna's wet cheeks.

"Violet is beside herself with concern."

"Aunt Vi?" Jenna sniffed, more perplexed than ever. "You've spoken to her?"

"She called via wireless, beside herself over your coming to the Amazon in your present mental state."

At her continued bewilderment, the man motioned for Jenna to sit down. "She felt you took your broken engagement a little too easily...said you were walking around like a programmed doll, canceling this, returning that, gracious to a fault. You were so remote, it frightened her. Then you found my wedding present, and I quote, *went over the deep end,* unquote."

Jenna laughed, fully able to hear the drama in Aunt Vi's voice.

"Well, I'm beginning to think she's right. I really knew my faith would see me through. Mama's verse—the one in her journals—it was like she and God were assuring me, even if at times it didn't *feel* like it."

"That's pretty common, unfortunately; especially if our perception of things working out and God's aren't necessarily the same. You learn that quickly down here. 'The best laid schemes o' mice and men gang aft a-gley'... well, mine went astray for sure. I'd hoped to meet you myself, but a baby got himself turned around the wrong way in the womb and needed a guiding hand."

Her father poured her a drink in a tall glass from a colorful matching pitcher.

"Tilda's own concoction," he told her, handing it over. "Since Adam bought her a new juicer, she's become queen of the fruit punch."

"She seems a gem."

"So long as we give her her way and remember that

106

she always knows best." Robert grinned, betraying his fondness for the housekeeper. "She practically raised Adam." Suddenly he sobered. "Perhaps if I'd had a Tilda for you, things might have been different. Your mother and I were living in one of the huts out back when you were born, and the outpost was primitive at best."

"Uncle Benjamin and Aunt Violet were good parents. You couldn't have chosen better guardians, I suppose." Jenna meant her words to soothe the graze of pain that deepened the lines of her father's face.

"But you want to know why I never bothered to contact you in all these years?"

Jenna nodded. Aunt Violet had given her so much background information, infused with opinion, that Jenna'd been lost in the diatribe. Dr. Marsten cut to the chase.

"I made a deal with the devil." He laughed at the surprised lift of Jenna's brow. "I needn't tell you that Violet Winston and I were not the best of friends; although I rather think she'd say it was *she* who made the deal with me as the devil."

"What kind of deal?" Her aunt said nothing of a deal.

"Bear in mind, Violet could have no children. She'd taken care of you when Diana visited her shortly after your birth and was caring for you when your mother was killed in the crash. She feared I might at some future point try to take you away, like I had your mother. Part of the agreement was that I was never to contact you, that as far as you were concerned, *both* your parents died in that crash."

Taken back in time, he sighed, as though his regret pulled breath from him. "I thought at the time that I'd done the best thing for you. What did I know about raising a little girl? I'd started the wheels working for opening the clinic. Others were involved; money was invested. I saw no other way." He sighed, as if the decision still weighed on his mind, and then shifted his gaze to Jenna. "Looking at the lovely young woman you've become, I am convinced I did the right thing for everyone concerned."

"Not exactly the picture Aunt Violet presented to me," Jenna reflected with a scowl. *How can you want to meet the man who chose his work over his own child?*

"Hah! I can imagine. But bear in mind, I'd already taken her baby sister away from her. Now I was in a position to take away the baby she'd become so attached to. Diana had decided to personally see through a windfall delivery of medical supplies she'd wangled out of the local hospital during her visit to Boston. She could raise money from a dry plank."

Robert eased into an upholstered bamboo chair next to Jenna and covered her hand with his own as the story of her past unfolded.

"Anyway, you had to wait for additional shots, so Diana was going to fly back for you, and…well, you know the rest. Violet blamed me for your mother's death. Not that she needed to. I blamed myself enough for the two of us. But she was grieving and afraid. She still is. I don't hold it against her and neither should you. Fear can make us do things we'd not ordinarily think of doing."

Maybe. Jenna teetered between anger at her aunt and the sympathy her father championed. The very mention of excerpts from Diana Marsten's journals would make Aunt Vi shudder. If Jenna hadn't discovered them one afternoon while playing dress up with a friend in the attic, where her mother's few belongings had been stored after her death, Jenna never would have gotten to really know the woman who was her mother.

Her father rested a moment in the recollection before shaking himself from the retrospection enveloping them both. "Save only good memories for the past, Jenna. The space in our minds is too precious to clutter it with bad ones." With a quick wink, he got up, as if that were the end of it. His eyes twinkled, all sign of the spirit-dampening subject banished. "Let me show you something."

With that, he disappeared into the house, leaving Jenna to her thoughts. Much as she regretted it, her father had made a logical decision; one that made sense to the head, if not the heart. Single fathers raised children today...but that was today, not twenty-odd years ago.

When her father returned, he carried two large scrapbooks. He spread one open on the table. There on the first page was her birth announcement, along with a few faded Polaroid pictures of a pink homecoming.

"Except for the hairstyle, you could be Diana."

Jenna warmed beneath her father's appraisal. "Except for a few missing hairs, that could still be you."

He ran his fingers through the thinning top of his head. "You have your mother's ready sense of humor too. She could find something bright to say about the worst possible circumstances. She lived by that Scripture. Those first few visits down here, we had lots to despair and distress over."

Yellowed newspaper announcements of this or that award for volunteer service or outstanding achievement, pictures and clippings of a Brownie troop selling cookies, favorite pets of bygone days—Jenna's growth from infancy to adulthood was portrayed throughout the pages.

"Violet never failed to send me any news of your achievements. I have to give her credit for that."

Jenna stared at the picture from her senior prom. She sat on a paper moon swing in front of Scott Pierson. Like the old saying went, Looks good on paper. She really hadn't dated anyone else, at least not seriously.

"Why did you break the agreement and send that little man?" she asked, steering away from that painful train of thought.

"You were getting married, and…what can I say, I was struck by a sentimental notion." He gave her a sheepish look. "Your mother helped me deliver the first caesarean baby here at the clinic. There was no light, save flashlights and kerosene, but the baby wouldn't wait for ideal operating conditions. Diana held the mother's hand and talked her through, soothing her in English and broken Spanish until it was over and mother and child were stable. She was like an angel."

Again the doctor drifted to another place, his eyes sparkling at what he saw.

"Anyway…" He cleared his throat. "The happy father carved the little man out of stone from the altar of an ancient mission and gave it to us as payment. He believed God had sent us to help his people again, as the original missionaries had come to protect their ancestors from the gold seekers. Most people hang their first dollar on the wall. I kept that statue on a shelf instead. Your mother treasured it."

"That would explain the mystery of the base markings being so old yet the carving relatively new. I had it analyzed at the museum," Jenna explained. "I mean, there was no card, no explanation."

"I shouldn't have sent it. I just couldn't get you off my mind, and this time, I caved in."

Jenna leaned over and gave her father a hug. "Well, I'm glad you did. I think coming here is just what the doctor ordered, no pun intended."

She meant every word. It had all been a part of God's wonderful plan, even if it hadn't seemed so wonderful at the time. Her fretting was her weakness; worrying about tomorrow was a wasted effort when it was already in good hands.

"Only if you've come here running *toward* something, not away from it." He studied her warily. Not that Jenna could blame him. She'd already proven herself a walking volcano of emotion.

"See this glass?" Jenna held up her drink, taking up her father's challenge. "It's half *full*...kind of like me. I don't know where the other half is yet, but I'm going to find it."

"Then here's to finding the other half!" Robert Marsten touched his glass to hers in toast.

"Here, here!"

"Something is missing?"

Adam DeSanto stood in the open screen doorway with a bemused expression.

"Unless, that is," he added quickly upon realizing he'd intruded, "it is nothing I need to know. My apologies." He inhaled sharply and glanced inside the house, as if looking for an escape from his blunder. "Ah...dinner is served."

Six

Adam waited inside the dining room at the end of the polished mahogany table, where one of the place settings had been pulled from the cozier grouping of three Jenna had seen earlier. She took the one next to her father, feeling at least *half* welcome. Why did it matter to Adam DeSanto whether she existed or not?

"Speaking of halves," Robert Marsten said, "Adam is my other half. He is my partner in the clinic. Actually, his father and I founded Santa Beliza. Adam took over after attending medical school in the States. Graduated from Hopkins with honors."

"Really!"

Jenna looked at the tall, dark-eyed doctor who acted as if his off-white linen trousers and open collared dress shirt were constricting him. The reputation of Johns Hopkins and Adam DeSanto just didn't seem to fit together. Unless he was like a chameleon, which managed to blend in with various settings whether he was at home there or not.

"He has a gift for understatement," her father remarked, tongue in cheek.

That explained her father and Adam sharing the house. Piece by piece, the brooding doctor was coming together. He was born and raised at Santa Beliza with a native nanny. He was a widower. Maybe he was just lost in grief.

"It is not so much that, señorita, as it is that I only speak when I have something to say. I do not rattle on like the soundtrack of a nature video." He mimicked a female voice. "Oh, look…a wild ginger…and there's a philodendron. Have you ever seen such intense color? Did you see that red macaw? Pictures just don't do them justice."

Jenna threw up her shoulders in her own imitation. "Ah, I was impressed not just by the beauty, but that I recognized some of the things from the guidebook I read on the way down. What can I say!"

"What is *this*?"

Tilda burst into the room with a platter of fried plantains, drilling Adam with her dark eyes. She put it down and, with an authority Jenna sensed only she possessed, dragged the place mat with Adam's setting to its original site on Robert Marsten's left, opposite Jenna.

"This is no formal table, Adam DeSanto! I will not run my legs from one end to the other to indulge your bad manners. You are all family, no?"

"Not exactly, Tilda."

Despite his wry protest, Adam followed. He sat opposite Jenna and raked his fingers through his wet, freshly showered hair. He'd shaved too, leaving his black sideburns just the perfect length to compliment the taper of his jaw. All in all the improvement was remarkable—a clean-cut Don Juan without the charm, but oh, those eyelashes!

"Nearly thirty and she treats me like I'm three," he muttered under his breath.

"I heard that!" Tilda shouted over her shoulder on the way out to fetch the rest of dinner.

"I think it's sweet." Jenna met Adam's dull stare with a grin. She definitely liked Tilda.

"Tilda keeps the peace around here. At least, that's what she tell us," her father observed to no one in particular.

Undaunted by Jenna's obvious satisfaction, Adam switched to another topic. "It was slow in the clinic, so I started laying aside the supplies for the trip upriver this afternoon."

"How short are we?"

Adam shrugged. "Not so bad as I thought. At least we have enough disposable needles and vaccines. I would like to have more antibiotics, but that would cut us short here."

"We're making our annual venture to the interior next week," Robert explained to Jenna. "The Black Lake tribes keep pretty much to themselves. They only bring someone here as a last resort."

"And by then, it is usually too late to help them. Their jungle medicine is pretty effective, if somewhat peculiar to Western standards." Adam exchanged a knowing glance with her father, as though they shared some secret humor. "But we do try preventive medicine and show them better hygiene."

"Are you up to a real adventure inland?"

Adam stared at his partner, incredulous. "*She* is going with us?"

"It's what I came for." Jenna informed him in kind. She reached over and squeezed her father's arm. "I'm looking for the other half."

"Of your mind, perhaps?" Realizing he breached the line of hospitality, the junior doctor changed course. "There are all manner of dangers...parasites, for instance. She gets bit by the wrong bug or eats the wrong fruit..." He finished with the all-inclusive shrug.

"I have insect repellent and I always watch what I eat."

"She doesn't know to drink enough water."

"Learned the hard way."

"Is there something you two aren't telling me?" Robert Marsten sat back in his chair, waiting.

Adam locked gazes with Jenna across the table. It felt like she had the proverbial bull by the horns, and to her astonishment, there was something about the challenge that she found more exciting than frightening.

"What is there to tell? Jenna is softened by her life in Boston, unaccustomed to the rigors of the jungle. You *know*, Robert, that I know of what I say. You know what happened to Marina."

The fierceness of the beast behind Adam's dark gaze nearly took Jenna's breath away. Gooseflesh rose on her arm. Marina? His wife?

"That could have happened to anyone, native or stranger."

"But it happened to *her*, the stranger, did it not?" Adam rose, leaning into the table, fists drawn.

"Besides, I got badges in wilderness camp," Jenna piped up brightly. "Shoot, I even took shop in school...made a hammer with screwdrivers hidden in its handle!"

"Good for you." Her father beamed proudly.

Adam was not nearly as impressed as her father.

"This is not a Girl Scout camp, señorita."

"Nor is it the den of darkness you portray, Adam. If I didn't know better, I'd swear you were trying to frighten Jenna away."

Adam's mouth fell open as if he'd been smacked. The muscles in his clean-shaven jaw practically snapped as he closed it and sat down.

"You have my apologies, Jenna. It was not my intention to..." He drew a deep breath, searching for the right words. "My wife died in the jungle. Perhaps I am just overreacting."

"I understand, Adam."

Jenna had an uncommon urge to get up and hug the man, yet the smoldering emotion just barely under control warned her it could do more harm than good at this point. *So much anger, Lord.*

"And I intend to listen to you and my father. I know you'll help me adjust just fine."

Although she meant her words to soothe him, a glimmer of panic grazed his eyes for just a second, then it was gone.

At that moment, Tilda reappeared with a glazed pork roast, beaming as she placed it on the table. It glistened in the light of the tiered candelabra hanging overhead. Surrounded by colorful yams and pineapples, it looked as though it belonged on a gourmet magazine cover.

"Oh, Tilda, it's too pretty to eat!" Jenna's stomach growled loudly in direct disagreement with her words, and the housekeeper laughed.

"Listen to your belly. It knows better than you, no?" Tilda handed a silver carving set to her father.

"Tilda worked with embassy cooks in Lima while Adam was away at school," he informed Jenna. "And Adam's mom was a bit of a gourmet cook as well."

It was hard to think of Adam as a boy. Men with an attitude like his seemed to have come into the world full grown, already hardened by life.

"After his father passed away, Tilda came back to the compound."

"Well, how could I leave his mama, a widow and all

118

alone, with no woman to confide in?" the housekeeper exclaimed.

"And I thought it was missing me that brought you back."

"Ah, listen to that man!" Tilda laughed. Despite her teasing, there was no doubting the affection in her gaze for the senior doctor. "Me, I was hoping that you and Adam's mama might—"

"Elizabeth was never in love with anyone but her Martín, like me with Diana."

"Still, it would have been nice," Tilda said dreamily. "Then these two could be brother and sister and—"

"It would also have been nice if Tilda was born with the ability to mind her own business," Adam injected, stopping that direction of conversation in its track.

The housekeeper was quick to catch up. "And if *you* were born with manners instead of good looks!"

Jenna was no less eager to shift to another subject than her brooding host. "So tell me about Adam's folks."

"Elizabeth was a New England schoolteacher," Robert said. "She came here on a mission trip, met Martín DeSanto, and never wanted to leave. They had this house here and one in Lima. Martín was the diplomat of the two of us, so he took care of getting all the clearances and keeping us in good grace with the government."

"So you grew up here *and* in Lima?" Jenna asked Adam.

"And occasional summers on Cape Cod with my

maternal grandparents." Adam relaxed again with the change of topic. Perhaps it took him back to happier days.

"It's a wonder we didn't meet. I lived there in the summer too!"

"I kept pretty much to myself and the boat."

"You like yachting?" It was hard to picture the jungle doc kicked back at the helm of a sailboat. Somehow, a machete belonged in his hand more than a boat's wheel.

"Canoeing is more to my liking. The jungle is in my blood."

"And steaming upriver is in mine," Robert chimed in. "We've converted a rebuilt steamboat into a hospital ship. She'll do ten knots on a good day."

"*Down*river," Adam teased. He helped himself to the plantains and then passed them across to Jenna with a devastating boyish flash of teeth. "He is the Amazon's own Steamboat Willie."

Whether it was the good food or the civilized setting, Adam DeSanto thawed as dinner progressed. When the conversation gravitated back to the upcoming river trip, he seemed reconciled to Jenna's inclusion. Past that, he became animated.

"It's the time of year when the eligible boys go through their initiation into manhood."

"A good time is had by all, even the boys," her father injected.

Jenna was afraid to ask just what the initiation was. Her imagination was as vivid as the nature shows she'd seen on television.

By the time they finished a light hazelnut brûlée, a concoction Tilda learned to make from a French chef, Jenna felt a contentment she'd not known for months.

Maybe even never, she thought happily, slipping between the fresh scented sheets of her bed that night. She wasn't sure when the housekeeper had remade the bed, but Tilda was everywhere in the house at once, anticipating needs before they were realized by those she served. Milk and delicious macadamia nut cookies were waiting on the table by Jenna's bed when she retired from an after-dinner interlude with her father.

While Adam did the rounds at the clinic, they talked as though to make up for a lifetime of missed conversations until the compound generators were cut off at midnight. Robert was like a favorite uncle to Adam, and then a father after Martín's death. He was the mentor who encouraged the young man through the grueling years of medical school. He spoke of Adam with a pride Jenna envied.

Heavens, she was jealous! The revelation brought her upright in bed. Despite all the earlier banter, could this be sibling rivalry? After all, Jenna had never had a brother or sister to vie for her aunt and uncle's attention.

Nah. She fell back against the pillow, dismissing the absurd idea. She envied the longevity of Adam and Robert's relationship, but no matter what, she could never think of Adam DeSanto as a brother!

Morning broke with the smell of fresh coffee blending in the wafting air with the fragrance of flowers in the courtyard. The birds welcomed the sun, which was peeping over the perimeter of trees as slowly as Jenna moved. Sleepily, she kicked off her morning prayers, thanking God for another day. Then there was her wonderful reunion with Dr. Robert Marsten, her *father*. He was everything she thought he'd be and more. She couldn't wait to read the journals he, too, had kept over the years, despite his insistence that her mother had had the way with words and not he.

She'd heard of people running off to "find themselves," but she never really grasped what that meant until now. She wondered how they knew they weren't themselves or weren't just, as she'd always thought of herself, hard to please. And how did one know where to look for his or her missing person?

After pulling on a pair of shorts and a coordinated T-shirt, she made her way to the kitchen by means of the arched passage skirting the courtyard. A fountain with three angels back to back trickled in the center. Tilda was nowhere in sight, despite the steaming coffee meaning that someone had been to the kitchen earlier.

Jenna helped herself to a cup and checked the dining room and veranda to see if her father was about. But he'd either already left for the clinic or was still in bed. Not quite ready to venture out into the medical compound alone, she chose the courtyard and found a nook with a concrete table and benches, almost enclosed by a trellis wall of bougainvillea. She didn't know about the rest of the jungle, but surely Eden wasn't much prettier or more serene.

Adam, however, could use some work. The corner of her mouth quirked as she inhaled the rich aroma of the black coffee. It penetrated her nostrils, clearing the steam hovering over the brim of the cup and the muddle of her wandering thoughts. In the distance through the open gate, the devilishly good-looking jungle doctor came striding toward her…or the courtyard itself. She was partially hidden in the alcove of waxen leafed, red-spiked blossoms, and he hadn't noticed her yet.

"Hey, you. Wait up! You wanna run my legs off?"

Jenna recognized the little boy she'd seen but briefly the day before, scampering after the long-limbed doctor. Adam stopped and laughed as the child ran headlong into him and latched on to his thigh.

"Ah, I have picked up a sloth!"

The little boy cackled, being dragged along as if the doctor didn't really know what was impairing his progress.

"A sloth who is going to be late for school!"

"Don't you want to see my homework?"

"So you have decided to apply yourself again, eh?"

"If it is wrong, I will tell la señora that it is on Dr. Adam's head!"

With an outraged growl, Adam collapsed in the dirt, drawing the boy down with him. Whether it was a wrestling or tickling match, Jenna couldn't exactly tell. All she knew was there was lots of laughing amid masculine grunts of aggression. Suddenly the little boy rolled away and threw himself atop Adam's back, wrapping his slender brown arms about the doctor's neck. Adam bucked and growled, but the kid held on for all he was worth, squealing with glee the entire time. Off to the side lay a scatter of what Jenna assumed was the boy's schoolwork.

Now she knew the reason her father said Dr. Adam DeSanto was so gifted in pediatrics. Adam was an overgrown boy himself.

"Aye, Pepito, *oncle!*"

Pepito giggled. "I give you a nubbin' on the head, you loco horse!"

Adam winced and climbed to his feet, forcing the child to use both hands to hold on, rather than perform a lobotomy with his knuckle. Pepito swung from the man's neck until his strength gave way and he dropped to his feet.

"Now, pick up your papers while they are still fit for your teacher to see."

Adam brushed the red-brown dirt off his formerly white scrubs. Pepito, folding his schoolwork under one arm, did the same with the other.

Enchanted by this charming side of the jungle doctor, Jenna leaned forward on her elbows, when her dreamy state was interrupted by the sudden appearance of a scrawny monkey with a white-tufted head and bright beady eyes. It dropped onto the table in front of her. The scream she swallowed sounded more like a yelp. Frozen, she watched the monkey skip about the table, chattering noisily.

"Ah! A stranger lurking in the garden! Nothing escapes Rita."

Adam put out his arm for the creature to vault up to his shoulder.

"She is our *huachiman*. That is Spanglish for watchman. Just a marmoset...perfectly harmless. Although," he admitted grievously, "very loud for her size. You are up early, señorita."

"When in Rome," Jenna managed, forcing the tremor from her voice.

"Pepito, tell Tilda we will breakfast here and that Jenna is with us."

Adam slid onto the bench across from Jenna.

"You do math, Jenna?" Pepito slapped the folder with his smudged homework in it.

Jenna drew her gaze from the mischievous marmoset, which now contented itself with digging through the dark mass of Adam's hair with tiny fingers.

"It's not my best subject."

"I will check your numbers. Now go! Vámanos."

Pepito darted off toward the house, exciting Rita, who promptly leaped after him. The marmoset caught up just in time to miss the door slamming on her tail. The way she chattered, however, one would have thought it *had* caught her.

"Ai, you get that nasty ape out of my kitchen!" Tilda exclaimed from inside.

"She's a marmoset, Tilda."

"Monkey, marmoset, chimp, they are all apes, and I will not have those animals in my kitchen!"

The door opened and Rita was tossed unceremoniously through. She landed easily on her feet and shrieked at the door in all her minifury.

"I get you a treat, Rita." Pepito consoled from the other side of the screen.

"All bark, no bite."

Jenna glanced at Adam. "Promise?"

"I promise…within reason," he stipulated. "You mustn't pull her tail or hurt her, just as you wouldn't do the same to a dog or a cat without risking retaliation."

"Of course not!"

As if she'd understood Pepito, Rita resorted to a quiet swinging pace by the kitchen door.

"She *is* cute."

"When she was a baby, she was no bigger…well, she and her sister would have fit in your cup. Alas, like Pepito, she became an orphan, another one your father took in."

It was ironic that while she lived without him, her father took so many children, both human and animal, under his wing. Was he trying to fill a void that giving her up left in his life? Jenna preferred to think so.

"So what happened?" she asked. The idea warmed her as much as she'd often imagined a fatherly hug might.

"Her mother became a meal for a jungle cat. Robert and I brought the babies inside the compound, but one died. Rita was a fighter."

"I meant to Pepito's family."

For a moment, it crossed Jenna's mind that there was more than friendship between Adam and the boy, that perhaps Adam and Marina DeSanto had had a child or…well, it wouldn't be unheard of for a man like the jungle doctor to have fathered a child by an Indian woman.

"Pneumonia killed both parents. His father worked here at the generating plant. Robert and I promised to see that the boy was properly schooled. He lives with cousins at the riverside village."

"And Rita?"

Adam smiled, a burst of white teeth against his sun-darkened complexion.

"Rita lives here in the compound; although she sometimes visits with Pepito's cousin."

"She just runs loose?"

The idea that the pesky marmoset could literally drop in on her at any time wasn't the most reassuring thought.

"It is her nature to, no?"

The door opened and Pepito came out, carrying a cup of hot, black coffee. Over his arm was a folded towel.

"Aquí, Dr. Adam. And you, Señorita Jenna, may I get more for you as well?"

He gave Jenna a sweeping bow.

"I'm fine, Señor Pepito."

The boy bobbed up with a bright expression. "You *must* call me Pepito."

"Me gusto mucho, Pepito. And you must call me Jenna."

"Are you married?"

"Pepito!" Adam chided, shaking his head in warning.

The boy, however, was determined. "But Dr. Robert sent her the little stone man for a wedding present. You got to get married to get a wedding present, no?"

"It's fine, Adam," Jenna intervened before her companion took further action to stop the curious youngster. "I was going to get married, Pepito, but then I changed my mind and came down here instead."

"But what about your *novio*? Your wanna-be husband. Did he let you keep half the presents?"

"Pepito, that is none of our business."

"But what happened to the stone man?"

Jenna laughed. The boy was precious. "My aunt has it."

This was obviously enough food for Pepito's inquisitive mind to ponder for a while. He spun and started back toward the kitchen. Then stopping at the door, he called out, "So *she* is getting married now, your aunt?"

Jenna cut off Adam's protest. "No, she's just keeping it for me, for when I do get married."

He digested this in thoughtful appraisal, hand still on the knob of the screen.

"The boy gets eighteen words to the dozen when it comes to questions," Adam mumbled over the rim of his hot coffee before taking a careful sip.

"Then that would make Jenna one good catch, eh, Dr. Adam?"

Jenna caught her breath, stunned by Pepito's frank observation. Adam choked on the coffee he'd almost swallowed. Putting the cup on the table, he covered his mouth and nose. His eyes watered as he dabbed the dribble from his face with the hem of his loose-fitting shirt.

"*Perdoname,* señ—" He coughed, still strangled by a remnant tickle. Finally, he was able to manage a stabilizing breath without another spasm.

"My apologies for the boy. He sees too many American videos."

"Frankly, I think he's charming."

Adam was saved the effort of a reply when the door opened and Tilda came through carrying a tray of fresh-baked pastries and assorted sliced fruits. Pepito followed with a carafe of coffee and another of juice.

"What have I told you about letting your coffee cool before you drink?" Tilda exclaimed, noting the stains on Adam's shirt. "He is always in a hurry."

Adam got up and grabbed a pastry topped with a baked pineapple ring. "That is because I am a busy man." He bussed Tilda on the cheek. "My favorite! Gracias."

"But I only just…"

"Sit, Tilda. Make our guest feel comfortable."

"What about my homework?" Pepito reminded him.

Adam took up the papers. "I will check them over. Pick them up in my office when you are finished with breakfast. Tilda…"

"I know, he needs a good scrubbing." The housekeeper sniffed indignantly, calling after the man loping off toward the long thatched-roof building. "Like someone else I know."

Tilda sat down on the bench next to Jenna and gave her the next choice of the assorted breakfast breads.

"Humph!" she remarked. "One would think he spills his coffee on his shorts the way he runs away from here. What do *you* think?"

Jenna halted the roll halfway to her mouth, caught off guard by the expectant gaze fixed upon her. Her mind tumbled blankly. Able to think of no adequate reply, she resorted to the universal shrug and sunk her teeth into the delicious confection.

"Is Father already at the clinic?"

It was after seven according to Jenna's watch. Somehow she thought he would be up and about before daylight. At least those were the hours described in her mother's journals.

"Some days, Dr. Robert sleeps later, especially if there is extra excitement. He does not manage the strain so, since his heart flutters."

"Heart flutters?"

Alarm diffused the growing heat of the tropical day, running cold along Jenna's spine. Her father looked like a specimen of perfect health! How could he have a heart problem?

"Oh, Dr. Robert and Dr. Adam both says it is not serious!" Tilda added hastily upon seeing Jenna's worried look. "They say peoples live for years with these flutters. Dr. Robert, he *just* have to rest more than before."

The woman patted Jenna's arm with kindly reassurance.

"Our heavenly Father, He say not to worry, just to ask. So I have asked along with all the doctor's many friends. He is in the prayer list at all the missions and churches. Dr. Robert, he is in good hands, no? Not to say that Dr. Adam is the best doctor in the world next to him. Straight A's in his *escuela de medicó*. The best!"

Beaming with pride, Tilda helped herself to another of her delicious fruit breads. "An' handsome too, no?"

"Very," Jenna agreed.

"The *dueñas* in Lima, well, Dr. Adam is one of the few *elegible* mens who both the girls and their...um, how you say, like a nannies...they all think Dr. Adam is the cat's holler."

Jenna chuckled. "So how has he escaped them?"

"He hides in the jungle." Tilda grimaced in total disgust. "But he cannot hide from God, and I know that my God has plans for him. He is a gift with little ones, and one day I will have little Dr. Adams to care for." Stern expression gave way to a glowing smile at the thought.

"He is such a good boy, with a heart big as the jungle. God will mend it."

"Over the loss of his wife?"

"Sí, pobrecito."

"He must have loved her very much."

"He a'worship her…more than she deserve, but Dr. Adam, he do what the Bible say and love her as he love his Savior." With a heavy sigh, Tilda crossed herself. "I am sorry, Lord, but You know I y'am right."

Jenna bit her lower lip, uncertain as to how to reply, when her father came through the kitchen door carrying a steaming cup of coffee. He wore casual shorts and a loose-fitting cotton shirt. With pilot sunglasses, he looked quite the tourist rather than the jungle doctor.

"So, here are my girls!" He motioned around, his blue eyes dancing with life. "Have you ever seen a more glorious morning? God has certainly outdone Himself this day in my own little Eden."

Jenna checked the *not exactly* on the tip of her tongue. As she looked around at the verdant surroundings, bursting with the colors of an intense rainbow, she could find no fault. She was here with the father she'd always loved vicariously through her mother's writings, except now that love was becoming real. Overwhelmed by the answer to a lifelong prayer, she offered a heart walloping *Thank You, Lord!*

Seven

———∞∞∞———

"Actually, I'm retiring," her father said later as he and Jenna ambled toward the village, picnic basket in hand. "Adam is doing a great job at the clinic, and I'm on hand in case I'm needed. I'll just be down by the river instead of in my office."

"So you wouldn't consider going back to the States?"

Robert shook his head. "A visit on occasion is the best I can do. This is my life. I can hardly remember the times it wasn't."

"Hola, Doctor!"

A man wearing a Coca-Cola T-shirt and driving an ox-drawn cart loaded with bananas passed them, eyeing Jenna curiously.

"*Esta es mi hija.* My daughter."

"Aiyee, qué *bonita!*"

"Gracias," Jenna called back.

From what she'd seen to date, denim, cotton, and commercial T-shirts were definitely the mode of dress for the river people, with sneakers for footwear, if they wore any foot covering. The women looked more native in homespun dresses, but their best work was saved for the market. Faded colors and wear betrayed a poverty level their cheerful waves and smiling faces belied.

The words of a song about one is only poor if one chose to be certainly rang a little bit truer in Jenna's mind. She waved back and met each "buenos días" with her own heartfelt one. It *was* a good day.

The church and schoolhouse shared a giant dome-shaped structure called a *churuata*. Almost a hundred feet in diameter and fifty feet high, it boasted a bell outside the door for calling school children and the congregation as well, depending on the function of the hour.

As Jenna walked by, a small voice heralded her from the open shutters of the building. "Señorita Jenna! Doctor Robert!"

A closer look revealed a boy's face plastered against the screen.

"Looks like a prison, doesn't it?" Robert mumbled under his breath.

Jenna waved as a sharp voice from inside commanded the delinquent back to his seat.

"Busted." She chuckled. She wondered how Pepito did on the homework Adam checked.

There were dozens more greetings and introductions exchanged before Jenna and her father reached the river's edge. It was like being introduced at a big family reunion, where everyone had been waiting to meet a new member—her. The warmth of her welcome, however, gave way to astonishment, when she discovered the river was not at the same level as the village. Unlike in Ichitas, where one could walk off the bank onto a floating pier, a body had to climb straight down a ten-foot drop on a ladder to get to the water level.

"The water's on its way down," her father informed her. "The rainy season brings it up level with the bank and more, sometimes." He pointed to the buildings near the river's edge, all of which were built on stilts about three feet or so.

"I imagine it's a job getting the supplies up from the river when it's low like this."

"A man gets his exercise, that's for sure. But everyone pitches in—helps pay off their tabs at the clinic."

The night before, her father had explained how hard it was for the people of the Amazon to afford medical treatment. The clinic itself worked off donations and grants, all of which took valuable time away from the patients to pursue and prove the clinic's qualifications. Jenna was astonished to hear records were still kept by hand, and gathering statistics was too time consuming. Things went from bad to worse after Adam's mother died, for she'd taken care of the bulk of the administrative work.

"And there is my pride and joy…next to you, of course!"

Down the length of the floating dock was a ragged-looking boat. Again Jenna was reminded of the *African Queen,* with its shabby planked sides and wearing paint.

"She was a *colectivo,* a river taxi. The owner donated her to the clinic when he moved to the city with his daughter. Truth is, he couldn't sell her," Robert confided. "But his loss was our gain."

Jenna wasn't so sure.

Her father nimbly climbed down the ladder and dropped onto the pontoon deck below. "C'mon. I'll spot you."

The wooden ladder creaked and swayed under Jenna's weight, the rungs a little too far apart for comfort. She made it to the bottom, however, with little trouble, glad she'd switched from sandals to sneakers and socks. Always socks, her father warned her, lest jungle rot set in. She couldn't help but wonder if jungle rot smelled anything like Scott's athletic club bag—and he'd worn socks!

"Diesel fuel is scarcer the farther upriver we go, but this gem burns wood for fuel. The natives are more than willing to supply us along the way as pay for treatment, so their dignity is preserved and the clinic has its own floating supply house."

"Sounds like an equitable arrangement." One man's junk was another's treasure—or something like that.

"I rebuilt her engine; it took forever to get parts. The mail service down here leaves a lot to be desired."

"What about the Net? I know Scott had a circle of

antique car enthusiasts and suppliers on the Internet. He got parts and all sorts of ideas."

"You mean the computer Net?" Robert snorted, shaking his head. "This is the Amazon, Jenna. We're lucky to have a phone here at Santa Beliza. And that only works when the lines aren't down somewhere, which is more often than not."

"Where is the phone?"

"At the government station house." Her father pointed up on the bank to a concrete structure with a red-tiled roof slightly downriver. It was surrounded by a dozen or so mini-block houses, which, according to him, had been built by the Peruvian government to entice more Indians from the interior to the riverfront and civilization. It looked more like a culture scramble than a clash.

"What do they do at the government station?"

"Keep the peace when the cachaça is too plentiful...watch for pirates."

"Pirates?" Jenna paused on the dock before jumping across the short expanse of water onto the rear deck of the boat.

"*Bio*-pirates. They go in and illegally strip the jungle of medicinal plants, which they sell on the black market to companies that will use them for research, or more likely, make them into medicines, vitamins, etc."

"Now *there's* a different kind of drug trafficking."

"Fortunately, we don't have that kind of problem around here. Too far upriver, for now anyway. Besides, the natives have enough natural hallucinogens and fermented concoctions to suit their needs without going beyond their backyard."

"So drugs *are* a problem then?"

"Nah. I'd say the alcohol was worse. The narcotic use is more for rituals and medicine. So what do you think?"

Her father pointed around the deck, which, despite the fact that it needed a good finishing, was tidy. At least the back part was shipshape. All but the small tip of the bow and the stern deck was enclosed by a modern fiberglass canopy and flap. The whole was a meeting of old world and new.

"I chose the hard roof instead of canvas. Canvas doesn't last long down here in this sun," her father said, reading her mind.

Jenna avoided expressing her opinion, but Robert didn't notice.

"And look at this! This is what I've been working on. Adam is going to help me hang it this afternoon."

He pulled aside a piece of canvas lying over a bench, which also served as a storage locker. There were two nameplates, each with the letters carved into the wood itself and painted: *S. L. Jenna.*

"S. L.?"

"Steam Launch Jenna."

A blade of emotion rose from nowhere, pressing against Jenna's throat. Eyes stinging, she threw her arms around her father and hugged him. "I always wanted

138

something that blew hot air named after me!"

"Hah! It's going to cost you, though." Robert Marsten cleared his throat as she drew away.

"Oh?"

"I need an extra pair of hands to mount a new pump."

"Hey," she teased, "I've got to live up to my name. What's your order, captain?"

The engine and boiler were forward of the enclosed area but still under cover from the sun. Thankfully, once the side canvas was rolled and secured, a river breeze kept the air moving through. Jenna spent most of the time admiring the milk chocolate water rushing by, keeping a watchful eye out for alligators and/or snakes and enjoying her father's company. They spoke of everything except the one thing concerning her most—his health. She figured when he was ready, he'd tell her.

Occasionally she had to crawl down amidst twisted pipes and intimidating valves and hold a mounting plate or pass her father a tool from a lovely dovetailed box made by a patient in payment for an appendectomy. Not that either he or Adam professed to be surgeons. It was just that in times of emergency, they were the most qualified to do what had to be done. The boat ride to the Posta in Ichitas was nine hours, and that could mean the difference between life and death with an appendix about to rupture or a woman unable to deliver naturally.

At noon, Jenna washed her hands in the water as best she could and put out the picnic lunch Tilda had prepared for them. There were ham and cheese sandwiches, far too many for Jenna and her father to possibly consume, as well as fruit and a half dozen bottles of Inka Cola. One taste of the Peruvian soft drink made her shudder. Yellow and syrupy, it smacked of bubble gum flavor, sweetened even more with sugar. With a horrible grimace, Jenna returned her bottle to the basket.

"Agh! No can do!"

"It tastes better with rum, or so the gringos say." Adam DeSanto leapt into the boat from the dock and reached into the picnic pack for the bottle Jenna abandoned. "It requires adapting a taste, no?"

"A *lot* of adapting!" she agreed wholeheartedly.

"How's the new pump going?"

"Like clockwork. My assistant engineer is a lot easier to work with than you." Her father worked his way around the engine and boiler toward the stern where lunch was being served.

"With *her,* you work in the morning when it is bearable," Adam rallied. "With me, I lie in the bilge and baste like a Thanksgiving turkey in the worst heat of the day. If the turkey could talk, he would be irritable as well."

"See what I have to put up with?" Robert grumbled, but his fondness for his partner was obvious.

Adam passed him a sandwich and a yellow cola. "You two look like monkey see, monkey do."

Jenna looked down at her grease and rust smudged clothes. Her white sneakers were smeared with a disgusting green, oily sludge. Her father, shirt unbuttoned and belly and legs smeared with dirt and oil, was no longer the pristine tourist, either.

"You do kind of look like Charlie Alnutt," she told him.

"Who?"

"Bogey on the *African Queen*," her father informed Adam.

"Ah yes. That boat sunk, didn't it?"

The younger man glanced askew at the engine and boiler toward the bow, his expression no more reassuring than his words.

"She was blown out of the water, Mr. Diesel Man."

"As a favor?"

Adam ducked the sandwich remains thrown at him and winced as they hit the water.

"Aiyee, don't feed the wildlife! I would as soon have no company when I go over the side."

"In *this* water?" Jenna hadn't seen any sign of wildlife, but that didn't mean something wasn't hidden in its murky depths. "Isn't this where there are piranha?"

"The books say they like the deeper water bottom," Adam assured her.

"Hmm…better you than me." She was not convinced. "I mean, have the piranha read the books?"

Jenna understood exactly what Adam was speaking about regarding working in the heat of the day. With the afternoon sun bearing down on them, the overhead canopy afforded little respite. In fact, she envied Adam, who, stripped to a pair of swim trunks, swam about the boat in the cool water. Either there were no caiman or piranha, or the man was like Tilda's meal the night before—just too pretty to eat!

It was amazing how many do-lollies and thingamajigs she found herself examining to keep from staring at his trim physique. She was reminded of the cliff divers in Acapulco, with powerful shoulders and legs, developed from swimming in the ocean currents and bronzed by the tropical caress of the sun. Except Adam was taller than the average cliff diver.

"Hand me the larger driver."

Her father had gone ashore with one of the river Indians to scrounge for a part. Introduced briefly as Arturo, the rivereño was the third male member of the *Jenna's* motley crew. Jenna, however, was not totally unfamiliar with tools, not after taking high school shop. Aunt Vi had been appalled, but Uncle Ben applauded her, insisting women should know a thing or two about tools and cars.

"Phillips, square, or slot?" she asked, peeping over the side of the bow.

Adam pulled himself up from the water, arms resting on the side of the boat. Ebony eyes twinkled with admiration as he handed her the tool he'd been using. "Slot. Like this, only bigger."

Jenna took it and turned to rummage through her father's toolbox. Sweat trickled down her face. She wiped it away with her arm and pulled what appeared to be the next size larger of the screwdrivers. She compared it to the one Adam gave her.

"Perfect!"

With the self-conscious notion that her companion wasn't speaking solely of the tool, she glanced over her shoulder to catch him staring.

"Not the oil stain on your bottom, the screwdriver," he told her quickly.

Jenna handed him the driver and checked her back-side. Sure enough, she'd managed to sit in some engine oil. So much for this outfit, not to mention the admiration. Not that she wanted it, she told herself.

"Hey, I wanna look the part," she responded.

Adam dropped back into the water.

"Okay, this is the last one. Can you hold the plaque in place till I get the screw started?"

Leaning over the side, Jenna grabbed the wooden nameplate. She could hardly see for the wayward strands of hair brushing across her eyes and nose. Adam helped her get it into place.

"There, hold it."

Hanging on with one arm from the rail like a pirate with a knife in his teeth, or rather screwdriver, he started the brass screw with his fingers. Then he finished twirling it in with the driver.

"Voilà!"

"I'm impressed." If it had been her, she'd have lost at least one screw overboard by now.

From behind his ear, Adam produced a second screw, which went in as easily as the first.

143

"Piece of cake, huh?"

Ignoring Jenna's dour remark, he handed her the driver and fell back into the water. "The holes were predrilled."

"What was she called before *Jenna?*"

"*Monolito*…little monkey."

Jenna tossed back her head and laughed. "What can I say? I'm flattered."

Smeared with engine oil and rust, blond hair falling limply around her sun-pinkened face, Jenna Marsten was as pretty as she'd been in her prom picture. Adam wondered what had possessed the fair-haired lad in the picture to leave her behind as Robert Marsten had informed him. He would have taken her with him, if the job was so important. But then, he'd done just that with Marina, and it cost him their marriage and her life. So maybe this Scott Pierson wasn't so foolish after all but unselfish. Perhaps his love for Jenna was more than Adam was capable of.

The lightheartedness of the previous moment dissipated, crushed by the heavy weight of the past. Stronger than the current of one of the world's largest rivers, it pulled Adam down. When he climbed back into the boat, he was exhausted, not from the swim but from wrestling to put the past out of mind.

"So, Jenna, what is it this fiancé of yours would say if he could see this grease monkey you have become?"

Adam dried his wet hair and then wrapped the towel about his waist.

"I don't think he'd know me, actually."

Her answer was reflective, as if she, too, had been drawn back to a less comfortable world, one in which she'd been hurt.

"I am sorry. I did not mean to pry. I only meant…to tease you." He looked away and swore under his breath.

"It's okay."

"I am not so good at this social business."

"Hey, I was raised to be society's darling and look what it got me!" She wiped greasy hands on her shirt. It was a stupid joke, but her smile was like a burst of sunshine from the inside out.

"I'll put up with your blunders if you put up with mine. How's that?"

Adam thrust his hand forward, relieved. "Deal."

"Deal." She shook it with the firm grip of a gal who knew her tools.

The shot of warmth from the contact between them went straight to Adam's belly. It twisted like a screwdriver, unleashing reactions far more potent than they had a right to be.

"I said Scott wouldn't know me. I think that's because I'm not recognizing myself lately."

"Oh…" Adam blew a dismissing breath through his lips. "The oil will wash off."

"No, it's not the oil. It's like I've changed." Jenna struggled, trying to find the right words. "Like, maybe there's more to me than I knew. I honestly believe Scott and I made the right decision to postpone the marriage."

Adam's attention sharpened. "Postpone?"

"Well." Jenna faltered. "He decided to do his thing and I decided to do mine. The rest is a wait and see. I think God wanted us to wait for a reason; that maybe I'm here for a reason."

"Ah."

The glaze in her eyes undermined her bravado, just as it undermined Adam's resolve to remain distant. "I used to believe in that too."

"Used to?"

"God does what He wants, regardless of how it affects us. If you are lucky, He favors you. If not—" He shrugged as if the raw hurt bleeding inside him could be dismissed with it. "I put my faith in me. Me I can depend on. God I cannot."

With a forced smile, he unwrapped his damp towel and dipped a corner into the water.

"What do mean by that? That you're more trust-worthy than God?"

"I don't want to go there, Jenna." Realizing the sharp edge to his voice, Adam switched tactics to keep things on a more even keel. "Here, cool off," he said, wiping her smudged face with the towel.

He had the uncommon urge to do more, to hold her in his arms and tell her everything would be fine. But that would be lying. He'd told Marina the same thing, and things were not fine. Her hatred of the clinic and his work turned to hatred of him. He'd prayed she'd have a change of heart, but even in death she blamed him. At least he felt the guilt.

No, life had taught Adam of the naïveté of Jenna's faith. It was as childish as the way she chewed the tip of her hair. Why did full-grown women still possess that vulnerability that could turn a man's insides to mush? Whether it was due to Jenna or the lure of that idealistic faith, Adam felt the closeness of the small deck closing in, making him all the more aware of his companion. Where the devil were her father and Arturo?

Adam glanced away toward the high riverbank and was relieved to see the mestizo who'd helped Robert Marsten rebuild the *S. L. Jenna* scurry down the ladder. It was the fastest he'd seen the old rivereño move in years.

"Dr. Adam! Quickly, hurry!"

Alarm froze the pulse Adam had barely recovered from his contact with Jenna.

"What is it, amigo?"

"It's Dr. Robert. His chest, he hurts."

"Oh no!"

Before he could move, Jenna sprang from the deck to the dock and raced toward the man. Adam followed on her heels, urging her up the ladder behind Arturo.

They rushed with the riverside villager to the marketplace, through the thinning crowd to a stall surrounded by all manner of junk and salvage. Adam put his arm around Jenna when she spied her father sitting on the ground, leaning up against the wheel of a cart.

"Stay back, Jenna. Let me see him."

"I'm fine!" her father declared, giving Arturo a stern look of reproof as Adam placed his fingers to the man's carotid pulse.

Another villager, a woman, handed the older doctor a jug of water.

Adam intercepted it. "Has it been boiled?"

"Sí, Dr. Adam. Just like you tell us."

Ignoring his order to stand back, Jenna dropped to her knees on the other side of her father and dabbed his clammy forehead with the wet end of the towel she'd brought with her.

"What happened, Dad?"

"I just got a little short of breath."

"Chest pain?" Adam asked.

Robert shook his head. "Just a little tightness. I get this way every time I get around steam. Gets the blood pumping," he told Jenna.

Adam rose to his feet and looked around. The village woman placed a hand on his arm.

"El medicó, he is okay?"

"May we borrow your cart to carry him back to the compound?"

"But of course!" the vendor exclaimed. "It is on my way home."

"I can walk," Robert protested.

"You can also ride, no?"

"I agree with Adam, Dad," Jenna spoke up. Her face

was drawn in concern. "In this heat, I'd welcome a ride back myself. We can sit in the back."

The canopy on the rough-hewn donkey cart snapped in the breeze off the river. Adam noticed a cluster of clouds gathering over the green horizon in the distance, beyond the village and the mist-cloaked mountains. Even as he helped Jenna up into the vegetable cart, other vendors were putting away their wares or packing up to go to their farms on the village outskirts. Stubborn to a fault, her father helped himself into the wagon. His color was returning more all the time.

"Did you have to take a nitroglycerin?"

Robert shook his head. "No pain, just shortness of breath."

Adam checked the man's ankles for signs of swelling. There was none. Chances were it was more the heat aggravating his condition rather than an attack of angina itself. In Boston the media would be warning senior citizens to stay inside in the air-conditioning. His friend had yet to turn on the ones Adam installed after the man's first episode with shortness of breath and the "flutters" as Tilda called them.

"Looks like we're about to get cooled off anyway," Robert observed, noticing the clouds in the distance.

Adam nodded. "Arturo, will you close up the boat?"

"Sí, Dr. Adam. She looks nice with her new name, no?" The mestizo looked at Jenna, beaming.

The donkey started pulling the cart toward the compound, instantly striking a deep rut in the dried dirt.

With a startled laugh, Jenna grabbed on to the side rail, to keep from being jolted off its back edge or slammed into her father.

Adam ignored the sly male-to-male look Arturo gave him and followed in the dust of the vehicle. On his heels was the vendor's dog, a shaggy mixed breed with no tail. A man would have to be blind not to notice Jenna Marsten, he mused grudgingly. If he noticed the young woman any more, he'd not be able to stay away from her.

Perhaps the best news he'd had was that her wedding was just postponed. That was another good reason not to give this ridiculous infatuation he had with her the slightest consideration.

Adam clenched his fist, furious at this confounding state of turmoil. His only comfort was the fact that she was just visiting. A week upriver would erase all her romantic notions about a new family in the Amazon, of that he was certain.

Eight

At the hacienda, Adam was better able to assess Robert Marsten's condition, at least to his satisfaction. Robert had not only been Adam's father's best friend, but he had given his mother a new lease on life after the passing of her husband. When Adam left for medical school, he'd worried constantly over his mother's state of depression. She'd lost weight, and the smile he remembered fondly from childhood had all but disappeared. That summer, she returned to work on the often neglected administration of the complex. Inviting her back to the clinic gave her a reason to go on, a place to lose herself and her grief.

After dinner, which Robert insisted on attending rather than being served in his room, Adam excused himself from the table.

"I have some paperwork to attend to from this

morning's ear infections and diarrhea—I mean *intestinal distress*," he added quickly, upon seeing Jenna put down the last spoonful of a light banana rice pudding. "I forget myself, señorita. I am not used to having nonmedical guests at our table."

She waved aside his apology. "Believe me, we used to sing about worse than that at our camp dining hall. I just needed a sip of water."

"Why don't you go back to the clinic with Adam?" Before either of them could object, Robert Marsten cut them off. "I myself am going to bed. Besides, Jenna had some ideas for the office records."

"Oh?" Adam wondered what a socialite with a degree in art could possible know about medical record keeping.

"Computer," she said brightly.

"Computer?" He tried not to scowl.

"Yes, *computer*. Systems are relatively inexpensive now, and if I entered your records into a database, you could compile all the statistics you need to qualify for grants."

"I was telling Jenna that the research facility has just *uploaded*—?"

"Upgraded."

"Upgraded," Robert repeated after his daughter. "Anyway, they offered us the old system."

"It will take forever to input the data, even if one knew what data to put in. And you may not be here that long, señorita."

"She could train Lola."

"The cleaning woman?" Adam said skeptically.

"Besides which, I'm not sure how long I'm staying. I just might get to like the place. The little cabin Dad lived in is still available, I've heard."

Adam felt as though he'd been kicked in the stomach. Fire flew to his face, bringing his tumbling thoughts and reactions to a full boil.

"The paperwork is fine, just as it is." If he didn't take a stand, he was going to be bowled over. By what, he wasn't certain, but it could be a tall, comely blond with seemingly endless optimism.

"I thought you were a man of the twenty-first century," Robert chided.

"I may be, but this country is not!"

Panic welled in Adam's throat. This was *his* world. What right did some happy-go-lucky art director have invading it? It was bad enough she'd worked her way into his home, his family, even his blood, but his *work?*

"You see these?" he declared hotly, holding up his hands. "These will work twenty-four hours a day, without electricity if necessary. And *this...*" He pointed to his head. "This works the same way."

"Ah!" He held up a finger, stopping Jenna from replying. "Now, I go to put them both to work. And I do not need your computer!"

Jenna stared openmouthed at the doorway where Adam disappeared. His angry footfall faded and ended with the slam of the back door. Just when she thought they might get along!

"Don't pay any attention to him. He gets that short fuse from his father's side. With Adam, you plant an idea and then give it time to grow."

"Looks like pretty hard ground to me."

"Hah!" Her father took her hand and squeezed it. "Something tells me that young thundercloud's met his match in sunshine."

Jenna considered the challenge in her father's gaze. "Maybe." She hesitated. "How did his wife deal with him?"

"Like two thunderclouds. I was glad his mother wasn't alive to see it. Always felt I was walking on glass with that girl."

Jenna licked the spoon of pudding thoughtfully.

"She was a beauty…his Spanish rose, he called her. But the rose didn't transplant from Lima's more glamorous social life very gracefully. She demanded Adam take her to the city every other week on his days off. He could keep up with her financially, what with his own share of the old DeSanto family money, but he was like the walking dead when he came back, shopped and partied out."

"What happened to her?"

"Snake bite—a fer-de-lance, we think, extremely poisonous. If we'd found her in time, we might have saved her, but she ran away to spite him after an argument. Her father had made arrangements for Adam to enter a pediatric practice in Lima."

"How could she run away? The only way is by boat." Jenna cringed remembering the trails Adam had led her through across land. Only a fool would try such an unfamiliar terrain alone. "Surely she didn't try to hike to Ichitas!"

"Adam had a motorized bike. Marina took that until she ran out of passable trails. Adam didn't know she was missing until almost sundown. Marina told Tilda she was going down to the market. The villagers mounted a search party for her, but the forest is dense and dangerous. Only a seasoned hunter dares go into the jungle at night, but Adam and a few of the men spent the night looking for her with lanterns. She wasn't found until the following afternoon, dead, of course. He blamed himself."

"So that's why he's so angry at God."

"He was a godly man—as godly as most young men his age. He'd been raised in the church and felt the calling to spend his life and fortune helping the natives rather than lavishing it on himself. He'd wanted so much for Marina to share the calling with him, as his mother had with his father, but Marina..." Robert shook his head. "She was young, beautiful, and eager to experience all her money had to offer. Perhaps in time she may have changed."

Her father's manner suggested he thought otherwise, even though he made a conscious effort not to speak ill of the dead.

"Adam worshiped the ground the girl walked on. So when his marriage deteriorated and ended with Marina's horrible death, his anger and grief drove a wedge between him and God, not to mention the church. He used to lead a Bible study, but he hasn't even attended a local service since."

Adam was not the only one who felt the burden of memories from the past. With a heavy sigh, her father shoved the chair away from the table.

Jenna stiffened in alarm. "Are you okay?"

"I'm fine. I'm just tired." He pushed himself upright on the arms of the chair. "I hate not being able to go like I used to, but the alternative leaves a lot more to be desired…especially now."

Jenna gave him a spontaneous hug.

"At least *you* don't mind my being here."

"Like I said, give Adam some time. I've never seen a doctor quicker on his feet professionally, but socially…"

"I get the picture."

At least she understood his hostility a little more. Given the circumstances of his wife's death, it was no wonder he was obsessive about Jenna's naïveté where the jungle was concerned. And wounded animals were often territorial, aggressive, irritable. Heaven knew Adam DeSanto had been hurt, more deeply than just a broken heart. His soul was broken.

After her father went to his room, Jenna helped Tilda clear the table and do the dishes, despite the woman's protest. Later, she was still too restless to sleep.

Seated at the table in the courtyard, Jenna saw the lights come on in Tilda's room and the shadows of a television show dancing on the open louvers of the shutters.

Yet it was the lights of the clinic shafting through the cleared woods that dominated Jenna's attention. Dare she venture into the dragon's lair? Twice she started to get up and walk out there. Twice she hesitated, twisting the pink cotton knit of the dress she'd changed into for supper. True, Adam made it clear he didn't want her around, yet now she had an inkling why. It wasn't her, but the anguish she reminded him of.

Somehow, she had to show Adam that she was no threat to him or his work, that she was not the least like his late wife. She had her own reasons for being here and they didn't concern him at all. She might even show him how God can and will mend a broken heart, a wounded soul, if he'd let God back into them.

Father, I don't know what to say or do, but You know my heart. Maybe You've allowed my pain so that I could recognize it in another. If I can help nudge him back to You, please show me, for I know he'll never truly be healed without You.

A peace filled Jenna as she rose a third time, this time continuing through the open courtyard gates toward the clinic. As she walked to the open door, she had second thoughts about carrying along a flashlight. The area inside the compound, however, was kept clear of growth, save a few manicured lawn areas. It was done specifically for the purpose of avoiding hiding places for snakes, according to her father. A shudder ran through her, as she thought of the horrible death Marina DeSanto must have suffered.

A single light bulb hung over Adam's desk. There was a wall of files on shelves to the right. Another wall boasted a credenza, long inundated with cardboard file boxes so that only its front showed. An unplugged coffeepot with contents of questionable vintage sat on another rusted cabinet near the entrance to the clinic itself. To the office's left were a long string of rooms she assumed were for patients.

No one was in the room. Jenna wandered in and looked into the adjoining one. It was piled high with supplies, many of the boxes open. She'd heard things were slow and wondered if there were any patients staying over. Perhaps that was where Adam was because he certainly wasn't doing paperwork.

At the sound of footsteps approaching from the outside, Jenna hurried back into the office as Adam stepped into the room, a stethoscope suspended from his neck. He stopped short.

"What are you doing here?"

Jenna shrugged. "Dad's gone to bed early. Tilda is in her room."

"Catching her television shows before the power is shut off." It wasn't a question, just a flat observation. "The satellite dish has ruined her."

"Who got it for her?"

"Me."

There was a smile. Well almost.

"Were you doing rounds?"

"In a manner of speaking. I was helping Lola light the kerosene lamps. We have one patient, an older man with asthma. We're rehydrating him with fluids."

The conversation died in awkward silence. Adam pursed his lips, as if he too were desperate for something else to say. He looked about the room, as if searching for a hint.

"Well, anyway," Jenna spoke up, "I just thought I'd remind you that I have two hands too...and a head! And they don't need electricity, although it helps the eyes. So what can I do to help out?"

"Nothing. Everything is in perfect order."

"Come on, Adam. Get real!" Jenna pointed around her. "It looks like a tornado went through here."

His jaw clamped, muscles twitching in protest. "I know where everything is, just as it is."

"It looks like Pepito's monkey did your filing."

"Marmoset."

"Like it makes a difference?" Jenna flushed, her indignation eroding away at her earlier more saintly intention. The man had an incredible stubborn streak. It was clearly a case of someone who'd been given his way too long. Hurt or no, it was time somebody told him he was not king of the forest!

Marching up to him, she tapped her finger against the hard muscle of his chest.

"Look, I know life hasn't exactly been rosy for you but that is no excuse to regress to a chest-beating

Neanderthal. You can mark your territory for all I care, but I am not leaving!"

The thick, black lashes above Adam's gaze twitched with an angry flutter. Jenna fully expected to see the ebony turn to a feral red glow, fanned by the deep breath he took.

However, her own annoyance, once unleashed, would not retreat.

"So you can either take my offer gracefully or…or…"

The overhead light flickered. In the background, above the hammer of her heart, Jenna heard the winding down of a hum she'd not paid attention to until now. Her eyes grew wide as Adam took a step toward her. The light went out, seizing them in darkness as Adam's hands seized Jenna's upper arms. Her mind went just as black with shock, uncertain whether or not to run from the beast she'd unleashed or scream. But neither was possible. What his grasp did not prevent, his lips did.

They fell angrily upon Jenna's, establishing possession, claiming dominion as no spoken word possibly could. They punished, and yet, through the numbing spell they cast, it was a sweet justice. Her breath flared short and desperate through her nostrils. Blood catapulted to her brain. At least, that's what it felt like, blood rushing, roaring in her ears, pulling her strength from her knees, so that the arm Adam slipped behind her held her suspended against him.

His body thrummed with the power it held over her, as if some magnetic force held them together, so that not even breath came between them. Their breath was one, his was hers and hers was his.

When he drew away, the field of energy surrounding them weakened. Jenna caught herself before she collapsed in a pile of pink skirt at his feet. Instead, she grabbed the back of the desk chair for support. It swung away, nearly dumping her, but Adam would not allow that. He'd stated his case, established his claim. He could afford to be a gentleman again.

When he simply helped Jenna regain her footing, she felt a nagging pang of disappointment, rather than the soar of indignation she would prefer. She didn't even slap him! Instead, she pressed her fingers to her lips, as if to be certain that what had happened was real and not some figment of imagination spawned from a vixenish side of her she never knew she had.

"You are not the only one who can issue ultimatums, Jenna."

Adam's warning was ragged as if the storm had ravaged him as well.

"It's no wonder Marina ran away!"

"What?"

Jenna gasped, realizing that she'd thought aloud. "I mean…I mean you're a bully!"

No, that's not what I meant!

As if to bolster her flailing state of mind, she drew herself to her full height. Jenna wished she could see more of him than his outline in the moonlit door behind him. On the other hand, maybe it was just as well. She put her hands on her hips.

"Well, you don't scare me one bit, Adam DeSanto! You might be bigger and kiss like the devil himself, but I'm here to stay for as long as I want to, so get used to it!"

Jenna turned sideways and skirted around her thunderously silent companion until she cleared the door and was outside, in the cool of the night. With marked steps, she walked back toward the open courtyard of the hacienda. In truth, she wanted to run, but that would be unthinkable. She'd sooner crawl than give Adam DeSanto the satisfaction.

With each step, however, the wind escaped her sails until her anger sagged with her shoulders. Instead of helping Adam, she'd antagonized him, blowing her original intent big time. Like her father said, the best laid plans of mice and men...

Lord, please help me control my temper, no matter how much Adam DeSanto irritates me. I'm so sorry, really. And Jenna was, miserably so.

The next morning, Jenna told her father what she thought needed doing around the clinic, and he helped her get started on her project. Together they determined which records were trash and which needed to be kept. Whether they got a computer or not, the organization still needed to be done.

Meanwhile, Adam accepted her presence with a grudging silence and an occasional glare as he went about his work, tending the patients. It was a cold war atmosphere, at least for Jenna. Conversation took place primarily between her and Dr. Robert.

If her father suspected anything more than a stubborn clash of wills between his partner and daughter, he gave no indication. In fact, it seemed to amuse him when Jenna volleyed one of Adam's challenges right back in his court. As for the work itself, Robert positively glowed with pride over her suggestions. When Tilda called them to lunch, Adam simply took his plate from the table on the excuse that he had chores to do and Jenna hadn't seen him since.

It wasn't like Jenna to go over an adversary's head, but Adam *had* left her little choice. He hadn't exactly played fair either. He was not going to bully her or send her scampering off like a frightened rabbit with his chest-thumping, territorial kiss. She'd show him that she was not the scatterbrained, spoiled debutante he obviously thought her to be, if she had to flay him with his stethoscope. If anyone was spoiled, it was Adam DeSanto—*wherever* he'd gone to sulk. At least he'd left the women to their work later that afternoon.

"I am *so* glad you are doing this! When one box gets full, they just make another box." Lola, the clinic's helper and housekeeper, threw up her hands. "Men!"

Jenna looked up from stuffing a trash bag full of invoices and shipping tickets for goods received eight years ago and older. She and the woman had made a showing since lunchtime cleaning and reorganizing. The patient files were in order on the filing shelves on the wall. Should her father and the jungle doc decide to go on computer, the most recent patients' records were available.

"I wanted to do this, but I just don't know where to start."

"Just dig in and do it," Jenna answered the young mestiza.

Lola had been educated at the village school, enough to read and write passably. More important, she knew how to alphabetize! She wasn't fast, but then neither was Jenna. At least the woman was more familiar with the Spanish names and what names belonged in the same files. They'd found patients with as many as ten separate files, where one of the doctors, unable to find the previous, just wrote up a new one. Her father was just as guilty as Adam and had just as little use for paperwork.

"Where did we put the patient logs?" Lola held up the contents of another box.

"We'll possibly need them for the database, so we put them—"

"Sí, I remember!"

Lola stepped over another pile of trash, contents of the rusty filing cabinet. Jenna was certain these were the clinic's very first records, never put aside to make room for current ones. She supposed she could consider it an accomplishment that the files were at least separated by alphabetical dividers.

"Holy moley! More trash?"

Jenna braced at the sound of Pepito's voice, certain that darned marmoset was going to latch on to her at any moment. It was as if Rita knew Jenna wasn't monkey-friendly.

"Hello, Rita!" she said brightly as the varmint scampered up on the desk and pulled at the trash bag Jenna stuffed. "Go ahead. Hop in and Pepito will give you a ride to the trash pile."

The boy broke into a wide grin. "Not today. It's Saturday. Dr. Adam and me, we go fishing!"

Tilda poked her head in from the supply room, where she'd volunteered to clean. "Good! Then we have fresh fish for supper tonight. Dr. Adam can cook!" The task was easier now that most of the supplies had been moved down to the *Jenna* for a Monday morning departure. "Me, I gonna go back to the casa."

"Oh, me too!" Lola exclaimed in dismay. "I forget today is Saturday and the little ones are home from school."

"I'll go put these on the burn pile and be right up, Tilda." Jenna looked at the bag she'd filled. It weighed a ton.

"You wanna borrow my wagon?"

"You gotta deal!" Jenna extended her hand to the boy, only to have the marmoset leap onto her arm. "But you can keep the monkey."

"Marmoset!"

"Pain in the butt!"

Jenna reached inside the desk drawer and drew out a bag of peanuts. One shake spilled enough on the desk to tempt Rita away and keep her busy long enough for them to load the boy's wagon.

It was a bright red mini flatbed with detachable rails, one of which was almost permanently detached. Pepito had devised a way to steer the wagon with the handle and kneel on it with one leg and propel it with the other in scooter fashion. He kept it polished and well oiled. It was cute to see him with his wagon upended on the dock, borrowing tools and oil while his doctor buddies worked on the *Jenna*.

"I will just add this to my bill," the boy said, as they started to pull the bag away. "Pays for the overhead, you know."

Jenna shrugged and suppressed a smile. "It's only good business."

Naturally, her father and Adam paid Pepito for his "services" in hauling boxes from the steep bank to the end of the dock, which she suspected was more trouble than it was worth. In truth, she wondered who had adopted whom where Pepito was concerned. Dr. Adam was more fun to play with, but Dr. Robert, according to the boy, told the most wonderful stories.

"It's such a pretty day! Why don't you come with us?"

"I'd better make hay while the sun shines." At the boy's confounded look, she tousled his shining dark hair with her fingers. "In other words, I'd better work while I have the help."

"I didn't think there was hay in the clinic."

A shrieking chatter drew their attention to where Rita, who'd discovered she'd been left, clamored after them. In her tiny arms were more peanuts than she could hold. On discovering she'd dropped one, she stopped and very carefully tried to pick it up without spilling the others. She was so desperate, Jenna took pity on her.

"Okay, Rita. You ride on the wagon. I'll get the nuts."

It wasn't until Jenna had picked up every peanut spilled and placed them on the wagon that the suspicious Rita hopped aboard and gave her a show of teeth.

"That's monkey for *thank you.*"

"You mean *marmoset!*" Jenna teased.

They were unloading the bag on the trash pile when Rita shrieked and pointed in the direction of the main gate where a family of natives entered. Upon seeing Jenna, they waved and started toward her. One carried a squalling infant.

"You better go get Dr. Adam," she told Pepito.

Her father had gone down to the *Jenna* after lunch with Arturo to work on some much needed maintenance.

Jenna recognized Yamo and Alma, as well as the brood of children following them, from the house call she and Adam made after her arrival. Both man and wife barraged her with their staccato mix of Indian and Spanish. The young mother, whom Jenna recognized as their eldest daughter, bounced the crying infant on her shoulder to no avail. Since she'd been pregnant the last time Jenna saw her, her baby couldn't be over a few days old. Jenna tried to make out what the adults were saying over the noise of the rest of the crew. The youngsters who chased a chicken they'd brought with them were oblivious to the gravity of the visit.

"*Mas despacio,* por favor. Mas…*slow-ly!*" Jenna demonstrated for them, raising her voice above the squeals of the children and squawks of the panicked bird.

Once again, even though more slowly, everyone tried to talk at one time. Dragging the empty wagon behind her, empty save Rita, who was not about to give up her prize treat to follow Pepito, Jenna led them to the clinic. She was more bewildered than ever at what they were saying, or rather, what she *understood* them to say. Once inside, the daughter shoved the infant at her with an unmistakable do-something look.

The baby was warm, although Jenna couldn't tell if it was from fever or from its fit of crying. And it was so tiny! She looked at the mother, wondering how she'd made the long walk to the clinic so soon after delivery. No wonder she looked exhausted and was on the verge of tears herself.

"No soy un medicó." Boy, was it true that if one didn't use it, they lose it! Her seven-year-old Spanish had faded more than Jenna realized.

"I am at least glad, señorita, that you realize *that* limitation."

Adam entered the examining room in a pair of cut

off denims. His upper torso glistened with sweat and was flecked with bits of grass, betraying his early morning activity.

"She says he has a splinter in his finger and can't urinate…I think." Jenna blurted out, glad to hand over the distraught infant to Adam.

He ignored her translation and turned to the baby's relatives. *"Qué es el problemo? Qué pasa?"*

Another torrent of explanations ensued. Adam nodded, his lips twitching as he laid the baby on the table with a darting glance at Jenna. After a bit of coaxing, he did a quick examination of the tiny, perfect fingers.

"Not a splinter," he announced smugly. "I think the problem lies in this little man's diaper."

Jenna colored as the doctor removed the cloth. The baby's umbilical cord was still a far cry from falling off. It was knotted rather than clamped, no doubt by a tribal midwife.

"Look, Castilian Spanish and mestizo do have their differences!"

"Ah, but Jenna, a finger is a finger," he chided, examining the baby boy's genitals. "And *this* is…well, it's—will you fetch me the Betadine?"

The infant had not been circumcised. At least that was Jenna's observation from her limited experience in baby-sitting for friends. Feeling awkward, to say the least, she feigned the same indifference as Adam, hoping for the sake of the little one, no splinter was involved on such a tender spot.

Adam finished swabbing the baby. "Are you capable of assisting me or should I call Lola?"

"In what?"

"A circumcision. The skin has sealed off the opening. See?"

Jenna nodded, not really looking. She could do this. It would make Adam's day for her to turn tail and run.

"I will get my instruments and some anesthetic, *if* it is still in the same place?"

Jenna dug in for battle. "I've only moved records." She was *not* going to be bullied again!

"Then bring me some gauze and stand by with a second pair of hands."

She couldn't resist a parting salute. While she retrieved the supplies, Adam explained the nature of the problem to the family and asked them to wait outside while it was done to spare the mother even more distress.

The procedure was as fast and painless as medication would allow. Jenna flinched inwardly as the doctor anesthetized the area while she held the baby's flailing legs and arms. The screaming infant wanted no part of any of them. While Adam conveyed his apologies in an unhurried velvet coo of Spanish syllables, Jenna prayed in utter desperation for relief, for both her and the baby.

Afterward, Adam gave the family a few doses of antibiotics and explained that the baby had not urinated yet because it needed to drink. The young mother had not fed the child because she feared it had no outlet.

Incredible as it seemed, Adam took the news in stride, drawing the new mother aside and patiently going over the needs of the infant while it hungrily fed beneath a cotton diaper.

Back home, in the sterile and civilized setting of a hospital or doctor's office, the scene would somehow have been inappropriate, primitive at best, but here, it was beautiful. Like her father told Jenna, things we take for granted in the States have to be taught down here. Adam spoke more like a father to a child than a physician to a patient.

Given the girl's tender age—Jenna guessed her to be no more than sixteen—it seemed right. She wasn't to give the baby water unless it was boiled. She was to use the boiled water and the small bottle of antiseptic solution to keep the incision clean until it healed. Again, these were things many young women would take for granted to do back home but not here.

It was Adam's romantic language and accent that affected Jenna more than his patience with the new mother. It was a shame it was wasted on clinical instruction. In that tone, Adam DeSanto could coax a female to do anything!

When the doctor was finished, Yamo snapped something at the children playing outside. Instantly, one of them appeared in the door, trying to smooth down the feathers of the frazzled fowl.

Adam turned to Jenna. "Do you wish to take the payment and write a receipt?"

She gave him a grimace. "*I'll* write the receipt. The chicken is all yours, Doc Doolittle."

Nine

⬡⬡⬡

A LITTLE LATER, AS THE *S. L. JENNA* PUFFED ITS WAY UP THE milky brown Amazon water, it was like a ride through the animal kingdom at an amusement park, except better! Jenna leaned over the rail and snapped a picture of a playful otter family frolicking near the shore. She'd brought along four disposable cameras. It was only noon and she'd already used one completely.

She had pictures of Pepito and his empty wagon, with Rita perched atop the boy's head like some exotic headdress. It hardly seemed fair that the boy couldn't go, but school was school. Besides, Adam promised him a weekend camp out on their return, where they would take nothing but a compass and bows and arrows into the jungle. Pepito asked in his excitement if Jenna could go too. He wanted to show off his fishing skills. Adam's response was so unenthusiastic, she'd had to laugh!

The younger doctor was no more excited when she'd stood on the dock and taken pictures of him, her father, and Arturo. He now reclined in a hammock, absorbed in a book, while Arturo piloted the boat upriver. Her father was in his glory feeding the refrigerator-sized firebox as if he were a mother bird stuffing its hungry babe.

"Oh, look!" Jenna pointed to a beautiful red toucan as it streaked across the verdant foliage of the overgrown bank. She snapped another picture.

"That should show up well. Look at the red spot. That's a toucan!"

Jenna turned and made a face at Adam, who'd given up his book to make fun of her. She brushed the hair, which had escaped from her floppy travel hat, out of her face and snapped a picture of his smart-aleck grin.

With Adam it was either dour fun or cold shoulder, neither of which put her at ease. Unless she counted his kiss. Nothing cold or dour about that! Bold and passionate were more like it. The very thought sent a rush of blood to her cheeks, tripping her pulse in the process.

Jenna dabbed her tank top at the valley of her chest, where sweat tickled, and reached for her water bottle. After a gulp, she licked her lips and put the bottle back in its niche, very much aware that her every move was being observed from under the brim of Adam's palm hat.

He looked like a beach bum in cutoff denims and a wrinkled cotton shirt missing several buttons. It didn't matter since he'd made no attempt to button it. It billowed from his waist, filled by the river breeze.

A loud splash near the boat drew Jenna's attention back to the water. It was a fish, a large one, by the sound of it.

"A river dolphin," Adam informed her.

Jenna knelt on the wooden bench, poised to catch a picture if it surfaced again. Out of an overhanging tree limb, an osprey streaked toward the ripple and veered upward as the fish jumped. She caught both in the frame, the dolphin and the startled bird, which decided that it had bitten off more than it could chew.

"Hah! Got a classic."

"You are very full of ants."

"What?"

"Ants in the pants," Adam explained. He eased out of the hammock and stretched lazily, scratching his flat belly. At Jenna's still blank expression, he proceeded to jump about. "Like a fish in the bottom of a boat, twisting first this way, then that."

Jenna gave him the all-encompassing shrug. Maybe he was hoping she'd flop overboard.

"I am going to spell your father. Try to talk him into taking a nap."

Robert Marsten's health was the one subject upon which Jenna and the younger doctor agreed. Adam actually tried to talk her father out of making the trip, but he was as stubborn and set on going as she was.

"People live for years with angina. But if I die, I'll die doing what I love to do! I don't know what more a man could ask for in this life," Robert declared, ending the conversation.

It was agreed that the older doctor would operate the clinic off the boat for the riverside dwellers while Adam went inland to the Black Lake village. Her father's words, however, weighed heavily on Jenna's mind after they retired early for the evening; early because they needed to get an extra early start. *What more could a person ask for than to do something they loved; better yet, something they were called to do?*

When her father came back from the midsection of the boat, his tank shirt was clinging to him, soaked with perspiration and soot. Despite his blackened face, his eyes sparkled like blue diamonds, clear as the sky overhead. His body may have aged, but his gaze was as bright as it had been in the wedding picture on Jenna's dresser in Boston.

"This may not be Eden, but it's as close as I'm going to get this side of life!"

Except for one disgruntled Adam, Jenna had to agree. A body felt closer to God here. At least *she* did. Perhaps it was because there weren't as many man-made trappings to distract her. Sometimes the more one had, the more trouble one had being thankful. In Boston Jenna had everything, or so she'd thought. Yet there'd been this troubling feeling that there was something more to her life than the golden plans laid out for her and Scott.

Father, thank You for bringing me here. Thank You for

*giving me the father I always dreamed of, for the knowledge
that I was abandoned out of love, just as Moses was abandoned. Coming here was no accident. I feel as though I have
a purpose here, that You have a purpose for me. I'm not sure
what it is. For that, Father, I wait for You, for Your hand to
show me.*

"Aye chi——!" The rest of Adam's curse was drowned
out by the hissing, snorting engine.

"I told you, use the gloves!" her father shouted over
the din. He cut a sidewise glance at Jenna and shook his
head. "That mule needs help, though he's too stubborn
to admit it."

Robert leaned over the rail and dipped a handkerchief into the water sweeping past the boat. Mopping his
forehead, he backed into the hammock abandoned by
Adam and swung his legs around with the practiced ease
of one who'd spent many nights in such a contraption.

"What do you think?"

The direct question caught Jenna off guard.

"About the mule?"

"My protégé."

She looked out at the riverbank where a caiman
basked in the tropical sun.

"Well, he seems very competent…and devoted to
you." She smiled over her shoulder. "But who can blame
him for that?"

"I see." Her father laid the wet handkerchief over his
eyes and forehead.

"See what?" It wasn't the answer she expected.

"Nothing. Just babbling."

Jenna waited for him to say something else, but he didn't. Torn between wanting to know just what he was talking about and knowing he needed to rest, she gave in to the latter concern and took up the camera. Okay, so Adam was right. She *was* excited. It was impossible to sit still.

The rhythmic puff of the engine began to falter long after Arturo steered off the main river onto a tributary, which took them deeper into the interior of the Amazon Basin. For a while, Jenna marveled at the way he managed to avoid the floating stumps and debris that fell off the banks from low growing limbs and vines. In some places, the passage was so narrow, the jungle canopy brushed them. Then the water would widen again.

At about midday Jenna unpacked some sandwiches Tilda sent with them and carried Adam his lunch. He'd removed his shirt and his body glistened from the heat of the fire. Jenna knew it couldn't be healthy for her dad to tend it for too long. It practically took one's breath away.

Adam took the sandwich in one hand while shoving a piece of wood into the firebox. "Thanks."

"No, thank *you*...for taking Dad's place."

That quirky little smile of Adam's could be adorable.

"You are welcome, Jenna."

And when he said her name like that, her brain scrambled.

"N-no, not for me. For him."

"No problem." A playful wink nearly took out her knees. "He is like a father to me too."

It was the heat, she told herself. Adam certainly wasn't flirting and she…well, she wasn't sure what was wrong with her. But whatever it was, Jenna hoped it would pass quickly. She returned to the stern of the boat as if the blaze had caught on to her shorts.

The sight of a cluster of thatched huts on a little bluff was a welcome one. The rivereños ran down the steep incline to take the lines Adam tossed to them. Jenna's interest, however, was torn between the fluster of activity and the presence of another boat, a much more modern launch, about the size of the *Jenna* but with a second deck on the canopy. There were a man and woman standing on the lower level, looking back, both mestizo in features.

"Hola, amigos!"

A man descended the steps set into the high bank carved out by rushing water. Ahead of him, the Indians lowered a gangway spanning the distance between the *Jenna* and the shore. As he took to the gangway, Jenna recognized Stefan Murillo, the photographer whose family owned the Posada Explorador.

Adam leapt onto it from the catwalk and shook hands with his late wife's cousin. After a rapid exchange in Spanish, the doctor stepped aside and swept his hand toward the boat in a help-yourself manner.

"Señorita, how good it is to see you again! We have been expecting you."

"Oh? How's that?"

"I knew that Adam would be here in time for the Orinca's fiesta."

"He didn't say anything about a party," Jenna glanced toward the top of the bluff where the natives warmly greeted Adam.

"It's not a party," her father informed her, emerging from the makeshift engine enclosure. "It's a ritual type thing where the young men of the village are initiated into manhood. Quite interesting. That why you're here, Stefan?"

"You read my mind, Dr. Marsten. And when I can incorporate sharing work with the pleasure of a lovely young woman's company, well…" Stefan shrugged.

Right, Jenna thought dourly. Her knit tank top and shorts were smudged and sweat soaked. Her hair, what wasn't concealed beneath her hat, hung in wet little strings about her face, which she was sure was hot pink despite the sunblock she'd used. What she wouldn't give for a shower and a fresh change of clothing! She'd almost envied Adam's going over the side. At least he was getting *some* sort of bath.

"You are being too kind." Her politely extended arm felt as if it were going to fall off from the workout the pump gave it. To Jenna's dismay, Stefan brushed her grubby knuckles with his lips rather than shake her hand.

"Careful, you could catch something being that gallant!"

"A lady is a lady on the inside, Jenna. Outer trappings cannot change that." The photographer raised his voice for the benefit of everyone on the boat. "But I came over to invite the crew of the *Jenna* and the lovely woman herself to dinner. Carla, the captain's wife, is an excellent cook."

"You go ahead, Jen," her father answered. "Arturo and I have to break down the pump and check the water lines to see if any of the sludge got into it."

"I appreciate it, Stefan, but I'm part of the *working* crew."

"You can go…"

"Dad! I'm not leaving you. If Arturo is going with Adam inland tomorrow, I'm going to need to get as familiar with the engine as I can, right?"

"Then I will bring the supper to you!"

Jenna and her father looked at Stefan Murillo in surprise.

"There is actually more room on the *Jenna* than my hired boat anyway," he explained. "Our decks are filled with barrels of fuel for the trip back, and my equipment takes up the most of the cabin space."

"You sure?"

"Dr. Marsten, I am certain. Carla is preparing peacock bass with her delicious corn cake and—"

"Sounds divine!" Jenna said, suddenly aware that unless she counted the chips Adam opened earlier, she'd not eaten since breakfast that morning.

She slapped at a sudden sting on her arm and

brushed away a dead fly. It was the size of the end of her little finger!

"My word, what a vicious beast!"

"If you have insect repellent, señorita, I suggest you put it on," Stefan advised her.

"Yep," her father agreed, glancing out at the sun setting over the western crest of the rain forest. "It's about time for the black flies' supper—*us.*"

Jenna made straight for the repellent in her small-wheeled carry-on. She debated whether or not to try to wash some of the grime off, but her father assured her the soot and smoke would be an added deterrent. Besides, the flies had swarmed in so suddenly, now that the boat was still, that she was desperate to cover herself from head to toe in it.

"So, amigos, you can see my dilemma," Stefan announced later after a delicious meal on the back deck of the *Jenna.*

His hired boat, *La Bonita,* was tied alongside, separated only by thick rope bumpers. It facilitated serving the meal. The cook lived up to Stefan's claims, although what she possessed in cooking skills was lost in communications. She spoke no English. However, she did smile a lot.

"And you want to accompany us to the lake village." Adam's look was as droll as his words.

If there was some bad history between the two, only

182

Adam seemed aware of it. Stefan's response to Adam's subversive wariness was totally guileless.

"Eduardo and I will be no problem, Adam, I assure you. We only want to film the ritual."

Stefan's guide fell sick just before they left Ichitas. The photographer, knowing of Santa Beliza's annual mission, continued ahead in hopes of convincing Adam DeSanto to bring him along, not to mention work out the details with the chief of the Black Lake village. Some of the interior tribes were reluctant to be photographed, but Adam had spent his boyhood visiting and learning the ways of the natives. They would listen more readily to him than to a guide. At least that's what Stefan was counting on.

"And of course, we will trail you back to Santa Beliza, given the troubles you have been having."

"That's sounding fair." Jenna took a sip of American soda, served with a twist of lemon. Murillo's expedition was certainly better funded than theirs.

Adam cut her a silencing look. "I think that is up to me to decide, Jenna."

"I wasn't finished," she said sweetly. "We are perplexed but not in despair!" She turned back from her smug quote to Stefan. "How much money did your company budget for the guide?"

"Thirty million *intis,* but I made a 20 percent deposit that I imagine I will never see."

"Then how about donating the rest to the clinic…in exchange for guide services?"

"Hah!" Robert, who was now helping Arturo dismantle the worrisome pump, slapped his knee. "She's got her mother's business sense."

"That would be about, what—" Jenna did some quick mental calculations. "A little over four hundred dollars."

"And I thought the fund-raiser for the clinic was not until the end of the month." Stefan's admiring gaze belayed his lamentation.

Representatives from major pharmaceutical companies, philanthropists of all manner, and the medical authorities were invited annually to Posada Explorador. It was as close as Adam and her father had ever been able to get the men to Santa Beliza. There the doctors worked the crowd, soliciting donations of all sorts. It produced considerable funding, but the majority of interest lay in the ethno botanical and disease research center in Ichitas itself.

"Or…" Jenna went on. "You could put it toward an excursion from your family's inn to Santa Beliza."

Adam shook his head and leaned back against the side of the ship. "Four hundred in the hand is worth more than twice that with the birds. We have tried for years to get them to come to the clinic, to see what we do."

"In the bush," Jenna reminded him. He did have a charming way of twisting idioms and sayings. "A bird in the hand is worth two in the bush." Jenna turned to her father. "It sounds reasonable—"

"Where would you put them up?" Adam inter-rupted. "They cannot make the trip up there and back in one day."

If only he weren't so stubbornly set against progress, or at least her ideas for it.

"The clinic beds aren't usually filled at night."

"We have a more immediate problem, folks."

Robert pulled himself to his feet and kicked the machinery in disgust. "Arturo and I are going to have to take her down. The lines are clogged."

"But that *could* take a couple of days, no?"

Jenna's father nodded, engrossed in thought. "I really need Arturo here," he said to no one in particular.

"Fine. I can take the clinic to the lake."

"An extra pair of hands speeds things along, and Stefan and his man will be busy setting up for the film-ing. You know it's a lot of hauling and unpacking," Robert pointed out.

"I could go." Jenna braced for Adam's outburst.

"I do not think so, señorita!"

"Oh, don't be such a mule! Most of the supplies aren't that heavy. I helped inventory them *and* move them," she reminded him. "And I know what they look like, for the most part. Unless you simply don't want me to go because I'm a girl."

"I have a tent you can use for privacy," Stefan offered, earning a glower from the jungle doc.

"She could be a big help."

Jenna turned her expectant gaze to Adam, waiting

185

for his reply. Clearly outnumbered, he gave her a mocking bow.

"In that case, señorita, I will be honored to have your company. But do not expect special—"

"Oh, I won't." Jenna tried not to look too triumphant. That guy was going to get used to her or bust! "I will have you organized to a fair-thee-well."

"I am certain I will wonder how I have ever practiced medicine before you came along."

Adam got up and climbed on the rail. "I will be back in a while. I wish to speak to the chief about the arrangements for tomorrow. Stefan, thank you for your hospitality."

"While you're up there," her father called after him, "see if you can find something to fit over the end of the intake, something to at least catch the big stuff from being sucked into the engine—a cone shape if possible to deflect the debris."

"I imagine all I will find is some netting; it should be wire."

A wire cone, Jenna mulled silently. She knew just the thing. Reaching behind her head, she pulled the pin out of the wire cagelike accessory holding her hair up off her neck in a knot.

"You mean like this?"

She handed it to her father, her loosened hair falling in disarray to her shoulders. There'd been no point in changing clothes, but she had managed to wash her face and do something with her hair before dinner.

"Is she a genius or what?" Robert took the hair cage and measured it with a rule. "By golly, I think it'll work. It will at least catch the big stuff."

"And I have some panty hose you could stretch over it to filter it better."

Adam leaned against the canopy, peering under it in disbelief. "You mean to say, you brought panty hose on a…a *camping* trip in the jungle?"

His expression made Jenna snicker. "A girl never leaves home without a spare pair of hose! Anything could happen."

"Ah, I had forgotten all the badges you won at your wilderness camp."

"Nylons will be too fine, I'm afraid," her father interrupted. "A hair net…"

"Those went out ages ago, Dad. But I do have a lingerie bag."

"A *what?*" Adam squatted on the side of the boat, genuinely intrigued.

"A net bag to wash my lingerie in. It has holes about the size of a hair net and it's stronger."

The young doctor shook his head in wonder. "I think I will go then, since Jenna has everything you need to fix an antique engine in her little flower bag on wheels."

At least he lost graciously, Jenna thought, as, whistling an absent tune, the doctor strode up the springy gangway to the hillside steps. Riding high on a wave of success, she fetched the small zippered bag for her dad.

"Just what the doctor ordered!" He gave Jenna a buss on the cheek and dropped back down into the lower midsection of the boat to share his good fortune with Arturo.

"So," Stefan said when she resumed her seat on the side bench. "All your worries were for nothing."

"What?"

"I recall a nervous señorita who was afraid her father did not want her. From what I see, you are up there on a pedestal, no?"

"Well, I don't know about that, but…" Jenna smiled dreamily. "It's been pretty wonderful."

"So you will be staying on at Santa Beliza?"

"I don't know. I think Dad and I need each other. I think we need to make up for some lost time, then…I don't know."

"Ah, but where else does the night descend like a blanket of stars, so close you can almost touch them?"

Jenna followed Stefan's raised hand with her gaze. He was right. The sky was like a diamond-studded blanket, bathed by the light of the moon. The river was no longer its muddy chocolate color but a silver ribbon weaving through the black thicket of the jungle cradling it. In the golden glow of the kerosene lanterns hung off the stern, it was easy to see why her mother had fallen in love with this place and its friendly people.

Later that evening, Jenna wrote as much in her journal, a makeshift spiral-bound office pad, before climbing into the hammock slung across the stern for her. The men had bunks in the bow compartment; although Adam chose to stretch out on the roof. He was obviously more immune to the insects her mosquito net protected her from than she.

As she closed her notebook, she noted with dismay the smudges of her fingerprints on its pristine, white pages. Despite having bathed as best she could from a bucket, Jenna felt like a sweaty grease monkey soaked in chemical repellent, and she envied the man sleeping overhead.

Just before Adam climbed topside, he dove into the water for a leisurely swim over to where the *Bonita* had moored for the night and back. The rope he used to climb back into the *Jenna* was still hanging over the stern.

Maybe if she just hung on to the rope, she could wash with a free hand. It was ungodly hot. If she saw something move in the water, she could simply shimmy up the rope like Adam and get into the boat. Jenna peered over the side at the inviting mirror smooth surface, as still as the surroundings. Then, making her decision, she fetched a bar of soap from her carry-on and slipped into the water, sleep shirt and all.

Her mind drifted back to her first "bath" in the jungle, during Adam's house call the night after her arrival in Ichitas. One thing was for certain, this wouldn't be the first night she'd dried out in a hammock.

Ten

A BATH OFF THE SIDE OF A BOAT SOUNDED SIMPLE IN THEORY. After all, a rope hung over the side for access and safety. Unfortunately, application of the theory was an entirely different matter.

First, Jenna lost her bar of soap. It slipped out of her hand while she was sudsing her hair and went straight for the river bottom, which she could not touch with her toes. But the water was heavenly, not too cool nor too tepid, like that of the club pool during a long, dry heat wave. She wished she could let go of the rope, but the current was strong and she was too tired to test her swimming skills.

Feeling fully refreshed, or as refreshed as one could in water the color of a malt chocolate shake, Jenna wrapped her feet around the rope and pushed upward. To her surprise, beneath the water surface the thick jute was slick, no doubt covered with the same greenish slime that coagulated along the nooks and crannies of the banks.

A fish jumped a few yards away from her and her breath seized. Reminded that she was not alone in the water, Jenna tried pulling herself up hand over hand. She could get her shoulders as far out of the water as the ship's rail, but there was no strength left to get her bottom half over it. Her bare legs scraped the cracked paint on the planking, searching for a knee, or even a toehold, but all she gained was sharp pain in the ball of her foot.

With a startled yelp, she slipped back into the water, panic growing by the heartbeat. Leave it to her to get a splinter *swimming!*

"Adam!"

And blood attracted piranha. *Oh, heavenly Father, please don't let it bleed!*

"Adam!" she hissed through her teeth.

A cartoon image of a skeleton clinging to a rope off the back of a boat flashed through Jenna's mind. She had to stay calm. *I won't distress!*

She didn't want to awaken her father, or anyone else for that matter.

And I won't despair!

As for Adam DeSanto, it didn't make much difference. He'd make fun of her regardless. Although, she thought, pulling on the rope again with renewed determination, she hated to give him more fuel for his warped humor.

There was a sliding sound from overhead and the light thump of elbows, or perhaps, knees. Adam's head appeared over the edge of the canopy, silhouetted dark against the moonlit sky.

"Jenna?"

He slid further over and peered into the darkness of the deck beneath him.

Jenna swallowed the last of her pride.

"Down here…in the water."

"Ah!" He looked at her over folded arms, head cocked sideways. "Are we skinny dipping?"

"In your dreams."

"In that case…" He yawned and rolled over. "I will just go back to sleep."

"I *can't* get back in the boat!"

Something brushed against Jenna's foot. It was most likely more of the flotsam, but she couldn't keep the panic from her shrill whisper.

"And there's something in here nibbling on my toes!" *Dear God, please, no piranha!* Although, they'd have made a meal of her by now, wouldn't they?

With a smooth acrobatic curl, the irascible doctor dropped down from the canopy and onto the stern deck light as a cat. He moved like he was born to the jungle, quick and quiet.

"Grab my arms, Jenna."

With no quirky smile or taunt, simply raw grunting strength, Adam hauled Jenna out of the water. Exhausted from fear as much as effort, she didn't resist when he pulled her to him and held her, trembling in his arms. He was warm, and his embrace felt as if nothing could harm or threaten her. She savored it, knowing full well the risk she took was all her own. But reckless was becoming a growing facet of her personality. For all she knew, it had always been there, leashed by the role of her former life.

Her nose twitched, tickled by the hair on his chest. Without warning, she sneezed. The captivating close-ness evaporated. Adam released her. The cool rush of air that filled the void between them struck Jenna at the same time her left foot protested from her full weight upon it.

She gasped and dropped onto the bench, remembering the splinter. Her foot cradled across her leg, she felt for the offending object. It had broken off when she stood up. She shook off a tummy swirl of nausea.

"Let me see."

Seemingly from out of nowhere, Adam produced a small penlight and shined it on her foot. Wrapped around her toe was a piece of river grass. He pulled it away and tossed it over the side.

"I did see a fish earlier," Jenna managed in self-defense.

Adam touched the stub of the wood and swore. "My next project is to scrape and paint this boat!"

"Can you get it out?"

"Have you got tweezers? My bag is stashed forward, and all I have is this."

He produced a pocketknife.

Jenna nodded toward her overnight case. "In the bag."

Ah, the leetle flowered bag on wheels! Adam didn't need to say it. His expression did. He picked it up and handed it to her. From an outside zippered compartment, Jenna took out a leather-encased manicure set.

"Have you any lotion or such with alcohol?"

"Will triple antibiotic ointment do?"

"For tonight."

Jenna contemplated the sharp, noble profile of the doctor's face as he went to work with the tweezers. He was so gentle, she hardly felt it when he opened the wound a little more to extract a piece of wood that remained behind. His application of the ointment afterward affected her far more than it had a right to.

Adam DeSanto might have the temperament of a jaguar, or *onça,* as Tilda chided from time to time, but beneath it was incredible tenderness. Jenna saw it when he was with patients, especially the children. Now he shared it with her.

"You continue to amaze me, Jenna Marsten." Adam shoved himself up from the squatting position in front of her bench.

"I'll take that as an apology."

"For what?"

"For trying to scare me away with that kiss."

Jenna regretted the words the moment they were out, not just because she'd admitted that Adam's kiss had

left its impression, but also because they brought the
onça back. Gone was the sweetness, the tenderness. In
its place was a predatory ebony gleam.

Adam tilted his head, like the cat contemplating the
mouse.

"You mean, you want me to apologize for kissing
you?"

Jenna rubbed her foot and slipped it into a pair of
canvas deck shoes. She could tell from the incredulity in
his voice that anything of the sort was out of the question now.

"Forget it. It was a dumb joke."

"Well, I am *not* sorry!" He glanced up at the canopy
and ran his fingers through his thick hair.

"Fine. It was nothing."

"In fact..." He swung back to her, jaw jutting in a
neck-stretching jerk. "I am so *unsorry*, that I will do it
again!"

Frozen like a cornered mouse, knowing there was
no escape, Jenna caught her breath. The caress of Adam's
skilled fingers along the taper of her chin moved her
head back to receive his kiss. If the possessive yet tender
claim on her mouth could be called that. Its completeness was intoxicating and relaxing at the same time, like
the brush of a tropical breeze through her hair.

And she thought feelings like these existed only in
romance books! She'd never known the like with Scott.
They begged her abandon reason and will. The only
course was to go into Adam's embrace. Jenna moved

closer, until she could feel the counterpoint of thundering hearts.

Then suddenly, Adam tore away, staring at her as if she'd grown two heads. He raised his finger at her and then dropped it, as if he had second thoughts about what he was about to say.

"For the love of Pete's sake, put some dry clothes on!"

Jenna almost corrected Adam's English, but considering the way his kiss still ravaged her senses, proper speech was the *least* of her problems.

Reaching up, he grabbed the lip of the canopy and curled up and over it. Jenna crossed her arms and shuddered, listening to the man settle restlessly on the deck above her. She wasn't cold. She was far from it. In fact, she didn't even feel the tenderness on the ball of her foot until she lay in the hammock, her scattered senses barbequed with ragged emotion and skewered by one thought—*heavens to Betsy!*

Maybe she shouldn't go, she thought the following morning as the natives moved the medical supplies in an assembly line from the gangway to the donkey drawn cart. Not that Adam did or said anything about the passionate interlude the night before. Manning the cart end of the line, he was his usual dour, all-business, no-nonsense self. He'd had little, if anything, to say to her all morning, which was fine, considering the quagmire of

Jenna's mind. She wasn't even sure she could manage a shrug.

Stefan and his soundman opted to carry what they'd need on a second, much smaller cart. The metal photography cases glistened in the sunlight, drawing as much attention as Jenna's little flowered bag on wheels. Several people gathered around to watch and to wait until the boat was unloaded. Once that was done, her father could start seeing patients.

A flat boat arrived loaded with various size stones. Two boats and the stone seller were enough to draw a crowd. Evidently stones for hearths and building were scant in this area.

Unlike the village near the clinic, this one was, for the most part, free of concrete and manufactured goods. The jungle and water provided food, clothes, and shelter. Enough and no more, Jenna thought, even for the authoritative man whom her father introduced as the chief. Respect set him apart more than his clothing or his home.

Jenna's wounded foot, ensconced in a Band-Aid, the mandatory cotton sock, and sneakers, didn't bother her all that much, which was good, considering they would be walking most of the way to the inland lake. She hugged her father good-bye.

"You're just like your mom, Jen," he told her proudly. "She loved adventure, trying new things, meeting new people."

"You sure you're going to be okay here?"

"More comfortable than you're going to be, I assure you. Now get going."

Jenna hugged him again.

"And don't let Adam intimidate you. He's a softy inside," her father called after her as she walked the bouncing gangway to where Stefan Murillo, always the attentive gentleman, awaited to assist her up the steps.

"Your water bottle is full?" Adam reminded her when they reached the ready caravan.

"To the brim."

Jenna looked beyond him where two village men took the lead, machetes hanging from the same thong that held up their loincloths. Slung across their bare backs by strips of leather were long tubelike things of wood and bamboo.

Stefan's camera clicked. "And now, señorita, we go into the land of the blow gun."

Scenes of *Tarzan* and other jungle movies flashed through Jenna's mind as the ensemble moved ahead on the hard-packed earthen road. It ran alongside a small stream that disappeared into the leaf-canopied jungle. Never in her wildest dreams did she ever expect to be a part of a safari like this. Oh, she'd fantasized about it, always the adventurer at heart, but this was real. Her heart swelled with a primitive excitement she'd never known on her art tours of Europe and the Orient.

Adam DeSanto troubled her, but the prospect of carrying medicine and help to the interior tribes overshadowed her distress. Her own reaction and feelings toward him left her perplexed, but today, in the bright light of God's sun, she could not despair. She earnestly meant it when she prayed, *Thank You, Lord, for this glorious day, for the opportunity to serve You and Your children, for this breathtaking Eden, and for the good company...even Adam.*

A born volunteer. That's what Aunt Violet insisted Jenna was from her candy striper days through all the campaigns for this charity or that, in which the Winston clan and its peers were involved. This, however, was more hands on.

Literally, Jenna thought later as she ducked low hanging tree branches that grew across the jungle pass. No air-conditioned ballrooms. No champagne. No sequins or black ties. Just jungle, a water bottle, and basic cotton.

Ahead, the men cleared a path for the carts by hacking away the undergrowth while the donkey plodded patiently along behind them. Although they widened the footpath, Stefan remarked that they would still have to clear new brush on the way back to the river.

"The jungle reclaims its own very quickly."

As he had on the airplane trip to Ichitas, the photographer made the journey more pleasant, telling stories and anecdotes along the way. As a sideline for his career in nature shows, he filmed advertising videos for various individually financed projects. The more he talked, the faster the wheels turned in Jenna's mind.

"How much would you charge to film the clinic?"

If the businessmen and grant administrators would not come to the clinic, why not carry it to them? They could take copies of the video back to their home offices to show the good their support would bring to the Indians and those who could not afford government health care.

"And we could send them out to foundations not in attendance. I have a vast mailing list of philanthropic organizations who might be willing to donate. I've built it over the years raising money for the art foundation." Jenna placed her hand on Stefan's arm, stopping him in his tracks. "You could be a godsend!"

Taken aback by her fervor, Stefan chuckled. "I have been called many things, señorita, but a godsend is not one of them."

"You could start at the lake! Adam is wonderful with the natives, especially the children. Everything we use is donated, like inoculations, preventative items like toothbrushes, over-the-counter aspirin. Have you got extra film?"

"What's the hold up?" Adam shouted from the back of the caravan.

Jenna turned to discover herself about to be rear-ended by the gray donkey.

Stefan ushered her ahead. "Let us not lag too much, Jenna, or we will have to walk *behind* the donkey."

"But the film!"

"I think we can arrange something," he told her with a conspiratorial wink.

"Great!" Jenna hugged the young man and gave him a hasty peck on the cheek.

"This is truly a first," Stefan said as she resumed her walk beside him, a decided bounce to her step that had not been there before.

"How's that?"

"I think I am having my purse emptied and enjoying it at the same time."

"Just so you keep walking, amigo." Adam DeSanto had caught up with them.

"Adam!" There was no way Jenna could contain her excitement over the good news. "You'll never guess what just happened!"

"Not now, Jenna."

Instead of falling in step with her and Stefan, the long-legged doctor continued moving ahead, a machete brandished in his hand. Jenna exhaled, her balloon of exuberance punctured by the sharp dismissal.

"Perhaps, señorita, it is just as well that he is swinging that blade *ahead* of us, no?"

"Nah! He'll be thrilled. He just doesn't know it yet."

Jenna winced as Adam assaulted the greenery with the flashing steel in steady but vicious swings and wished she was as certain as she sounded.

Father, I feel this is what You sent me for. Just help me deal with the temperamental onça.

It made perfect sense to Jenna. Her coming here wasn't just to find her father. It was to pick up his work, or rather, facilitate it. With her contacts and vision, she could make up for what his partner lacked in social skills. For the first time in her life, Jenna was really excited about what lay ahead for her. It was a conviction of the heart and the soul.

Godsend his feet! Adam thought hotly, taking off a low hanging palm branch as if it were Stefan Murrillo's head. The man wouldn't even be here if Adam had not agreed to show him the way and bargain with the Indians for him. So he was going to take a few pictures for the clinic. That made him a godsend? If Adam had taken the position offered him by Hopkins, there most likely would not even be a clinic to take pictures of!

If Jenna kissed anyone, it should be him, not the photographer. What did she even know of the man? Hah, the things he could tell the doctor's daughter about her "godsend." Stefan was a womanizer! She would mean nothing to that picture taker—unlike Adam himself.

Adam stopped suddenly, shocked by his unexpected conclusion. In an instant, Jenna stumbled against his back with a startled exclamation.

"Hey, Doc, your brake lights aren't working." She stepped backward, alarm infiltrating her voice. "Did you see a snake?"

Adam ground his teeth to hold back his frustration. "Yes," he hissed through them. "A very dangerous one."

Murillo glanced around warily. "Where?"

Glaring at the man, Adam shrugged. "It must have slipped away. Even so," he told Jenna. "Perhaps you'd best stay close."

The young woman closed the distance she'd placed between them. "Like a second skin, Doc."

Ignoring the photographer's suspicious look, Adam turned to the path ahead, the corner of his mouth twitching in satisfaction.

Eleven

SLEEP HAD BEEN INTERMITTENT THE NIGHT BEFORE, SO IT FELT to Jenna as if they'd been walking for days when the small caravan finally broke free of the green hothouse air and emerged at a vast clearing. The lake shone like a dark mirror in the late afternoon sun. Some half naked children squealed and splashed in delight along the edge of the water, while some sort of jungle pet, which resembled a pig with a rodent's head, raced in and among them.

A black water lake. It was hard to imagine, but there it was, with water that looked like a strong tea in color, clear as opposed to the milky translucence of the Amazon. Once a hairpin bend in the river, the constantly rerouting water built up enough silt and soil that it was eventually cut off. Its water color came from the tannin of the vegetation rotting at the bottom, the clarity from lack of current.

Stefan told Jenna about the abundance of wildlife with which he hoped to supplement his filming of the coming-of-age ritual, including a bizarre bird that was thought to be a throw back from prehistoric times—the hoatzin. Its young was born with tiny claws in their wings with which to climb back up the bank, should they tumble out of their nests into the water.

Feeling a bit like an explorer at the edge of time, Jenna stayed close to Stefan and Adam as curious children and wary adults surrounded them. Only the visitors' camp itself was allowed to be unpacked until Adam parleyed with the chief.

The jungle was cleared around the village, with its open long houses of palm and thatch. There was a large *molucca* in the center where they were received in a stoic manner. Sitting on the ground around a large square hearth, a stone perimeter filled with sand, Jenna endured lingering stares from the council of elders while Adam spoke to the chief and shaman using grand gestures and few smiles.

She picked up on a few of the words, but the intonations of the conversation and body language told her more. Adam was welcome. The village men spoke to him as an old friend. Stefan on the other hand was the recipient of suspicious, skeptical looks on the sly, all the while being talked about. She felt more like a curiosity, especially when she removed her hat and reclamped her hair.

The sun was going down before Adam was able to convince the chief that there was no harm in Stefan filming the ritual. He managed to convince the Indians that many people would be fascinated by the custom and impressed by the strength and endurance of the tribe's young men. He asked the shaman to bless the project so that no evil spirits would invade the film, and the true courage and integrity of the Orinca would be made known to the outside world.

"And the chief would like to keep your tent," Adam informed Stefan as they left the council house. It was an open structure, which allowed those inside to watch the setup of the guests' campsites, where Stefan's modern tent of lightweight material captured the chief's fancy. "Your Swiss army knives will serve for the participants in the film. They will make the young men happy."

"Fine. For a moment, I thought the devil was bargaining for Jenna."

Jenna cracked a smile, not so certain herself. There had been many gestures during the negotiation directed at her.

"I merely insisted that Jenna was to occupy the tent until we left…and explained that, while she is a stranger, she is Dr. Robert's daughter and interested in the well-being of his people. You are both welcome as *my* guests."

"How come you're in so good with them?"

Adam removed his palm hat and wiped his forehead with his arm. His attention was on the two hired men, who were working with Stefan's assistant.

"I spent a year with the tribe, studying medicine under the shaman."

At Jenna's disconcerted silence, he turned and winked.

"Not to worry, señorita. I did not learn the practice of the black magic…but of the value of the native medicines."

"That's why the doctors at the research center always call Adam when they discover something they are not familiar with," Stefan added. "I don't think he wore shoes on a regular basis until he went away to school in the States. I remember the first time Marina saw him, he'd just returned from a season with the Orinca—"

"I have work to do. We will have dinner with the chief tonight," Adam informed them over his shoulder. Clearly uncomfortable as the center of conversation, he left Jenna with Stefan to help the men set up the medical canopy. While she really wanted to hear the rest of Stefan's story, Jenna excused herself as well.

"Guess I'd better earn my keep!"

The canopy was a dirty white canvas with a faded red cross, twice as heavy as the lightweight material of the newer tent. Once erected, it served as a cover for the cart. Flaps, rolled up on all four sides, stood ready to tie down in case of inclement weather, but according to Adam, they were rarely used. Jenna held the hammock posts while Adam drove them into the sand with a mallet.

"It is just as well you have a cot," Adam remarked, upon putting his weight on the hammock. The two poles immediately pulled inward. "It is almost impossible to string a bed in this sand."

"Why not string it from the cart wheel to the tree?"

She watched as the idea took root in Adam's contemplative gaze.

"Humph!" he grunted in agreement. "You untie that end. I'll get this one."

Singing inside at Adam's approval, Jenna did as she was told. The idea worked perfectly. In fact, the open canopy looked more inviting than the enclosed tent…until the flies started in on their evening meal of human flesh.

Inside her private "room," Jenna bathed from a bucket and smeared on the last of her over-the-counter insect repellent. Tomorrow she'd have to resort to kerosene and avoid campfires, she told herself, nose wrinkling in distaste.

"Hello? Jenna, may I come in?"

"Enter."

Adam unzipped the front of the tent and poked his head inside.

"I came to make a house call."

As he ducked under the opening, he held out a fresh bandage and disinfectant as proof. The ceiling was still too low for him to stand upright. It brushed the top of Jenna's head at its peak.

"You were starting to limp when we left the molucca."

She laughed, startled that he'd paid her any heed at all. Perhaps his intense focus was just a facade for morbid curiosity.

"I can clean it up, you know," she offered, as he settled on his knees. "Although I kind of like the idea of you on your knees at my feet."

"In your dreams, señorita."

There it was, that quirky little twitch at the corner of his mouth. Its mischief infected his dark glance as he removed her sneaker and sock.

"So tell me, did you wear one of those little native diapers?"

"Loincloth," he corrected, dabbing Betadine on the open wound. "And yes, when I lived with the Orinca, I dressed as they did; I became one of them."

"Ritual and all?"

"Sí, ritual and all."

She leaned over, watching as Adam worked more ointment into the ball of her foot with massaging fingers.

"So what did you have to do, walk over hot coals?"

"Not in this country."

"Well what *do* they do?"

"Fire ants."

He finished securing the Band-Aid and sat back on his heels.

"They very carefully weave a sleeve of palm with live ants fastened in it. It is meticulous work, but there are hundreds of the insects with pincers fastened inside. The young men then thrust their arm into the sleeve like so—"

He cupped his hands on either side of Jenna's arm to demonstrate.

Jenna winced at the thought. "Ouch!"

"Oh, I am sorry."

"No, you didn't hurt me. I was just thinking about how awful the pain must be. I mean hundreds of fire ants at one time..."

"It is painful," the doctor assured her. He looked over at the open suitcase. "So, what are you going to do without your panty hose tonight?"

"Have to shave my legs, I guess."

This time it was Adam who made a face, as if the very idea were repugnant. "I hope you have your own razor, señorita, because you are not ruining mine."

"Sounds like the voice of experience," Jenna teased as he backed out of the tent.

"I am never twice burned, chica."

The flap closed, sealing his hasty retreat.

A spontaneous yawn assaulted Jenna, taking her by surprise. She wondered if she had time to take a short nap before dressing for dinner. The hot pink tank dress from the same travel outfitter her hat came from had more than paid for itself since embarking on this adventure. Although she was probably overdressed for an open-hearth meal.

"Oh, by the way..." The tent flap moved aside and Adam stuck his head back in. "I hope you like monkey."

"Does it taste like chicken?"

Her companion shrugged. "It tastes like monkey."

Jenna's stomach did a complete turn, but she hid it behind a bright smile. "Looking forward to it!"

Twelve

MONKEY DEFINITELY TASTED LIKE MONKEY. HARDLY TASTING
the stew, Jenna filled up on a package of crushed cheese
crackers, which Tilda had thoughtfully tucked into her
bag. She blessed the woman time and again—although
the stew wasn't really bad. At least it didn't have little
hands and humanlike skulls floating about in it, like she
imagined. It was just the thought that made her shudder.

Adam and Stefan, however, had no problem with it.
While she picked at the cassava bread, something she'd
come to recognize as a native staple, they helped themselves to seconds. The tinned meat they'd had that afternoon with bread had long since been burned off by the
day's travel.

She listened to the men talk, picking out words here
and there, until their voices became a drone somewhere
in the back of her mind. She didn't realize she'd fallen

asleep until she keeled over into Adam and awoke with a start.

"If you wish, I will walk you back to your tent."

Jenna shook her head. "I can find my way. Just explain to the chief for me. I didn't really sleep well last night."

"Neither did I," Adam said with a thoughtful curl of his lips. "Something in the air, perhaps?"

"Insect spray, no doubt!"

Her companion gave her regards to the chief for a pleasant evening, paving the way for Jenna's "Gracias, señor, y mucho gusto." Unsure of just how much the native understood, Jenna backed up her thanks and pleased to meet you with a strong handshake.

"Are you certain you do not wish company to your tent?"

"It's within shouting distance if I need you, and the grounds are grass free."

Hence, snake free, Jenna told herself as she made her way back to the tent with a flashlight. The moon was bright enough to do away with the light were she back home, walking along the dunes of Cape Cod. Here in the Amazon, however, there were so many exotic creatures to avoid.

After dousing the kerosene lamp on a post set outside the tent, Jenna opened the flap and ducked inside. The beam of the flashlight illuminated the floor of the small enclosure, assuring Jenna it was vermin free. *Almost.* Dropping to her knees, she thrust the light beneath the collapsible cot where she'd stashed her little flowered bag.

The first thing that caught Jenna's attention was her clothing, strewn about and smudged with mud and dirt. That was followed immediately by a dual red glare. Her light reflected a large pair of eyes staring back at her!

A scream lodged in Jenna's throat, as frozen as every muscle in her body. Neither she nor the animal, whatever it was, moved. She had to be calm! Wild beasts responded aggressively to panic, even beasts with a shredded pair of jeans hanging from their mouths. Her only pair…

"Oh no!"

Her high-pitched wail broke the stalemate. The creature charged her, its back rippling the cot like a shark fin breaking water. Jenna screamed and slung the flashlight at it. With an ungodly shriek of its own, it retreated back, upending the cot as it tried to butt its way through the back tent wall.

"Adam!"

Jenna threw herself on the cot to hold it down, not to mention getting her feet and legs out of biting range. Or clawing.

"Adam!" Incredibly the animal was bucking beneath the cot, practically lifting her off the ground. Incoherent terror tore from Jenna's throat, only her silent prayer made sense. *Dear Jesus. Oh, Jesus!*

The muffled thunder of footsteps outside assured her that someone was running to her rescue, or was it the racking and thumping of the cot? The animal moved beneath her, driving Jenna to the end, as far away as possible.

"Jenna!" Adam's light flashed inside the tent. "What the...?"

At the same time the forward end of the cot flew up in Jenna's face. She tumbled off the back. Certain the animal was upon her, she kicked and screamed, clutching the flipped bed as a shield between her and certain savage death.

"Jenna!"

When Adam pulled away the cot, he brought Jenna up with it. Upon realizing it was he and not the beast, Jenna let go, sprawling back against the corner of the tent. Her feet were entangled in the open case. Her clothing, or what was left of it, lay strewn about.

"What was it?" she whispered, too weakened by sheer terror to move. "A jaguar?"

Her eyes glazed over, blurring the hands that grasped her by the arms and hauled her to her feet. "It...it lifted my bed and ate my clothes!"

Shredded was more like it. *And if it could do that to denim...* Turning away from Adam's open arms, Jenna examined her legs for any sign of bites or scratches.

"Are you hurt?" Her rescuer squatted, running his hands up and down her exposed limbs in hasty examination.

A commotion outside the tent generated more amusement than terror, distracting Jenna almost as

216

much as Adam's impassive touch. It struck her odd that a big cat would cause the natives to laugh, but then they ate monkeys, so…

"Adam?"

Her voice shook almost as much as she did. Locking on to his shirt with balled fists as he rose again, she leaned into him. A sob erupted against his chest, where she buried her face.

"Shush, chica. It was just the children's pet capybara."

"That big p-pig-looking thing?"

Pressed close, she felt his deep-throated chuckle. "Yes, the pig-looking thing. Believe me, from all the shrieking we heard, you scared it as much as it scared you."

Jenna wasn't so certain. Her chest hurt from the beating her heart was giving it.

"You must have left the tent flap unzipped, or it nosed the zipper up. They are quite mischievous and innovative creatures—a lot like a certain young lady I know."

He was laughing at her! With an angry shove, Jenna struck Adam.

"I do *not* go around rummaging through people's suitcases with dirty feet and—" She bent over and picked up the shredded jeans. "And eating their clothes!"

"What do you want me to do? Take it before the fashion police?"

Jenna jerked her hand toward the tent flap. "I want you to leave. Wait!" she added hastily.

He turned, crossing his arms with a condescending air.

"Will you fetch me a stone to put over the zipper?"

Jenna had never wanted to strike a soul in her entire life until now, but the crooked grin Adam gave her begged to be knocked off. Only her most supreme self-control saved him. He leaned down and pointed to a strap that was used to hold the zipper in place. She hadn't seen it before, not that she'd thought securing the tent was necessary.

"All you must do is—"

"Okay, I see it. I'll try not to be a bother now."

"Ah, chica, I don't think that you can help yourself."

Adam slipped through the flap, but not before Jenna whipped him on his way with her torn jeans.

Feeling somewhat avenged, she turned to the task of putting her things back to order. She sorted the dirty from the clean, the torn from the intact, uprighted her cot, and fell into it exhausted and fully dressed. Jenna couldn't recall when she'd ever felt more drained, emotionally or physically.

Her earlier bright sense of purpose flickered dangerously near going out. Had she read God wrong? At that moment, it sure seemed like it.

Lord, I need Your strength. Right now I feel like David going up against a giant—and Lord, I'm just about out of stones! And speaking of stones, I know Adam isn't stone-

hearted, he's just…well, he's stone-headed. Jesus, he needs a heavenly thump of some kind. I just don't know what or how…but You do. And please, Lord, keep that pig thing away. In the name of Your son…

Her prayer gave way to much needed sleep.

"So, the great capybara huntress emerges!" Stefan called out to the girl stepping through the opening of the tent the following day.

Adam didn't find it so amusing when the photographer found grounds to tease Jenna Marsten. Yes, it had been funny at the time; that is once he knew she was in no real danger. Prior to that, he'd aged a year for every step he'd taken between the molucca and Jenna. His imagination ran as wild as Jenna's, overriding his common jungle sense. Even when the spooked capybara charged between his legs, he'd not really seen what it was. His attention was focused on the young woman wrestling with the cot atop her. He'd had to pry her fingers from its frame.

Then she was trembling and clinging to him, driving what little presence of mind he held in reserve completely away. It took sheer will not to keep her there, not to smother her with reassuring kisses. Of that, his fear was as real as Jenna's. He would not be burned twice. He couldn't bear it.

Jenna took a seat at Murillo's portable table and thanked the photographer for a cup of coffee.

Adam had already had his caffeine boost at daybreak, after a wildlife wake up call—a caiman thrashing a fish to death on the water's bank. Dawn was as breathtaking as it was deadly. Love was as inviting as it was painful. He wasn't willing to pay its price.

Let Stefan Murillo flirt to his heart's content. It didn't matter.

Suddenly Adam's ears burst with a high-pitched squeal. Jerked from his brooding, he pulled his stethoscope away from the baby he examined and wiped the drool on his shirt.

"I am sorry, *niñito!* That is what I get for not giving you my undivided attention."

Like most of the natives, the baby was basically healthy. Mother Nature provided a good diet plan with exercise. The biggest threat to the locals were parasites, infections, disease from poor hygiene, and traumas, such as snake or caiman bites. The allergies, heart and lung problems, and ailments of civilization, which Adam had treated during his internship at Johns Hopkins, were practically unheard of here. Childhood diseases, however, were not.

He filled a syringe and wiped the baby's fat thigh. Regular inoculation during the past fifteen years had substantially increased the survival rate of the native children. What had been pure curiosity up until this point, changed to screaming despair when Adam delivered the injection. It was quick, but not quick enough for the little one.

"Ah, I am so sorry, amigo!" He threw the disposable needle down on the ground and stomped it. "Bad, bad!"

Distracted by the strange antics of the doctor, the baby's scream reduced to a hiccoughing breath.

"You are all finished!" Adam picked up the baby and jiggled him playfully. The baby's quivering lips broke into a large, round *O* of delight. Quickly, the doctor turned his head just in time to avoid a dropping glob of drool.

Jenna approached him, teasing. "Boy, the hazardous material police would be all over you like ugly on an ape!"

With a cursory glance at her, Adam handed the assuaged babe back to his mother.

"Did you sleep well, señorita?"

She still looked tired to him, not enough sunshine in the blue of her eyes.

"Like a log. Having the life scared out of one does that, I guess. Speaking of which…" She cast a look around. "Where is the critter?"

"Probably sleeping like a log somewhere."

She snickered. It was as charming to Adam's ear as the baby's laugh. Something told him Jenna Marsten would always be part child, wide eyed in wonder and adventurous in spirit. At least, he hoped she would. He didn't want to see the jungle put out that special innocence and replace it with bitterness and resentment. Sooner or later, she would get her fill, and like a child, wander off to new experiences, leaving him behind.

"Okay, so besides making certain all the needles get into the proper containers, what do you want me to do?"

"How about writing down what I tell you? That will free my hands for the patients. We will need the patient's name, the family name, the tribe…"

"They aren't all Orincas?"

"I mean the village. There are many lake villages. This one is the most central of them, so many of the natives here today are from places further inland. I will give you an abbreviation."

Jenna took up the clipboard Adam handed her. It was filled with the forms she and her father had made up to record data on the trip. A beguiling thrill of satisfaction swept over her face.

"One small step for Jenna, one giant step for Adam DeSanto."

Adam ignored her feisty jibe and placed a toddler on the makeshift examining table. When it came to shots, this child was no more receptive than the last one. It took him and the mother to hold the child.

"Okay, señorita, where is it you wish me to film?"

Surprised, Adam glanced up to see Stefan Murillo setting up a camera. "Film what?"

"Stefan is going to film some of your work for a video to show just what you and Dad are doing here in the jungle."

"And who will watch this video?" The idea of being on film did not appeal to Adam at all.

"The people attending the seminar at Posada

Explorador," Jenna informed him in an enthusiastic burst. "And I intend to make copies to send to the various philanthropic clubs and organizations on my art foundation list. We may actually be able to set up the minilaboratory you and Dad have wanted, not to mention—"

"And Jenna has talked me into filming it for free."

"Enough!"

Adam held up his hands in surrender. It was a good idea, one that never crossed his or his partner's mind. He was beginning to think the meaning for the word *resourceful* was Jenna Marsten.

"Just stay back and use discretion," he told Stefan.

The mother of his next patient complained of a toothache. Adam told her to wait until all the children received their shots. Then he would look at the adults. Since it was a fiesta day, most of the families would be staying for the celebration and ceremony that evening. It was like a giant family reunion and clinic combined.

While he spoke to the woman, he caught a glimpse of Jenna traversing up and down the line initiating some sort of game with her broken Spanish. She would thump the little ones with her finger and then allow them to do the same to her. And they loved her hat, the way the brim could be folded up in the front or down to hide their face for peek-a-boo.

When the next child, a little girl of about five, was brought before Adam, Jenna plopped her hat on the little one's dark shining hair. While Adam filled the syringe for the vaccination, Jenna alternated between thumping on the child's arm with her finger and peek-a-boo. The little girl giggled at the woman's crazy antics, forgetting what lay ahead of her for the moment.

"Ready? Where's the target?"

Adam pointed to the child's upper arm. His unorthodox helper promptly stung the arm with a snap of her finger and tugged the brim of her hat down on the little girl's face. Following her lead, Adam delivered the shot. When the hat brim came up, it revealed two wide, round brown eyes and a large grin, which broke out as he withdrew the needle, as if the child was stunned and delighted that it hadn't hurt.

"That's it! Finished." To Jenna, he said, "Let her pick her own Band-Aid."

Jenna gave the little girl a choice of assorted colored bandages. The child chose a red one and wore it like a badge of honor for her friends to see.

And so the day wore on. To Adam's surprise, there was nothing Jenna turned up her nose at. In fact, she seemed genuinely interested in the cases, plying him for answers to intelligent questions, especially regarding parasites.

"The human body is the perfect medium for such things to grow, and there are so many here that it can be expected."

"You mean I could have some sort of worm larvae in me right now?"

"It's possible but not likely. We take precautions

with our food and water that the natives do not. That is why this is not only a treating excursion, but an educational one as well."

After three tooth extractions, too many inoculations to remember, not to mention treatments for parasites and administration of antibiotics, the line finally dwindled to an elderly gentleman and his daughter. Jenna took down the information while Adam examined a long gash on the man's thigh that had become infected. It needed to be lanced and drained.

"Although this is not the first time," Adam observed. He spoke to the man in the native's language, discovering the shaman of the tribe had treated it. The daughter believed her father was not healing because a *bruja* had cast a spell on him.

"They think it's witchcraft causing the infection," Adam informed Jenna as he probed the wound with a needle of local anesthesia.

"A witch?"

"Sí, señorita," Stefan spoke up. "The natives are very superstitious, despite the missionaries efforts to combat it."

"This is the jungle, Jenna," Adam explained. "It is why we must combine the best of modern medicine with jungle medicine for the good of the patient. I am working on a thesis for the medical journal with that theme. Much of what we discover during our work helps advance knowledge and treatment."

"Are you getting all this on film?"

"All of it," Stefan assured the young woman working at Adam's side.

Adam wondered if the film would do justice to the way the sunlight played in the tumble of hair clipped haphazardly atop Jenna's head.

"Better put your hat back on," he observed. "And write this down: purulent material, possible anaerobic bacteria. Treatment: metronidazole."

He prepared to trim away the black, dry necrotic skin.

"Ah, see this?"

Jenna looked at the piece of debris he plucked from the incision. A thick fluid began to drain from it, the stench of which drove her back a step. Adam wouldn't have blamed her if she'd retched, but she didn't.

"What is it?" She was genuinely interested.

"This is one of nature's dissolving stitches—the pincers of jaguar ants. This technique was recorded as being used in India for centuries before modern medicine."

He removed two more remnants of the shaman's surgery.

"The shaman holds together the flaps of skin with tweezerlike tools and puts in the ant, pincers first, so that it latches on to both sides of the skin. He then cuts the ant off, leaving the pincers locked intact. Barring infection—"

"Do I need to write this down?"

"Only if you wish to remember it."

Adam noted again that she looked a bit pale beneath

her golden tanned complexion, but her expression was like a sunbeam on a cloudy day.

She practically bubbled with enthusiasm. "What can I say? Monkey meat, ant pincers, pig-sized rats—this place is more than I ever dreamed!" She turned to Stefan and laughed. "You *can* edit this, I hope."

"Most assuredly."

Adam had to admit, Jenna Marsten was a trooper. She took things in her stride and came back for more. But how often would she do this before she reached the point where she could no longer stand it?

He pondered that question over and over as he watched her check their new records against the inventory while he finished treating his last patient. They'd worked through siesta—the hottest part of the day—and she'd made no complaint, aside from chiding Stefan when he packed up his camera to set up for the ritual filming.

Some of the children came back, laughing and begging her to come play with them. Instead she took some blank forms and drew pictures on the back, quite good ones actually. Her pen nailed the image of the capybara, which was no doubt indelibly etched in her mind for eternity.

When the donkey cart clinic officially closed, most of the supplies had been used or doled out with instructions. All were accounted for, in legible writing on a coherent form. Adam was again taken with the young woman's seemingly bottomless pit of resourcefulness.

She was too perfect, a dreamer hung up on lofty ideals and God-ordained purposes. Yes, she was more resilient than Marina, but time and the jungle had destroyed men and women of equal or stronger ilk than the naive debutante from Boston.

"I think I'm going to rinse off and take a short nap…too much *mal dormido.*"

Adam's attention snapped to. "What?" He knew full well that what Jenna meant to say and what she said were not the same thing.

"I said I didn't sleep well—*mal dormido*—bad sleeping."

But she was so adorable! Life would never be dull around her.

"Jenna, Jenna…*mal dormido* this is an idiom, that means, um…" He searched for a softer word for the term. "Lovemaking."

"Ah!" She winced in dismay and walked off, shaking her head. "No wonder that woman was laughing at me. The whole blasted tribe probably thinks…I don't dare take a nap now!"

Mal dormido. The Indian idiom pricked at Adam's mind, raising thoughts he had no right to consider. He exhaled heavily, as if to rid himself of them.

"No, amigo," he resolutely argued with himself. "Don't even go there!"

Thirteen

———⦿⦿⦿⦿———

JENNA SPENT THE REMAINING PART OF THE DAY ON THE LAKE-side, watching the children play. Up near the molucca, great goings-on were taking place. The men mostly talked and drank cachaça, a beverage made from sugar cane rum. Jenna refused the offer of a cup and kept her water bottle close by. That and a dash of lime juice, courtesy of Stefan, were sufficient for her. Besides, she already had a headache.

Adam, now stripped of shirt and shoes, sat cross legged with the men around the square stone hearth of the long house, until a group of boys spirited him off to fish. Watching from the shore, Jenna rubbed on a home-made concoction of diluted bath oil—a parting gift from Aunt Violet. Its strong perfume was said to work well against mosquitoes, so Jenna was counting on it for the flesh-biting flies as well.

The sun hung low over the cathedral canopy of the jungle on the opposite shore of the lake, streaking the dark water with incredible shades of orange, red, and gold. Adam's silhouette stood tall amid the pint-sized fish prowlers. Waist deep in water, they waited for a likely supper candidate to pass by. With thin, sharp spears raised, poised and ready, they presented a primitive picture, beautiful in its simplicity. Jenna snapped it with the throwaway camera, hoping it would turn out.

It seemed as though every muscle in her body ached. She took a couple of aspirin, determined to watch and participate, if possible, in the fiesta. No one liked a party pooper, and she was not going to be accused of being one. Leaning against her arms as a prop behind her, she continued to watch the great fishermen, her eyelids growing heavier and heavier.

It had to be the long journey yesterday, coupled with lack of sleep rather than too much lovemaking. She laughed at herself. These people must think her some kind of floozy, traveling with two men and complaining of too much bed and not enough rest. This was definitely another one for her journal.

Her head seemed to lift, lighter than air, taking her with it. It was only when the sensation was doused by the very real drip of water that she came back to earth. Jenna opened her eyes to see Adam standing over her, water shedding off his sun-darkened skin and raven black curls.

"Jenna, why don't you lie down before you fall down?"

"No, I'm fine!" Climbing to her feet, she admired the nice sized fish still moving on the end of the sharp spear in his hand.

"I thought I would roast a fish for supper to go with the specialties our hosts are preparing."

He looked like some proud Robinson Crusoe or Tarzan. Of course, Jane should be admiring his fish not his physique. He just looked so…so wild and rugged and…*lead me not into temptation.*

"That would be heavenly." Jenna's enthusiasm for his offer was real, especially after last evening's monkey du jour. "Can I help do anything?" *That,* she didn't mean. She was feeling worse, and a bed was seriously starting to look better than a native party. This wasn't like her at all.

"After all your help today, the least I can do is see you well fed. Just go. What is that smell?"

Clearly from Adam's wrinkled nose, Aunt Vi's bath oil did not make a good impression.

"Insect repellant. At least, they say it works like one."

"It certainly has a repelling scent," Adam agreed with more candor than was necessary. "Like a perfume factory gone bad."

Jenna grimaced and snapped her fingers in exaggerated disappointment. "Darn, and I was hoping it would sweep you off your feet."

"The night isn't over yet, chica." Adam shot back with a ornery grin. "It might work better than *yoppo!*"

At her bewildered expression, Adam pointed over to where the shaman and some of his companions were grinding a root in to some sort of dark powder.

"That stuff will clear the sinuses *and* the brain."

"Cocaine?"

Adam shook his head. "Yoppo is a root…big medicine. Makes you think you can wrestle a jungle cat with one hand tied behind you."

"So that's how the young men get enough nerve to stick their arms in a sleeve of angry, biting ants."

Earlier, one of the patients showed her how the intricate weaving was done. Someone would have to be on hallucinogens or painkillers to shove a bare arm into that thing! Having stepped on a hill of fire ants on the way inland, Jenna had a taste of what they could do— besides make one dance frantically with a floral suitcase! The idea of the weaving wasn't much more appealing.

"Don't eat or drink anything I don't okay."

"Aye, aye, sir!"

Actually, Jenna didn't feel like eating at all. All she wanted to do was sleep. To fight the lethargy, she walked along the shoreline, surrounded by Indian children with their puppy counterpart, a little capybara. In the daylight, the animals didn't look ferocious at all, just strange. They frolicked like a pet, chasing and being chased. Of course, the one in her tent the night before had been the size of one of those hogs she'd seen at the county fair!

A smile tugged at her lips. Maybe she could publish

her journal someday as a comedy of errors. Don't stand on a hill of fire ants while admiring wild orchids. She could fill pages with that sort of hard-earned advice. A hundred yards or so away, a seemingly listless log came to life and dove into the deeper water, leaving a decided wake in its path.

And for her next chapter, *Woman Outruns Alligator!* Jenna turned back promptly toward the village. There, lanterns and torches were being lit as substitute for the sun, which was sinking faster and faster toward the tree line on the horizon.

Of all the native spread served that evening, which Adam approved as nonintoxicating or hallucinogenic, Jenna liked the *panetón* best. It was a sweet bread with dried fruit. She also enjoyed a break from water with a nonfermented concoction of nature's fruits, which many of the women and children enjoyed.

One of the little girls gave her a wild orchid. Although Jenna left her hair down to protect her neck from the incoming insects, she did brush one side back over her ear and fix the fragrant blossom there with a clip. With it, she felt quite the native on fiesta in her trusty cotton tank dress.

After the initial feasting, the telling of tales of the past, of great deeds and wars ensued. Sometimes for emphasis, an elder carried a six-foot bow and a quiver of long spearlike arrows. Some took a red paste and smeared it on their faces, symbolizing war. Jenna was reminded of an exotic western Indian scene.

"This is how they prepare for battle," Adam explained. It appeared important to him that she understood what was going on. He hovered about her all evening like a guardian angel, yet his *protection* made her feel anything but safe.

"War? You mean they still fight like the Indians of the Old West?"

"Or like the quarreling factions all over today's world. Usually the trouble starts with the kidnapping of women and children by one tribe or another; it insures healthy propagation."

"Oh."

Not that Jenna felt she was in danger from any outside sources. It was the uncommon thoughts and stirrings he provoked within her that left her discomfited and bemused. He'd definitely gone *native* now. Clad only in white boxer like shorts, the jungle doc was streaked with black paint like his Indian brothers.

"Don't worry, no one would want you. You're too pale and thin."

Jenna chuckled. "Did I ever tell you what a charmer you are with words?"

The young men of the tribe were primed with something called spit wine, a fermented drink made from chewed manioc root and served in gourds. They cheered at the tales of bravado, growing bolder and bolder with each cup and story.

Jenna watched in quiet wonder at the strangeness of it all. It didn't seem real, for here was man as primitive as those she'd read about or seen on the nature shows. It was infectious, enticing a civilized soul to identify with it, as though some ancient part of her had been awakened.

To be included among the men in the malucca was an honor, according to Adam. It was afforded to Jenna because she was a medicine woman and daughter of Dr. Robert. The village women were gathered around the fringes of the long house, keeping food and drink available.

Although weather wasn't cold by any means, a sudden chill raised the gooseflesh on Jenna's arms. How could a body be hot and cold at the same time? Because despite the sun having set and the enclosure being open she was. Worse, the aspirin had not done the trick where her headache was concerned. The accompaniment to the stories and impromptu dancing by drums and gourds wasn't helping, either.

The closeness of the bodies and the saccharine scent of her homemade insect repellent made Jenna increasingly queasy. She sat, torn between really wanting to stay, to bear up and witness the ritual, or giving in to her headache and threatening stomach. Finally, she decided that it was better to catch the festivities on video later, when she wasn't about to heave her guts out or blow a head gasket in front of the chief and the prospective young men-to-be.

"I have to go," she whispered to Adam.

"You are sick?"

Jenna shook her head. "No, just need some air. Gonna wash off this oil, now that the flies have had their fill and gone."

It even hurt to smile at her pitiful joke. She tugged on a long-sleeved shirt she'd worn over her dress earlier to fend off the sunset insect invasion and pushed herself up from the ground. Her leg muscles fairly screamed in protest. With a startled gasp, she fell back.

"Jenna?" Adam leaned over her and placed his hand on her forehead. In an oath's breath, he leapt to his feet and scooped her up. "How long have you had this fever?"

"I took aspirin." She didn't realize she had a fever. That would explain everything.

"Well doesn't *this* look interesting," Stefan exclaimed when Adam stepped around the carpet of natives and into the open air beyond. "Is this part of the ritual I shouldn't film?"

In no humor for Stefan's poor jests, Adam snapped. "Enough, Stefan! Jenna is sick."

Jenna is sick. The words swept over Adam like a wave of weakness. Nothing could happen to Jenna! He could feel the blood drain from his face with each step as he carried her toward the tent. Her body was burning up, literally trembling with fever. Just when he'd let his guard down the slightest, when he was enjoying being around her, this happened.

"I just need more aspirin."

"I am the doctor, Jenna, not you. Remember that."

He brushed the top of her head with his lips. There was no doubt that she suffered from a type of jungle fever. As to when she'd been infected, who knew? While she complained the last couple of nights about the flies biting so savagely, this could be from an insect bite a week ago.

"Do you ache all over, like with a flu?"

"Like every bone in my body is broken," she mumbled against his chest. "What is it? What happened?"

"I think perhaps you have been bitten by the wrong mosquito or fly at the wrong time, chica."

It was impossible to carry the young woman through the narrow tent opening without unzipping the flap completely. Gently, Adam set Jenna on her feet, supporting her with his arms, lest she fall. She tried to smother a cry of pain from carrying her own weight, but the pitiful whimper that strangled out clawed at him mercilessly.

Anger tangled with fear and guilt in his mind. Why had he let Robert talk him into bringing Jenna here? Why had Robert let her come in the first place? It wasn't as if the man didn't know how cruel the jungle could be, especially to those not accustomed to it. He could speak of God's will and protection all he wanted, but Adam did not believe in a God who cared. It would be nice to believe, to share that unshakeable faith Jenna and her father possessed. Adam just knew better.

Although you used to believe as they did. The Lord once had a home in your heart. Adam shook the contradiction from his mind, but the tightness it spawned in his chest remained.

"I'm sorry to be such a bother."

She was on the verge of tears. The little that he'd known Jenna, he knew she wasn't the crybaby sort. If she cried, she had a reason. He couldn't bear her tears. He was distracted enough as it was. Again Adam forced the impromptu appeal from his thoughts. It was an expression, *not* a prayer he argued, not really understanding just whom he argued against. He inhaled a tortured breath. Besides, he didn't believe in prayer.

"You are no bother, Jenna." Adam stripped off her shirt and eased her back on the cot. Jenna's condition needed all his thought, his concentration. "Now rest here. I am going to fetch my bag."

"You'll be back?"

"Yes, I will be back." He started for the tent opening.

"Adam!"

He stopped short. "Yes?"

"Don't let that pig thing in here."

Another time, he would have laughed. Instead, Adam practically strangled himself by running under one of the tent lines in his rush to get his medical bag. In a minute or so, he returned to Jenna's side. A thermometer confirmed his suspicion. Her fever had shot up dangerously high and quickly. True she'd looked tired, but she'd given no sign of actually feeling ill that afternoon. He attributed her wanness to lying awake all night waiting for the return of the capricious capybara.

Rifling through the remainder of his medicines, he chose a vial of powdered concentrate and shot saline into it so that he could effuse it.

"This will help with the pain, Jenna. Then I will give you something to bring the fever down."

"Umm."

Her breathing was noticeably rapid now. While jungle fevers weren't usually fatal, they felt that way to the patient.

Adam took a pink sponge out of the water bucket beside the bed and squeezed the excess water out. Gently he began dabbing her face and neck. After a second dip, he worked his way around the scoop of her neckline and taper of her bare arms. An ice pack would be helpful, but since one was not available, he improvised by soaking her shirt and wringing it out. He wrapped it about her neck and forehead, covering the pulse points as best he could.

Her skin, when pinched, failed to resume its shape—the elasticity impaired. He hadn't paid much attention to whether or not his patient drank water steadily through the day, but she showed the signs of dehydration.

"Adam, *con permiso*, por favor?"

The doctor was so concerned with his patient, he'd not heard Murillo approach the tent.

"Come in." He took a mental inventory of the supplies

they had left. Fortunately, he still had a few bags of saline.

"Dengue fever?" the photographer guessed, squatting down beside the cot.

Jenna's hair was damp from the wet compress as well as the fever. Her face was increasingly ashen beneath the gold of her tan. She appeared to be sleeping until her eyes flew open at Stefan's diagnosis.

"Have I got jungle fever?" The helpless, frightened look she gave Adam twisted his insides.

"You have, I believe, a type. I could tell better if I had the proper equipment to diagnose, but it is nothing to take lightly."

"What about my foot? Can that be it?"

Her foot! Adam swore at himself for forgetting. Immediately he peeled off her shoe and sock. There was no sign of infection or redness. Whatever this was, it was in her blood, not parts specific.

"The foot looks good," he assured her. "But I am going to put in an IV because it looks like either you have not been drinking enough or the fever is dehydrating you. You will let me do that, no? No crying or shouting into my stethoscope?"

She responded to his teasing with a weak smile. Improvising, Adam hung the fluid from the ridgepole of the tent. When he inserted the needle, Jenna flinched slightly, but not enough to impair finding a good vein. It was a good thing he didn't treat the doctor's daughter every day, because the way Adam was feeling her pain and symptoms, he'd have to give up his practice. Gently he taped the needle in place, so engrossed in his patient's care that he'd all but forgotten Murillo.

"Well, call for me if you need anything. I really must get back to the taping."

Stefan rose and, after kissing his forefinger, he planted the kiss on Jenna's cheek. "Rest, chica. You are in good hands. You will feel better soon."

Stefan's compliment to Adam's skill took the doctor by surprise. Adam blamed himself for Marina's death. How could her family not blame him just as much? They were always polite, but Adam assumed that was all it was. He didn't have to imagine the hatred the civility veiled. He hated himself. How could they not hate him as well?

He winced as a pang of guilt over his earlier condemnation of the photographer struck his conscience. When he rose, Jenna reached for him.

"Please don't leave!"

Jenna spoke to Adam not Stefan, who disappeared through the tent opening. She smeared the paint on his arm, a look of panic on her face.

Adam tore himself from the past. "No, I will not leave you, querida...even though you are going to be fine. I only wish to light the lantern and bring it in, so as not to run the batteries down in the electric one."

"Promise?"

The plea in her voice told Adam how badly she felt. He ached in sympathy, having suffered this sort of malady himself. It was part of jungle life. At least he knew that even the dread dengue would be short lived with the treatment he gave.

"I give you my word, Jenna."

Once the lantern was lit and hung inside, he rummaged around, looking for something else to use as compresses on the pulse points in her ankles.

"Adam?"

"Yes?"

On tugging her suitcase out from under the cot, he found the dirty knit shorts and top she'd worn the day before wadded up beside it. They would do perfectly. If he had to, he'd carry her to the lake and dip her in the water; although its temperature wasn't much cooler than the human body's.

"Why don't you like me?"

Freezing with his hands in the bucket of water, he glanced over to see her watching him.

"I *do* like you, Jenna." For something he felt so strongly about, it was hard to admit. So help him, he liked her too much!

"Now *that's* convincing."

He didn't want to like her so much. Certainly he dared not tell her that. Adam proceeded to wring out the clothing, taking out his frustration on it.

"I believe God sent me here for you and the clinic, Adam."

The girl was clearly delirious. There was something about delirium that either brought a person in touch with her God or put her at odds. Rarely was the reaction impartial to the Creator. Was there a guardian angel standing over Jenna at the moment, as some of his patients claimed after a high fever or serious illness?

An acute awareness fell upon him like a blanket. Everything was clearer, sharper—his sight, his hearing, his touch. If there was such a creature, it no doubt wore a tattered robe from keeping up with her! If he were her angel, he wouldn't mind.

Adam rubbed her soft, hot cheek with the tips of his fingers.

"You are so good with patients," she mumbled against his palm. "It's almost worth being sick when you're this nice."

He withdrew his hand, but his senses had already committed the contact to his memory.

"We make a good team, don't we?"

They complemented each other. Out of her head or not, Adam had to agree with that. He moved away and settled against the wall of the tent, arms folded over his knees.

Better he didn't even think of them as a team. It wouldn't hurt so much when she tired of roughing it and went home.

"Get some rest, chica. We will talk tomorrow of this."

"It's so cold!"

Adam retrieved a blanket from the foot of the cot and covered her with it. To him, it was hot enough in the tent to roast eggs.

"You're just a softy inside, aren't you?" she murmured sleepily.

"Like the mushmellow, but don't tell a soul."

A silly smile settled on her mouth, a pretty purse that invited a kiss. "That's *marshmallow!*"

Adam couldn't help himself. He kissed the *marshmallow* from her lips and then backed away, lest he be tempted beyond reason. Like the campfire treats, a taste only made him want more. In fact, it would be easy to become addicted to it, to everything about Jenna.

She closed her eyes, her mouth tilting up dreamily.

His arm resting on the cot beside her, Adam leaned his head against the tent wall. He was more tired than he'd thought. Within fingers' reach, Jenna's hair shone soft and golden in the light of the kerosene lamp, despite the dampness from the fever. Adam could not resist. He touched it, twirled a lock around his finger, losing himself in wishes and what ifs, yet knowing some things were just impossible.

Outside, the music of the drums and gourds reflected the growing fervor of the celebration. It wasn't anything he'd not seen many times before. He'd once treated a young man who went into shock, apparently allergic to the insect bites. Were that to happen again, the villagers knew where to find him. A wide yawn took him by surprise. Adam covered his mouth with his hand a bit too late.

"Adam!"

Jenna's upright bolt startled him from the lethargy seeping into his system.

"Here, Jenna. Right beside you."

He placed a hand on her arm to reassure her, but that was not enough. She rolled off the cot before he could stop her. The blanket tangled in her legs, and she crawled up to him and laid her head against his chest.

"Jenna, I do not think…"

"You're so warm." She slipped her arms around his waist.

The sweet entrapment rocked Adam to the core. He tried to ignore the gallop of his pulse and ease her away, but her nails bit into the flesh of his back in protest.

"Okay, okay. Just let me get your pillow."

After wedging the pillow between them for the sake of decency, he allowed his patient to settle onto his lap, curled against him like a babe in arms. Once she was asleep, he would move her back to the bed. For now, he tugged the blanket around her as best he could and watched the flickering glow of the lantern overhead.

He wasn't sleepy anymore. Every part of him was wide awake, clamoring for action. At that particular moment, shoving his arm into a sleeve of biting ants would be a relief compared to the torture of holding Jenna this close, knowing she was so far out of reach.

God, if this is Your idea of punishment, You have made Your point. I know I am guilty for Marina's death. I brought her here. I kept her here. I did not listen seriously to her cries to go home. But this one, I will not keep. I cannot bear another such burden. I will not!

Fourteen

"BUENOS DÍAS, AMIGOS!"

Adam's eyes flew open as the tent flooded with sunlight. Squinting, he saw Stefan poke his head inside. With a groan, the doctor pressed his head against the side of the tent.

"I checked on you last night, but the two of you were sleeping so soundly…"

"I was more tired than I thought."

Adam shifted and tried to stretch his neck without waking the sleeping young woman curled on the linens and pillow on his lap. At the sight of a long shapely thigh exposed almost to indecency, he hastily drew her skirt down. If he hadn't had time to appreciate it, Murillo certainly wasn't going to! Although judging from the man's crooked smile, it was too late.

"So, shall we break up camp or—"

Adam grimaced. "Break it up. I'll be out in a moment."

He waited until Stefan was gone before gently shaking Jenna. Asleep she looked both the woman and the child, a disturbing combination of seduction and innocence. Her eyelashes fluttered, a dark golden fringe battling her lethargy briefly and losing.

"Jenna, chica…"

He leaned over and touched his lips to her forehead. It was warm, but not as bad as it had been the night before. He tested again to be certain. Her skin was soft, inviting more than he dared offer.

"Wake up, *chiquita.*"

Her lips pursed in a pout of protest. Instead of opening her eyes, Jenna snuggled even closer to him. Thankful for the pillow she dug her knee into, Adam grabbed her shoulders and shook her as easily as possible. He hated to awaken her to the fact that she was aching from tip to toe. It was the nature of the fever. Even the skin hurt.

"Nooo…!"

Adam groaned with her. Given a choice, he'd hold her all day, but that wasn't possible. If they did not return to the boat as scheduled, Robert would become worried. They could make a bed on the cart of wood bound for the steamboat's boiler. The passage would be rough, but she'd not be able to walk. When she put her weight on them, she'd think both her ankles were broken. He knew from personal experience.

Postponing the trip a day would do nothing, save provide another sleepless night for Adam himself. It took a couple of days for the fever to run its course. The best option was to get Jenna home as quickly as possible.

Home. It was his home, not hers! When had he started to think of her as a part of it? He'd brought her here, hoping that she'd see that she didn't belong, but somehow his plan was backfiring—big time! For most of the night, flags of surrender waved in his mind, keeping him awake as much as his concern for his patient's welfare.

Twice Adam tried to move Jenna. He was becoming too comfortable for his peace of mind. Twice she dug in like she did now, clinging to him, protesting, pouting in a way that drove him insane. She twisted in such a tangle of blanket and pillows that it was all he could do in the early hours of the morning to remove the IV after the bag had run out.

"We must go, chiquita. I must take you to your father."

Adam was determined. The temptation to stay like this was too great, and he dared not push his limit. Not that he'd take advantage of her. That was unthinkable. It was just…torture. He did not like being the battleground between morality and desire.

"Jenna, you must wake up!"

"But I love you."

Her sleep infused voice was a little girlish, but its effect upon Adam was not.

"What?" Adam's voice cracked with disbelief. The spot on his chest where she'd mumbled the words felt as if someone had laid a hot iron there instead of fevered lips. No longer was there a sheet between them. It was her cheek against his chest.

Adam went suddenly dry. He'd have to rehydrate himself if he allowed this to continue. He tried lifting her away.

"Hold me, puh-leezzz…"

She was dreaming, he told himself, sliding his hand between his skin and where she scratched her nose. He was probably going through all this torment while she was thinking about some other guy. Perhaps that idiot fiancé of hers!

Adam couldn't allow himself to think otherwise, that Jenna Marsten was speaking to him! He would not even consider making the same mistake again. Love hurt too much. If not for his own sake, he had to keep his distance for hers. She was the daughter of a man he much admired and respected, both as a colleague and a friend. What Adam was feeling, thinking, in spite of himself, was not conducive to maintaining that relationship.

"Come on!" he said, giving metal to his voice.

"What…?"

Unceremoniously, he rolled Jenna onto the tent floor and climbed to his feet. Sunlight flooded in as he tied back the tent flap.

She moaned, blinking. He could actually feel the pain making her chin quiver.

"Am I going to die?"

If he really thought God would listen, he'd ask for help.

Adam lifted her to her feet and eased her onto the cot. Tucking her hair behind her ear, he whispered softly. "No. You just feel like you're going to."

"My head hurts…" She rubbed her temples, eyes closed against the morning light. "*All* of me hurts."

He stood abruptly. "It is the fever, chica. It will pass."

"Did I do something wrong?"

"Nothing. You are just sick."

"I mean, to make you mad at me."

Her wounded expression dealt a fatal blow to Adam's heart. At least that's the way it felt, like a battlefield fully engaged with conflict. Despite his own pain, Adam couldn't bring himself to make her a casualty as well.

He softened his voice and lifted her chin. "No, Jenna. I am a grouch. I did not sleep much last night and I am sorry I snapped at you. But we must get back to the boat or your father will be worried."

Her lower lip trembled. "Oh, Adam…I don't think I can stand to walk!" Fever and panic rendered her hapless and befuddled. "Can't you just strap me to my suitcase and pull me?"

As frustrated and angry as Jenna Marsten could make Adam, she could also make him laugh under the most confounding circumstances. It always took him by surprise.

"I am going to make a bed in the medicine cart for you. It is mostly empty now."

She made a childish face and poked out her tongue. Her hair stuck to it, and she spat it out, slapping it away. He longed to touch it again, even if, at that moment, it looked like she'd combed it with an eggbeater. Instead, he focused on the present quandary.

"I know it will be bumpy but—"

"My mouth tastes like bad...like—" She searched the fog of her mind for an adequate word. "Yoppo."

If Adam didn't know better, he'd swear she really knew the bitter taste of the root.

Sitting on the edge of the cot, shoulders slumped and her elbows resting on her knees in a less than graceful pose, he'd never seen Jenna look more kissable.

Adam managed a smile, stiff with mustered resistance. Even her shoulder beckoned a tender affection. Instead of heeding instinct, he tugged the strap of her tank dress up from where it had slipped off.

It was better when they argued, he decided, until he remembered the kisses he'd stolen in a fit of unadulterated exasperation. Either one would have been worth it if she'd knocked his lights out. No, with Jenna it was best to keep things on an *even* keel.

"I will fetch you some water to freshen up with, then rustle up something for breakfast."

"Not hungry." She put her head down on her lap, arms folded beneath it.

Not angry, not friendly. Not too far but not too close.

Adam spun on his heel, dogged by confusion. If he had to, he'd get one of the Indian women to bathe her and coax her to eat. Right now, his best option was to get out of that tent before he broke the rules he'd just made and—

Enough! Adam ducked outside as though the devil were on his heels.

Most of the men in the village were still sleeping off the fiesta. The children played around them quietly. Already loaves of cassava lay baking in the bright sun, proclaiming the early start of the women's workday.

Adam made arrangements to take some fruit and bread with them for the return journey. After explaining that Jenna was sick, he asked one of the women to check on her.

His conscience relieved where Jenna was concerned, at least for a while, he returned to the campsite, passing Stefan and his assistant. Stefan waved at the air in front of him and remarked to his companion, "My, but doesn't someone smell *lovely* this morning?"

Adam stopped, perplexed by the private joke the two men shared until he caught a whiff of it too. *"Aunt Violet's bath oil…works like an insect repellent…"*

"Some kind of insect repellent," he mumbled irritably.

Changing direction, he headed for the creek. Jenna had so thoroughly coated herself with the strong perfumed oil, it must have rubbed off on him when he was holding her. Considering Adam was accustomed to baby spit up and worse, it shouldn't really bother him, but it did. Everything about the doctor's daughter affected him one way or the other. An even keel was impossible!

Stefan and his assistant were ready to move out when Adam returned from a quick bath in the lake. With their new tent to be left behind for the chief, there was little for them to pack. Ignoring the pair's irritating grins, Adam gave instructions to his rivereños to get busy breaking down the medicine shelter.

The river-dwelling mestizos had thoroughly enjoyed themselves with their pureblood Indian cousins the night before and moved about like zombies, slow but methodical. The bright daylight made them wince, as though it allowed in not just light but pain as well. Adam took pity on them and gave them each aspirin. He'd had a hair of that dog once and remembered too full well the nasty headache too much jungle juice could cause.

An hour later before the small caravan was ready to leave, Adam bade his farewell to the groggy chief and his elders and helped Jenna into the back of the cart. Fully awake now, she suffered in stoic silence, even though he was certain her bones and muscles objected painfully to every move she made. He gave her more medication, part modern and part a jungle concoction the shaman mixed just for this sort of malady.

The latter tasted vile, but Jenna took it with a look of complete trust.

"Thank you."

It was the weakest gratitude he'd ever heard expressed. He watched as she chased the medicine with water from the bottle he'd given her.

"Now keep nursing that along the way. I'll be checking on you."

"Thanks."

That wasn't much stronger.

"Ready then?"

With wood for the steam engine piled around her makeshift bed, Jenna nodded and laid down.

"At least nibble on the fruit," Adam encouraged as the donkey pulled cart pulled away. "And drink lots of that water."

A little later, despite the jolting cart, Jenna was soon asleep. The mango he'd given her was still in her hand, missing one tiny bite. Little Rita, the marmoset, could have made a bigger showing. Adam wished he had another IV bag, but the logistics just weren't feasible even if he had one. Instead, like a mother bird with its young, he kept stopping long enough to coax swallows of water into his patient before moving on.

The trip back should have been quicker, but frequent water stops and a midday rest offset the advantage of having the jungle path ahead of them mostly cleared by their previous passage. Jenna awakened for a short time, during which she finished the water, the mango, and a few bits of coconut. Then, as if the meal had been a triathlon, she collapsed back on the bed and was asleep again before the group moved out.

Sleep was the best medicine. Between it and Adam's treatment, the journey was likely harder on the doctor than the patient. The sight of the riverside village was one of the most welcome ones Adam had seen in a good while. Not only were they at their destination, but his responsibility for Jenna would be alleviated by her father's presence.

It was almost with relief that Adam filled his associate in on Jenna's symptoms, their onset, and his treatment. Together, they helped Jenna into the hammock, making her promise to call if she needed to get up.

Spared temptation and torment at last, Adam threw himself into helping Arturo make the boat ready for the next morning's early departure while Robert Marsten tended his daughter. The sound of father and daughter conversing between her naps and the tinkle of her laughter now and then as the fever diminished was as soothing to Adam's ears as the balmlike song of the jungle. It sounded like home. Adam hadn't heard it in years. It triggered yet another type of longing, for better, happier days.

After working through the evening with Arturo reinstalling the intake pump by kerosene light, he was so tired he could have slept through war drums. Lying atop the canopy of the boat beneath the stars, Adam listened with sharpened ears for any sign that Jenna might be stirring below.

Not that he needed to. Her father made a bed on one of the benches. Robert was determined to stay with her despite Adam's offer to take the shift. There was no arguing with the man. Besides, Adam didn't really want to argue. Who would have guessed that pining after someone who was dead was easier on the heart than longing for someone alive but just out of reach of his empty arms?

"Good night, Adam."

Adam smiled. Jenna's voice was a bit stronger now. "Good night, Jenna. Good night, Robert."

Robert Marsten answered with a gruff, "G'night."

"I love you, Dad."

Adam was instantly jerked back to that morning when she'd mumbled *I love you* against his chest. His heart beat hard enough to fracture his ribs. Reminded of the softness of her cheek against his chin, the cute way she burrowed against him, it stepped up its cadence even though there was a fiberglass canopy between them now.

Feverish patients said some of the most ridiculous things. But of all she might have said, why *I love you?* The least she could have done was talked to her dead mother or some relative who wasn't there. As it was, Jenna was loving everybody!

He closed his eyes, shutting out the spread of stars above him. God's canvas, his mother used to say. But like God, stars were for dreamers. They put crazy notions in people's heads if one paid too much attention to them. Adam had stopped dreaming; he'd given up crazy notions. He subscribed to the bird-in-hand philosophy.

If it was in his hands, he could count on it. He'd given up most of life beyond his work—the proverbial Jack of all work and no play.

Unless he counted Pepito. Children had a way of making Adam forget the pains of living. Through their eyes, he shared its joy. There was a time he wanted a house full of babies. But those were in his foolish, lovestruck, dreaming days. Pepito would be enough for him. He could adopt the boy. Tilda could mother him. That was all the family Adam needed.

It *was*, he insisted to himself, tossing over on his side. He and the boy were enough to make the happy sounds of a home. He tried to picture them together, camping and hunting, reading in the evening—the things families did. Yet each time a picture came to Adam's mind, there was another face in it. It was not Pepito's or Adam's or Tilda's or even Robert's. It was Jenna's.

Adam slammed the canopy with his fist in frustration.

"Everything okay up there?" Robert called out.

The younger doctor groaned, embarrassment adding to the heat wave of his bedeviled emotions. Jenna Marsten was driving him crazy!

"Yes. I just banged my elbow. Other than that, it's just like heaven up here," he added in a laconic drawl. Or *some* such place.

It was a pleasure to brush one's teeth without pain. Jenna stood in front of the bathroom mirror, counting her blessings. Two weeks ago, it would have been agony. She'd had the dreaded dengue and survived, thanks to the care of her new family. Her father or Tilda was there whenever she emerged from her fevered stupor, forcing liquids in her, bathing her brow, seeing to her every need. Even Adam was sympathetic, although at a distinct distance. For the life of her, Jenna couldn't fathom what she'd done to put it there.

The back screen door slammed, shocking the morning birds' song into abrupt silence. That is, if one could call a macaw's hawking cry a song. A few weeks ago, it stood out, dissonant to Jenna's ear. Now it added a new section of harmony to the jungle chorus.

Another voice replaced it; the one of the little boy who'd just barged into the hacienda.

"Dr. Adam, Dr. Adam…wake up! It's Saturday!"

The door between Adam's bedroom and the bathroom popped open from the boy's entrance into the master bedchamber, revealing the large rumpled bed with its fan-shaped headboard. Adam was sprawled in a tangle of sheets, seemingly deaf to Pepito's entrance.

The boy bounded onto the bed and the startled doctor came up like a shot. Jenna nearly choked on toothpaste. Hurriedly she rinsed her mouth, and shelving her toothbrush, went to close the door to restore Adam's privacy.

Upon seeing the energetic intruder was only Pepito, Adam fell back against the pillows with a muffled oath.

"Pepito, go away. I was up all night waiting for a new baby to come."

The boy bounced up on the bed, not the least deterred by the grumpy reception. "Why didn't you just cut it out and get some sleep?"

"That is only done as a last resort." Adam broke off with a yawn and raised his head from the pillow. "What time is it?"

"Time to get up!"

Jenna smiled when she heard the pillow slam and Pepito's startled yelp. She hated to close the door but knew she should. But what if it made a noise?

"It was in the mama's belly, right?"

"Right." Adam clearly wasn't into this, or any conversation, for that matter.

"What took it so long?"

"Some babies are faster than others."

"Why?"

"You can run faster than your cousin. Why is that?"

"Because I am faster."

"Voilà! *That's* the reason." The mattress creaked as Adam shifted on his side and burrowed into a pillow. "Now go see what Tilda is doing and—"

"Tilda is cleaning at the church, remember?"

"Then go find Jenna or Dr. Robert."

"That baby was an egg, right?"

"Umm."

"How did it get there?"

The door creaked when Jenna tried to close it. She froze, breath held until Adam answered.

"Females are born with them."

"How many?"

"All they will ever need."

"How many is that?"

"Hundreds, thousands…I *don't* know!" Adam pulled the pillow over his head.

"So a woman can have a hundred or a thousand babies?"

Oh, poor woman, Jenna thought, biting her lips to keep from laughing.

"Not all of them will work. Now go fix yourself some cereal and watch Tilda's television till I get up."

"Can Jenna have a hundred or a thousand babies?"

That little rascal! What on earth made him—

The sleepy doctor growled. *"Pepito!"*

"Can she?"

"How should—" Adam checked himself. "Even though a woman—" He stopped again before taking the easiest course out of the corner he'd painted himself into. "Yes, I imagine. Now get out of here!"

The boy scampered off the bed, avoiding the threatening swing of Adam's backhand.

"The men say Jenna is one fine lookin' mama. Guess they know all about eggs, huh?"

"Yes!"

Adam pushed up from the bed on all fours and

261

must've given the boy one of his drilling glares. Jenna couldn't see his face, only the snarling lump of covers with a disheveled head of black hair, but she could picture it. Thank goodness he couldn't see hers!

"Now get out of here before I have *you* for breakfast!"

Pepito darted to the hall door.

"Do *you* think she's a fine lookin' mama?"

"If I answer one more question, will you go?" Exasperation rang in Adam's plea.

Jenna didn't hear a response but assumed it was a nod. She dared not move now, not when she waited as anxiously for Adam's response as the boy.

"Yes, Jenna is beautiful. Now go!"

Okay, so the compliment was extracted by virtue of torture. She'd take it!

"How many good eggs do you think she has?"

Oh no! Jenna leaned against the wall of the shower behind the connecting door. Part of her wanted to giggle, the other to sink through a crack in the tiled floor. Only a child...

"I *think*," Adam warned, "that a certain nosey pain had better run while he still can."

The sleep-scruffy doctor rose on his knees and threw a pillow. The bedroom door slammed and Pepito charged off down the hall, skipping in triumph that he'd escaped the jungle cat's den without a scratch.

Jenna held her breath as the bed creaked with Adam's movement. He got up and retrieved the pillow.

Then tossing it on the bed, he sat down on the edge, his weary head in his hands. Just when she thought it safe to relax, he called out.

"Be a *good egg* and close the bathroom door, will you, Jenna?"

Her shoulders sagged. Busted! How long had he known she was here? If only she had just left the room, but no...

She tried to explain. "The door flew open when Pepito—"

"I know."

"I mean, the latch doesn't always—"

"I know."

"I didn't mean to eavesdrop."

Adam shot up from the bed again. In two strides, he peered through the crack at her, his voice a low rumble.

"Of course you didn't. It just takes you a long time to close a door!"

With a loud click, he closed it himself, and from the jolting sound on his side, dove onto the large mattress. Not the least offended, Jenna breathed a sigh of relief. Now she could stop trampling all over her tongue and slink away to suffer her humiliation in peace.

An extra hour's sleep did not improve Adam's temperament very much. Later that morning, he stood impatiently in the clinic, biceps bulging with the weight of boxed medical files.

"Okay. So where does this go? I can't believe the clinic has accumulated this many old files."

He'd found Pepito helping Jenna in her quest to organize the clinic office and could hardly refuse to help. Jenna and the boy were struggling to move the heavy boxes by transporting them from the office to the back room on Pepito's wagon. There was still, however, the lifting and stacking, which required them both.

"Are you certain we're not moving the same ones over and over?"

On more neutral turf than the jaguar's den, Jenna was unruffled by Adam's complaining. She glanced up from where she and Pepito were color coding the current files. They used magic markers instead of the smart stickers found on her own physician's shelved folders.

"Same place as the others," she told him, "but—"

"I know, I know. Be certain they are stacked in alphabetical order. If I need help, I can call Pepito."

"But *I* am helping Jenna!" the little boy protested. "I am better at coloring than alphatizing."

"Alphabetizing."

Pepito ignored Jenna's correction. "Rita can help." The boy pointed to where the pesky marmoset had given up slapping at their markers. She now slept atop the old filing cabinet, where Jenna had lured her with peanuts. Like Jenna's relationship with Adam, hers with Rita had developed into a peaceful coexistence, sometimes friendly, sometimes not.

"You're a traitor, Pepito!"

Adam slipped into the back room where he'd insisted on laying salt treated lumber down to keep the files off the floor in case of a flood. It was the price of his help—complicating what started out as a simple process.

He sounded as though he were peeved. These days, it was hard for Jenna to tell. He'd been attentive yet detached as she recovered from the insect bite provoked fever. She was used to an Adam who ran hot or cold. When he was hot, he was very hot. Jenna warmed, recalling his impassioned kisses. If he kissed that good in anger...

"How many more of these do you have?"

And when Adam DeSanto was cold, sweat froze! Her allotted time was obviously up.

"Pepito and I can get those if you have something else to do."

Looking thunderstruck at her annoyance, he shrugged.

"No, I was just..."

"Being a grouch?" Pepito piped up helpfully.

Adam pointed a stern finger at him. "Mind your own business."

He pulled up a box and sat on it, propping his arms on the desk. "I was thinking of going fishing this afternoon."

Jenna's peeve melted beneath the wistful glow of his boyish expression. Pepito, who'd been perfectly content to help her color, was suddenly infected by the same whimsy. The desertion rate in her army was getting desperate.

Her dad was working on the *Jenna*. Tilda was helping at the church, cleaning for a special graduation service.

Lola, their cleaning lady, had to take her eldest daughter, one of the graduates being honored at the mission school, to Ichitas to mail off her application for a mid-wifing curriculum in Lima.

"Aw, come on!" Jenna protested. "You guys know Stefan will be here today to finish up the video."

She hadn't wanted anything filmed on the clinic site until she'd straightened up after her organizing. There were even three patients in the infirmary, a father and two children of a family suffering from dysentery. Not that she was glad they were sick, but it would look good on the tape to have someone using the clinic.

When they came in the day before, Adam was furious to distraction that the natives had not heeded his advice about boiling their water. The same creek that provided food and water was also the village's septic system. While he treated the patients, Jenna called the mother aside. It was clear the lady simply didn't understand what Adam was saying about bacteria living in the water. After all, many things lived in the water and they didn't make her family sick.

It had been a long time since lab in college, but she managed to show the woman of the house a microscope slide of the bacteria in a canteen they'd brought with them, versus another of what existed after boiling it. The woman was much more impressed by Jenna's show than she was with the doctor's temper.

"Actually, I was thinking you might like to join us," Adam suggested. "I will show you how to catch piranha."

Jenna was stunned. Maybe she'd impressed Adam as well. First he offers to help her put away the last of the files. Now he was asking her to go fishing! What on earth had gotten into the man?

Okay, yes, it was for man-eating fish, but still…here she was, a mere female being asked to go into the wild by the jungle doc himself! Or maybe it was because he thought that she was one fine lookin' mama.

"So what do you say?"

Adam tapped the desk with an impatient finger. Waiting was clearly something he was not accustomed to, but he was trying. Upon realizing what he was doing, he wiped the recalcitrant finger on his pants with a self-conscious grimace.

For the first time Jenna had an inkling of hope that Adam was actually warming to her taking part in the clinic. Granted, it was lukewarm, but better than his previous iceberg resentment. Like her father said, seeds had been planted in Adam's stubborn mind. Jenna just had to give them time to grow.

"All work and no play makes Jill the dull girl."

She groaned inwardly. And when he teased like that, his eyes twinkling, his idioms slightly twisted, his mouth curled in that *Kiss Me, Kate!* pose…

Her resolve teetered. Jenna glanced from the shelves she'd yet to do back to that face—*those faces*—for Pepito's now pleaded the same case.

At that moment, the steam whistle from the *S. L. Jenna* pierced the air, announcing the arrival of Stefan

Murillo's boat with a prearranged signal. Her dad, who was no doubt now knee-deep in engine oil and soot, promised to let her know the moment the photographer arrived. Adam had even made her forget that!

"I can't," she whined in genuine regret. "This is so important for the clinic."

"Well, I can!" Pepito closed his marker and tossed it on the table, not nearly as disappointed by Jenna's declining as she was.

"Traitor!"

"Hey, I'm just a kid, remember?"

Adam veiled his reaction with the all-encompassing shrug. "Perhaps another time."

"It's a deal!"

She gathered up the folders they were working on to return them to the shelves. Stefan would just have to film them half done. Most likely the colors wouldn't show or mean much difference anyway. She just wanted to put their best foot forward.

"We'll take a dugout and get some lunch at the market," Adam told Pepito. "You run and tell your aunt where we are going."

Pepito went over to where Rita lay curled in a tiny ball of brown and white fur and picked up the marmoset. "Can Rita go too?"

"If Jenna hasn't worn her out with all this working."

The marmoset sprang to life as if she'd understood the criterion Adam imposed. Climbing atop Pepito's head, she chattered back in absolute proof that she was not only able but also most willing to go anywhere, so long as it was with her pet boy.

"You see," Adam teased, after Pepito dashed off toward the village. "Even the monkey needs a break."

Jenna gave him an impish grin. "You mean *marmoset*, don't you?"

She could hardly contain her excitement as Adam accompanied her on the walk down to the village. Even though she was still sick when they returned home to Santa Beliza, Jenna had asked Stefan to fax a message from Posada Explorador to her office requesting they send her laptop air express to Ichitas.

On it were mailing lists and contacts—a great start in compiling targets for the clinic's video. From them, she and the photographer could get some idea of how many copies to be made. His studio was even willing to make them free of charge, since Adam had been so instrumental in dealing with the natives to allow the filming.

God was bringing it all together so perfectly that Jenna was in awe. With luck, Stefan would have her laptop too. And now that Adam was beginning to thaw toward her work at the clinic...

Well, she supposed all this offset the depressing aftereffect of what she supposed had just been a feverish dream. At least Jenna *thought* it was a dream.

She remembered being sick, aching all over. Adam held her in his arms, soothing her with little kisses to the top of her head, her forehead, her nose, her cheek. It hadn't lifted her fever, but the tenderness sent her heart and mind soaring. It was as if she'd sampled the yoppo powder, or was like she imagined it would be. She floated, secure in the strength of his arms, the closeness of him. He was her anchor in the delirium of fever and ecstasy. When she blurted out that she loved him, she hadn't been able to help herself.

Then suddenly, *literally,* he dropped her on the floor! She'd never felt such pain, either physical or emotional. Where dream had stopped and reality began was still a mystery.

Wondering, she cut a sidewise glance at her companion, who walked and whistled tunelessly beside her.

"What?" he asked, catching her in the act.

"Just wondering what you were whistling."

"Nothing, just…" He shrugged.

They walked a little farther.

"A person can whistle without a tune, you know. Do you whistle a tune when you call a dog?"

"You really need to get a life, Adam." He was so literal sometimes, it made her want to scream. Other times, when he looked troubled, haunted by his past, she wanted to hug him.

"I *do* have a life."

He was doing it again!

"It may not be the best in your eyes, but—"

"There's Stefan!" Jenna interrupted. "Looks like he brought his assistant too."

Below the village bluff, a sleek speedboat was tied

up next to the *Jenna.* There were two men on the boat, both clad in traditional khaki safari wear, even up to the Aussie-like hats. Adam held Jenna's hand to steady her as they made their way down the steps from the red-brown bank to the floating dock.

"Hola, señorita!" Stefan walked ahead of his companion. "I have a surprise for you."

Jenna rushed toward her friend, staring hopefully at the box he carried.

"My laptop?"

"Yes, but that is no surprise," the photographer chided with a sly smile. Stepping aside, he pointed to the man behind him.

"Hello, Jenna."

"Scott!" Jenna's breath deserted her, leaving her mouth hanging open in shock.

The fair-featured, tanned young man closed the distance between them and took her into his arms.

"Wh-what are you doing here?" Her mind plunged into an utter chaos of mixed feelings.

"I came here to keep from making the biggest mistake of my life."

Scott Pierson looked deep into Jenna's gaze, his blue eyes as earnest as hers were astounded. The silence surrounding them was thunderous. The jungle had never been so quiet.

"I've come to my senses, Jen. I've come to claim my bride."

Scott sealed his fervent declaration with a kiss.

Jenna swayed in his arms, her strength robbed by shock. Instead of the thunderous pulse that Adam's kisses evoked raging in her ears, Jenna overheard Stefan's sly aside to Adam as if the words were amplified.

"So, amigo, it looks as if we both lose."

Fifteen

JENNA FELT SICK, BOTH PHYSICALLY AND EMOTIONALLY, BY THE ice-age effect of Scott's declaration. Before her eyes, Adam's demeanor changed abruptly from playful and teasing to guarded and cold. She wanted to deny Stefan's observation, but hospitality required otherwise. She had to introduce Scott, especially to her father.

"Dad." How could Scott think that she'd go back to him after what he'd done? "This is Scott Pierson...my *former* fiancé."

Schooled since birth in charm, Scott acted as if he walked on thin ice every day. He leaned across the span between the *Jenna* and the dock and shook her father's hand.

"Dr. Marsten, I presume?"

His joke fell short. Jenna forced a laugh.

"And this is my...my father's associate, Dr. Adam DeSanto."

Jenna now knew what it felt like to have an icicle driven through one's chest. Adam's expression gave a new dimension to the word *frigid*. He stared at Scott's extended hand for a moment. When it didn't break off, he took it with a short, dismissing squeeze.

"I have heard much of you, señor."

"Not that good, huh?" Scott glanced apologetically at Jenna. "Well, I deserve it, but I'm ready to get on my knees. Jenna is worth it. I didn't realize what I'd lost till she left."

A few weeks ago, those honeyed words would have been palatable, but not now.

"Scott…"

Scott pulled her into his arms again. "I'm not letting you go this time, Jen."

Adam turned abruptly to Robert, reminding her of some mechanized robot. "Pepito and I are going fishing. I will be back when you see me."

When the younger doctor swung his attention back to them, Scott stiffened instinctively, but he didn't loosen his hold on her waist.

Nothing was said, but somehow, Jenna felt like a bone of contention between a big cat and a rambunctious dog. And the cat looked like he could devour both the dog *and* the bone.

"*Hasta la vista*, Jenna." The parting was more akin to a growl than "see you later."

Jenna groaned silently, torn between running after Adam to stop him and running after him to kick his shins. She remained with Scott instead.

"Is he always this friendly?" Scott turned a suspicious gaze on Jenna.

He knew. But that was impossible. Neither Scott nor Adam could possibly know her feelings, when she hardly knew them herself.

The hours that followed passed in a daze. The perfect hostess, she introduced Scott and showed him around the compound. A rollaway was set up in her father's office to accommodate him since she occupied the guest room. It was just as well that Adam had left, or it would have been unbearable.

Thankfully, her father was more polite than his colleague, both in word and manner. She sensed his doubt about Scott Pierson more than the actual hostility Adam had so thinly veiled.

"So how much did Violet plead and bribe to get you down here, Mr. Pierson?" Robert asked Scott later that evening.

"Scott, please, sir," Jenna's dinner partner insisted.

"I'm certain she's given you an ear full about how Jenna is destined to hellfire and damnation on earth or worse for coming here."

Scott brandished one of his photogenic smiles. "Well, you're right about the ear full and damnation part. I take it you two aren't on the best of terms."

"Hah? That's a mild appraisal, young man." Her father bowed his head, pointing to the top, which had been generously thinned by age. "But as you can see, I have no horns nor surgical scars from having them removed."

Jenna laughed on cue. Across from her Stefan Murillo gave her a wink, as if he alone sensed the true nature of her quandary. Not that that was possible either. She couldn't even get a handle on it.

Once again, however, the photographer was a godsend. His presence helped ease the awkwardness Jenna felt, at least somewhat. She was able to speak enthusiastically of the work she'd been doing since her arrival, and used the excuse of Stefan's filming for the clinic to keep from being left alone with Scott. She just needed time to sort out the quagmire of emotions bouncing off the walls of her brain.

At least Stefan hadn't abandoned her to them like Adam had. His place next to Stefan had been set, but Tilda removed it when he was not there in time for dinner. Evidently, he and Pepito were going to make a long day of their fishing trip.

"Jenna has a lot of her mother in her," her father remarked after Jenna stopped for a breath.

She'd been running on about the endless possibilities for the mailing lists and contacts she had on her laptop. She knew she was babbling, a reflection of the activity in her brain.

"I can't wait to see her in action at the seminar this coming weekend," he went on. "Her mother could raise money out of a plank, you know."

Scott threw up his hands in surrender. "Hey, I don't

need to be convinced. I've seen her in action. It's just a matter of time before she replaces her aunt as queen of Boston's charities."

Now *there* was something to look forward to. Jenna winced inside. She'd had a taste of the hands-on approach here at Santa Beliza. Boston seemed like another world now. This world needed her more. Her father needed her; the clinic needed her. Maybe even Adam needed her. He just didn't know it yet.

"Do you think we'll be able to add the film you shot today of Dad at the clinic?" she asked Stefan.

With Adam gone, her father had to shower quickly and dress for the part of the doctor to Tilda's nurse during the shoot. The woman was in a stoic fluster the entire time, eyes as wide and body as stiff as a spooked statue. Now, however, Jenna could hear the housekeeper in her kitchen domain, clucking in Spanish to herself, as though a fox had come into her henhouse.

When the dinner dishes were cleared, everyone retired to the veranda. The heat of the day had been blown away by the night cooled river breeze. The open room was a perfect place for viewing what Stefan had edited of the video shot upriver on their trip. He hooked up a small television/VCR combination and put in a copy of the tape.

Jenna watched as the natives eagerly pitched in to set up the medical camp. Stefan's assistant even caught a shot on the sly of the council debating with Adam about the filming. Looking wilted in a cotton short outfit and floppy hat, Jenna stared at Adam in sheer wonder, as if enwrapped in the language she could hardly understand. It was almost embarrassing. Fortunately, she was the only one who seemed to notice.

"Stefan, you've captured Adam's essence perfectly!" she commented, when the scene switched to Adam working with the children. "He is such a wonder with his patients."

"Doesn't look like the same person I met today," Scott drawled at her side.

"It takes time for Adam to warm up. It's just his way."

Funny, Jenna recalled her father telling her the same thing. Although she doubted there was much chance of Adam and Scott becoming fast friends. They were as different as night and day.

"My word, Jen! Don't tell me you actually ate monkey! What did it taste like?" Scott asked, amazed and repelled at the same time.

Jenna borrowed Adam's expressive shrug. "Monkey, what else?"

When the last of the video ran out with a clip of Jenna playing with the children, keeping them occupied while Adam saw their parents, her father applauded.

"You and Adam remind me of your mother and me. She had such a way with the kids! They adored her."

"Jenna will make a wonderful mother," Scott agreed.

She ignored the comment, more moved by the nostalgic twinkle in her father's gaze. It told her just how much the film had affected him. She reached across the table and squeezed his hand.

"It's perfect, isn't it?" She turned to Stefan. "You can put my name down for a recommendation anytime."

But the video wasn't all that was perfect. She and Adam had made a perfect team. She didn't realize Adam had laughed so much at her antics, nor had she seen the way he looked at her when she wasn't aware of it, with a warm mixture of amazement and approval...definitely approval, if not more. Was it possible that Adam *was* attracted to her? Males weren't always the most clever at showing their feelings.

Jenna picked up her napkin and fanned herself, flustered at the direction of her thoughts.

"Did you bring the film of the ritual?" She was genuinely interested in seeing it. But it also gave her more time to compose her thoughts and postponed the inevitable time when she and Scott would be alone. Heaven knew she'd need to sort things out by then.

"Ah yes, that is right. You and Adam missed—" Stefan cleared his throat suddenly. "It is not edited, señorita, but—" he added as if he'd picked up on her silent plea—"I *can* fast forward it to get to the most interesting parts."

"Wonderful! You are *not* going to believe this," she told Scott.

"What, did you and your friendly neighborhood doctor treat patients all night too?" he asked with a skeptical lift of his brow.

"Jenna got seriously ill," her father explained.

"Adam had to treat her. I'm just grateful he was there, if I couldn't be. She needed IV fluids…"

"Jungle fever," Jenna picked up. "I don't think I've ever hurt so much, not even when I took that spill in Vermont at the ski lodge. The wrong bug bit me."

"You sure it wasn't the jungle doc who did the biting?" Scott whispered in her ear as the video flashed on the screen.

She laughed and settled nervously in her chair to narrate.

"The first shots are of a hoatzin nest at the river village. We left the camera on all night, hoping to catch some activity."

"It's a bird born with little claws on its wings," Jenna told her former fiancé, ignoring his comment about Adam. "If it falls from the nest into the water, it can claw its way back up. It's kind of a throwback from prehistoric times, which makes it great for Stefan's—"

Stefan jumped up from his chair in disbelief as the scene abruptly changed. "What the…?"

He stopped the fast-forward. The focus was no longer on the hoatzin nest. Something had jerked it around 180 degrees toward the *S. L. Jenna*.

Stefan smacked his forehead in dismay. "I forgot to lock the camera in place!"

There slipping over the side of the steamboat was a nightshirt clad Jenna. With soap and cloth in one hand, she clung to the rope hanging from the side like the lifeline it was.

Jenna felt her stomach drop somewhere to the floor beneath her chair.

"This is a surprise, no?"

She could knock Stefan's mischievous grin off his face. As it was, her father was now leaning forward as Adam curled down off the canopied roof of the steamboat, dropping lightly to the deck. He peered over the side at her.

The camera was far enough away that no one could really make out their expressions, and thankfully, the sound equipment was still focused on the bird's nest.

"We can just fast forward, can't we?" Jenna cleared her throat. "I mean, it was bad enough that Adam had to see how dumb I was, without showing the whole world!"

"Aww, let it be," her father objected. "This could be interesting."

"Indeed," Scott closed his hand over hers.

Stefan waited for her instruction as Adam hauled her up into the boat on the video screen, holding her longer than he needed to. She stumbled when he did let go, reminding Jenna of the splinter she'd picked up in her foot. But it wasn't the splinter or Adam's tender removal of it that made her jump up and grab the remote from Stefan's hand.

"Oh, honestly, this is enough!"

She hit the fast-forward button. The scene still showed on the screen, unfolding like an old silent movie until the part where Adam kissed her. Jenna tried finding the stop button, but her fingers just wouldn't work. It finally stopped it all right—on *pause*.

The silence in the room was so thick, it could have been sliced and served on a plate. Jenna wanted to run for all she was worth. Now both her father *and* Scott looked at her as if they'd seen something past Adam's kiss, something that definitely had not happened. If anything, Jenna had made matters worse.

She stood like a spotlighted deer, unable to move, much less speak. Stefan busied himself with retrieving the remote she'd inadvertently dropped, shutting the frozen picture off in the process. Thankfully, her father broke the silence.

"Well, enjoyable as all this has been, I need to get my beauty sleep now that I'm a film star."

He got up and gave Jenna a good-night peck on the cheek.

"Besides, the electric will be turned off for the night soon."

"You're kidding!" Scott thawed from his shock.

"No. It saves fuel for emergencies."

"And there's not even a stoplight or street to roll up."

Jenna rallied at the sting of the engineer's jibe. Their relationship might be in shambles at the moment, but there was no reason to criticize Santa Beliza.

"Actually, it's quite nice. I've come to love this place."

"Señores, señorita," Stefan announced. "I bid you good night." He picked up his portable system. "I am off to my *guest* bed at the clinic."

Leaving like a rat on a sinking ship, Jenna thought. She couldn't blame him. She'd bail out too if she could. But she couldn't.

She turned to Scott, hoping she could explain. To her surprise he was smiling.

"If you like it here, then you won't mind Arabia at all. At least we have electricity twenty-four/seven." Scott circled her waist with his hands. Leaning over with the wariness of an animal about to steal food from the table, he planted a kiss on her neck.

"That's an unusual scent," he said, nuzzling it afterward.

It took Jenna a moment to realize what he was talking about. In the rush to shower and change for dinner, she'd used her father's soap.

"I told you I've changed." What was she going to tell him? How?

"Either the jungle agrees with you more than Boston, or I've just been away from you too long. But I swear you're more beautiful than ever. You just have this glow about you. Tell me it isn't love, Jen."

Scott knew...or thought he did.

"Oh, Scott, I...I just don't know. What I do know is that I've changed myself." Jenna chuckled without amusement. "I know it sounds cliché, but I really think I found where I belong."

"Not here, Jen! I know I did a rotten thing, but don't settle for anything less than our dreams. You belong with me."

283

He kissed her, enveloping her in his embrace. His lips were warm, but they did not burn sweetly. His embrace was strong, but it didn't make her feel secure and on the very edge of temptation at the same time. Instead of swaying with a bone melting rush coursing through her body, Jenna tensed as though someone had showered her in cold water.

Scott felt it too. He released her; his expression as utterly devastated as she felt.

"I'm sorry, Scott. It's just too late. I think we'd be making a terrible mistake." It was hard to believe that she was turning away the opportunity she would have jumped at a few weeks ago, turning toward something that might not even exist, at least on Adam's part. But Jenna was tired of going with the flow. It was time to answer the call that had haunted her all her life and now had an identity—Santa Beliza.

"I thought we had something special."

"We do," she told him quickly, "but not till-death-do-we-part special."

"So what do you want to do, stay here with that stethoscope Tarzan and then decide or what?"

He was getting angry. She couldn't blame him. Even though Scott deserved it after what he did, Jenna couldn't help but feel guilty.

"I believe I could make a difference here." She did. She loved the people, the work…

"Do you love him? DeSanto, not your dad." Scott clarified at Jenna's startled look. "I know you adore your father…and vice versa. It shows. I'm glad for you there, honestly, Jen."

"I feel…fulfilled here, Scott. Back home, I was just going through the motions. Here, I'm really living!"

"I guess you can call it that."

At one point, she might have said the same thing, in the same way. "Scott, I'm so sorry. It's just too late…for *us.*"

There, it was out.

Scott's mouth thinned to a flat, white line. "Fine. I guess I deserve it. But you haven't answered my question. Do you love this *jungle man?* I mean, cover him all over with hair, put him on all fours and, so help me, you got a jaguar!"

Jenna couldn't help her nervous giggle. Scott had Adam pegged and he'd only been with him a few moments.

"He didn't even make noise when he stomped off in such a snit!"

"He was barefoot, Scott."

"Is he housebroken?"

She and Scott were much alike when it came to hiding behind a sense of humor. Jenna knew what the young man was doing and she appreciated the effort.

"Most of the time."

"Wonder how he'd look in a black tie."

Jenna's relief stalled. Adam would be miserable in a formal wear, but that was more than putting the cart before the horse. She wasn't sure of his feelings toward her.

"So do you love him?"

Her friend was not called the bulldog of the university debating team for nothing.

"I enjoy working with him."

"Does he feel the same way?" Scott switched tactics. "I mean…look, I hurt you enough. I don't want to see you hurt again. The guy is kind of…intense," he finished, for lack of a better word.

Jenna wondered which would hurt more, not knowing for certain how Adam felt or finding out. What good was Eden without Adam? Would she want to stay and work at the clinic if Adam didn't return her feelings? *Could* she?

"You love him."

Out of her confusion, a watershed of doubt built in her eyes until Scott wiped away a renegade tear trickling down her cheek. Jenna could hardly focus on his face at all.

"I have an idea, Jen."

She hadn't answered him in words, but Scott knew. That was one of the wonderful things about their relationship. They knew each other so well, one could finish what the other started. They were a phenomenal team at anything they attempted, as if they'd been made for each other.

Lord, I'm so confused!

Jenna went into Scott's arms, taking the comfort she so desperately needed.

"Jen, don't make a rash decision. Stay. Take as long

as you need to be sure. I'm willing to wait."

"Oh, Scott!" A sob caught in her voice. Here was reliability, not volatility, doubt reminded her. Here was comfort, the known, versus edginess and unpredictability. The debate between her head and heart intensified. She wanted to grab her aching temples, to shout for some kind of release.

"But for heaven's sake and all of Boston's, *please* come back with me to the eco-lodge tomorrow and call your aunt."

Scott ruffled her hair like Adam always did to Pepito's.

"You needn't think *I'm* going to tell her you're not coming home, at least for now. I may actually want to return to Boston to live someday. And if you do decide to stay here permanently with the jungle man, I'll be a safe distance away in Arabia, till the dust from the blast settles."

Jenna collapsed, laughing and crying, letting the steam of her emotions erupt against Scott's shoulder until she had nothing left. Once drained, she pulled away.

"Thanks, Scott. You've been a real…*sport.*"

She winced, wishing she'd not used the same dismissal he'd given her a few weeks ago. Although, maybe he'd been as relieved then that an ugly scene was avoided as she was now.

"Hey, we're still on the same team, right?"

"You bet." Jenna walked Scott into the house to her

father's office where the rollaway bed was set up for him.

God had helped her weather this storm. She would face tomorrow knowing that somehow He'd see her through future ones as well. For now, she would simply wait on the Lord to sort out this quandary.

The smell of a storm brewing the following morning gave Adam just the excuse he needed to cut the camping trip short; although Pepito challenged his decision the entire way home. After all the sun *was* shining. Adam wasn't certain how to explain to the boy that this was an instinct one learned if they lived in the wild for any length of time. The air had a different texture, a different scent.

But it was more than that. Adam *had* to see Jenna. Faded chambray shirt open, his pants cut off above the knees, he made his way barefoot along the path after dropping Pepito off with his uncle and aunt. Occasionally, he broke into a little skip, like the overgrown boy he appeared. The natives just looked at the doctor strangely as he passed them by without speaking. Oblivious to his surroundings, he practiced intently on the eloquent proposal he'd put together during the previous night away.

"My dearest Jenna, I did not think it was possible for my heart to love again, but you, my beloved, have changed that. I must, therefore, ask you to marry me because—"

He slipped on a rut, gouging it with his knee, but kept right on walking in a world of his own.

"Because—"

He repeated the speech again to that point.

"Because my heart cannot stand to be broken again."

Adam winced. It sounded better last night when he said it over and over to the moon while Pepito slept a few feet away. *My heart cannot bear to be broken again* sounded entirely too selfish. And he thought his doctoral thesis was hard!

"Because your love is the only medicine to heal my heart."

Why didn't he just write out a prescription?

"Marry me because I love you and…and…that's it! I just love you. No, I can take care of you too. I *want* to take care of you."

Never had words that came so hard to him sounded so inept. Ahead was the hacienda, its red-tiled roof strewn with leaves given up by surrounding trees to last night's wind. Adam broke into a run, his thoughts scrambling hopelessly with every step.

"Jenna!" He shoved the back door to the kitchen open. He hesitated, awaiting an answer, but all he heard was the slam of the screen behind him. "Jenna, are you here?"

Tilda's voice rose from another part of the house. "Adam, is that you?"

But Adam was too excited to answer. Instead, he

hurried down the hall toward the bedrooms. At Jenna's, however, he stopped short, his heart slamming against his chest. The door was open and the room was empty. He was too late!

No, Adam refused to believe it. Rushing in, the young doctor yanked open the closet doors. The breath frozen in his lungs escaped in relief. No, it was not too late. Jenna's clothes were there. She was still there! He still had a chance to tell her how much he loved her, even though he never intended to fall in love again, ever!

Marina had broken his heart, but Jenna had stolen it completely with her selfless love of life and her eternal determination not to despair, no matter what life threw at her.

Tilda appeared in the doorway. "Adam, it *is* you."

He spun away from the closet. "Where is she, Tilda? Down at the dock helping Robert secure the boat for the storm?"

"What storm? The sun is shining—"

"I can smell it! We're in for a big blow, *mi queridita.*"

"But she is not here! She left with Stefan and that Scott boy."

The intonation of her last words told Adam what the woman he called his "little dear" thought of Scott Pierson, but the doctor took no satisfaction in it. He narrowed his gaze, his brow forming a slash across his forehead that was worthy of his growl.

"She what?"

"They have gone on Stefan's boat to Ichitas." The

housekeeper frowned. "So you think maybe they run into a storm?"

"She's marrying Pierson?" He sank down on the bed, trying to catch up with his heart. "But her clothes…"

Tilda walked over to him and embraced him with a smug grin. "I could be mean and let you think that, but I would hate to see my grown man cry. Thank goodness, you have come to your senses!" She planted a loud kiss on the top of his head.

Adam pulled away from the mother hen in frustration. "So she's *not* leaving with Scott?"

"The Lord, he taketh away, *mi hijo,* but he gives too! I know in my heart, it was no *accidente* that she come to us. She is a gift from God just for you."

God? Adam wondered. A week ago he'd have brushed aside Tilda's opinion, except that both Robert and Jenna believed her coming was no accident, either. It was like they were all tuned to the same station, one he couldn't quite hear. Regardless, Jenna was not here, not now. He ran his hands through his hair and stared up at the ceiling, uncertain what to think.

"Our Jenna has gone with Stefan and that Scott boy to spend the night at the Posada Explorador. She wants to call her aunt and reassure her that she is happy right where she is and that she loves it here." Tilda beamed at him. "And *I think* she loves a certain doctor who is not her father and doesn't deserve her with his stubborn onça temper."

As if to prove her point, Adam exploded. "How

could Robert let them leave? He should know better!"

"Well, the speedboat is very fast—"

He leapt from the bed and to the door in a single stride. Maybe if he could make radio contact, he could warn Stefan to come back before they were caught in the impending and unforgiving weather.

Sixteen

THE AMAZON RIVER GREW WIDER AHEAD OF THE RED SPEED-
boat and the surface roughened to a lumpy expanse. Yet
the sun overhead was bright and encouraging. With the
canvas canopy of Stefan's speedboat tied down, Jenna
rubbed on sunblock. While she tanned nicely for her fair
coloring, this *was* the tropics. As Aunt Violet and Adam
warned her, it just isn't the same sun down here.

Adam. He hadn't returned the night before. She listened for him between intermittent bouts of sleep to no
avail. Her concern was assuaged that morning at the
docks. One of the natives reported that the younger doctor and his *boy* had made camp for the night further
upstream and might not be back until tomorrow.

The image of the two campers—one small boy and
one overgrown one—put a smile on her lips. At the front
of the boat, Scott smiled back hesitantly, jarring Jenna
from her retrospection.

Grateful he'd accepted her decision with a degree of grace, she decided the least she could do was see Scott off and call Aunt Violet to check in. Although Jenna had sent a letter just before leaving for the interior, she hadn't spoken to the woman since leaving Boston. The phone in Ichitas was more reliable than the one at the government house, which never seemed to work when it was most needed. The Murillo family was better connected, both literally and theoretically, than remote government officials.

Besides, she and Stefan were going to edit the rest of the video, so that he could have copies made in time for the impending seminar. And get rid of a certain scene! The idea of a group of media specialists watching her and Adam was almost as bad as those who had already seen it.

The diesel engine purred beneath her feet, and Jenna turned her face toward the milk chocolate-colored water ahead. It had begun to get a bit choppy, which made her recall her father's objection that the rivereños were talking of a possible storm and hadn't gone out that morning. He finally relented to Stefan's own experience and his assurance that the speedboat would be in Ichitos well before the bad weather approached, if any came at all. The river taxis were slow and took the better part of a day to make the same trip his boat could make in two hours.

And they were moving swiftly. Floating islands of vegetation that had broken away from the floodplains drifted by them. One was larger than the boat, a mat of beautiful floating hyacinth and coarse grass. It was alive with frogs, which dipped in and out of the water at will, not the least perturbed that their destination depended on the whim of the tide.

In the scheme of the river, which had widened significantly, Jenna felt about the same size as the amphibian seafarers. The boat was hardly much bigger than the mat of plants. She could barely make out the bank from which it had likely come. On the other side of the boat, there was only the horizon where the sky met the café-colored water.

Armed with an expensive thirty-five millimeter camera, Scott snapped pictures of four dolphins that raced alongside the speedboat, surfacing, diving, then jumping out of the water in spirals and somersaults. A few seconds later, they rushed to catch up and start all over again. Hair whipping about her face, she laughed at the antics, but her knuckles had turned white from holding onto the rail.

"Uh-oh, I don't like the looks of that!" Stefan shouted from the helm. He pointed to the north side of the river.

Jenna's heart skipped at the sound of his voice, and again when she saw what he was talking about. While the dolphins distracted the speedboat crew, the black clouds that had been at their stern had somehow slipped around to their side and nearly passed them. It felt like the boat was skipping over rocks instead of water, propelled by the same wind that moved the storm so quickly. Ahead, the closest bank of the river curved, heading on a direct collision course with the churning black sky.

"Think we ought to turn back?" Scott shouted above the din of the engine and crash of the boat on the water.

Uncertain, Stefan looked ahead and then to the rear. The storm had actually split, as if to block either path of escape. Adam's words about the Amazon owning up to no rules ran through her mind as she waited for the captain to decide. Like he assured her father, he grew up on the river. He knew its ways well.

"We will look for a tributary and wait this out."

A tributary! Jenna scanned the forested lining of the river on one side. It was one continuous run of green, the top rolling with the various heights of the trees. Beyond and above the tree line, like a faraway world in its own right, rose mist-cloaked mountains. Jenna found herself feeling more and more like the frogs, except that she was aware of her danger.

Stefan maneuvered the boat closer to the bank, running a parallel course. The decrease in speed left the boat more subject to tossing and rolling. Wide and low to the water, it was designed for calmer water.

"Do you know where a tributary is?" she asked him hopefully. *Don't panic, Jenna. Stefan knows what he's doing.*

"There are many offshoots, señorita. We will have to look closely because most are overgrown."

Of the same mind, Scott took a pair of binoculars out of their case and started studying the shoreline with meticulous slowness.

Jenna mimicked Adam's pat answer. "Ah."

Had he and Pepito come in yet? What was the man thinking, staying overnight and not sending word, especially after all his lectures on how dangerous the jungle is at night! For all her annoyance, she wished Adam were with them now. Not that he could avoid the approaching storm. She just wanted him to hold her.

To hold her. She wanted that with a ferocity she'd never known. The realization took her by surprise. She *was* in love with Adam DeSanto, head over heels, hopelessly, completely. If only he felt the same.

The boat struck something hard in the water and careened sharply on its side. Jenna grabbed Scott by his belt just in time as the young man pitched dangerously toward the water. The binoculars and the pricey camera would have gone over too but for the strap securing them around Scott's neck.

Swearing a blue streak in Spanish, Stefan cut the engine back and peered off the stern counter. Submerged in the milky brown water, a fallen tree was barely visible in their wake. Upon spotting it, the young man rushed to open the bow locker. To her horror, water spilled slowly over the bottom of the opening.

Stefan turned on a pump. While it hummed dutifully, he cleared out the locker of its life jackets and contents. Sticking his arm inside up to his shoulders, he felt around the interior, his eyes closed as if that might increase the ability for his hands to *see* where the problem was.

"Found it!"

Jenna was almost afraid to ask. "What?"

"There is a puncture, one of the tree limbs broke off and is still jammed in it."

"Here, put this on," Scott barked, tossing her a life jacket.

They were going to sink! The idea paralyzed her at first. With hands and fingers still numb, she managed to get the vest on.

"Get me your clothes!" Stefan unzipped his duffle and took out a handful of wadded clothing. "I'm going to pack the break. Then we'll try to get to shore."

It was starting to rain. One little black cloud puff of advance warning sprinkled them lightly, but the increasing wind made the droplets sting. Jenna unzipped her leetle flowered bag, wishing she had some sort of miracle in there instead of T-shirts and shorts. Not even her all-occasion tank dress could bail her out of this one. She gave it to Stefan anyway.

He somehow reshaped his body to crawl headfirst into the opening while Scott squeezed a flashlight through one corner so that the photographer could see.

"What if I pack it from the outside?"

Jenna couldn't hear Stefan's answer to Scott's offer, but she gathered it was a negative. Helpless to do anything else, she resorted to the one option she had left.

Father who calms the sea, please make this work! There is so much left to do for all of us. Please God, take me home to that so-irritating-I-could-throttle-him doctor! For better or worse, I think I'm in love.

It had been a terrible storm, typical of Amazonia. The telephone at the government station was down, and the radio airwaves were full of static and ghosting messages. Now a soft rain fell, as if to apologize to the landscape for the earlier ravaging.

Adam felt like an onça, a caged cat, full of fury and fear, yet helpless to do anything about it. He'd been trying since he discovered Jenna's departure to reach Stefan Murillo on the marine band radio to no avail. Then the hope spawned by the news that Jenna was not going to marry Scott Pierson crashed as quickly as it soared—except this time it was with twice the force. The news that the speedboat had not reached the eco-lodge launched Adam into the past.

Adam paced back and forth listening as Robert tried to renew their brief radio contact with Posada Explorador. All they knew for certain was that Jenna and Stefan had not made it to the inn. Then the power went out in Ichitas. Obviously the backup generator at the inn was giving them trouble.

"Madre de Dios!" Tilda broke her rosary in half in her fervent prayer, sending beads spilling like her hysterical tears. Adam rushed to the housekeeper's side and kept her from dropping to her knees to pick them up.

"Tilda, Tilda!" He gathered the plump woman into his arms. "You must not cry so. Come, I will give you something to help."

"No, no, no!" Tilda gulped a calming breath. "I need

to pray! We *all* do," she added, squeezing Adam's arm pointedly.

He knew that look. It could heap guilt on a soul, child or adult, more effectively than any biblical chastisement. It could have done away with torture in the Inquisition and lie detectors in modern day. One look from Tilda and a victim would come clean. Adam knew the housekeeper wasn't blaming him for this, but she was certainly reminding him of what he should do, what he'd been raised to do.

"I'll clean this up."

To his surprise, she agreed.

"If it will get you on your knees, fine! Me, I will be in my room *praying*. Call me if you hear anything."

Adam fetched a broom and dustpan from the kitchen. When he returned, Robert was speaking to someone on the radio. Adam's initial elation collapsed when he realized it was not the inn but another operator farther down river, where the storm now wreaked its havoc. The message came across in bursts, blanketed in static.

"Lost 'em!" Robert leaned back against his chair and stared, unseeing, at the ceiling.

"I can't believe you let them go!"

Adam instantly regretted his hasty accusation.

"I can't either." Robert shook his head from side to side, looking as forlorn and frustrated as Adam felt. Worry had drained him of color, just as it had everyone. "I guess I was so glad to hear she wasn't leaving that...I don't know! I thought the sooner Pierson was on his way, the better."

"But of course you did." Adam grimaced. He was only making things worse. "I am sorry. I didn't mean to sound so judgmental. Pepito and I barely made it back in time."

"I'd feel a lot better if Jenna were with you out there than Stefan and a Boston engineer."

Adam should have felt complimented. Instead, the gnaw of an old guilt intensified. He sat down before his growing fear took out his knees. His clothes were still wet from having run into the village after the storm to try the telephone at the government station house. It was a futile attempt, but at least it had kept him busy. This waiting drove him insane. He was a man of action not prayer. There had to be something he could do! As it was, night crept upon them earlier than usual in the overcast sky. This far upriver, no one ventured out on the Amazon at night.

He glanced over to where Robert sat, head bowed, hands folded in his lap. A terrible anguish ripped through Adam's chest, tearing a path through his throat, but he held it in check. He wanted to cry, but he couldn't. Anger was the only emotion that came naturally since Marina.

"Father, thy will be done," Robert prayed. "All I ask is that if I must give her up, let it be to her other life in Boston…or to Scott Pierson. Deliver her Father, not for my sake, but for the life she has ahead of her. Father, I pray in the name of Jesus! Don't take another angel from me when I've only just come to know her."

Robert's desperate plea echoed in Adam's mind, tormenting him even more. He had prayed the same thing for his wife. He'd been willing to give up his jungle practice, to go to the city, anything, if God would spare her. But God hadn't. So what good would prayer do now?

Again, guilt rose like bile in his mind. He should have stayed, not run off to sulk. Then this wouldn't have happened. It might have been torment to entertain Scott Pierson, but at least Jenna would be safe. At least she'd be here at the hacienda, if not in his arms.

"The Lord, He taketh away, Adam, but He gives too! I know in my heart, it was no accidente that she come to us. She is a gift from God."

Adam *wanted* to believe this, but Tilda's prophetic words were no competition for the horror, the sick fear making itself at home within him as if it had never been gone. He found Marina in the jungle, too late. Would he even *find* Jenna? The river was more savage than the jungle. It could swallow a boat and its occupants without a trace. It could…

The sampler on the office wall Diana Marsten had made of her favorite verse grabbed Adam's blurred gaze and came into focus. *"We are troubled on every side, yet not distressed; we are perplexed, but not in despair."*

Ah, Jenna! They were the words she and Robert lived by. They had served them well. They made her the beautiful resilient person she was, against all odds. Did

Adam dare hope they'd work for him too after condemning them for so long?

"Come on, son."

He didn't even see Robert get up, yet the man stood next to him, his hand clasped on Adam's shoulder.

"Are you up for a moonlight cruise?"

"There is no moon tonight. Surely…"

"I'm going to look for my little girl. I know Arturo will go if I ask."

The river was always dangerous after a storm, and particularly at night. Floating debris knocked loose from banks by the tempest could not be spotted as easily and was deadly to an unsuspecting boat.

Yet the deep furrows of concern on Robert's forehead had smoothed, as if wiped away by some miracle antiaging creme or surgery. He acted as though he were on some sort of tranquilizer. Gone was his earlier despair. In its place was a quiet, almost peaceful resolve. For all Adam knew, he might have been suggesting a fishing outing on a sunshiny day.

"Yes!" Adam choked on his fervor. "I will swim if I have to."

His friend gave Adam a grateful squeeze and released his shoulder. Theirs was not a demonstrative relationship, but it was strong and heartfelt, just the same. This time, however, Adam needed more. Like a child seeking the reassurance of his father, he rose and hugged the man tightly before releasing him just as impulsively.

"We will find her, amigo," he swore solemnly. "We must!"

A faraway look lit Robert's face and then was gone as quickly as it came.

"I know, son."

The lights were on in the church-school building. There were no secrets in the small community. As soon as word was spread that the doctor's daughter was missing, the people started gathering of their own accord. Poor in earthly goods, they were rich in faith. It enabled them to rebuild their lives each time a storm or some disaster struck. Adam had seen it over and over again. He'd once been one of them in spirit as well as body. Now he was a distant cousin rather than a brother or sister in the fold, removed by his lack of faith.

He didn't think it was possible to feel more lonely, but with each wish for success in finding the pretty *gringa,* he did. It wasn't just Jenna, the woman, he longed for. It was her body and soul, her bright outlook on life, her faith.

God's gift. Tilda's words began to have more and more meaning. Was Jenna God's way of telling him that it was time for healing, time for forgiveness, time to love again? Would God even want Adam back?

"Dr. Adam!"

Pepito scampered down the steps to the dock, Rita perched atop his head, squalling in excitement. The boy latched on to Adam's leg as he untied the lines at the dock.

"You will find Jenna, I know! I have already prayed!"

"I appreciate that, Pepito."

"And I know Jenna will make a good wife for you *and* a mother for me. Trust me."

"*What?*"

The boy grinned from ear to ear, pleased as punch with himself. "Well, I *hope* you were not asking yourself to marry you last night."

Adam hadn't realized Pepito had heard his pitiful attempts the night before to convince the doctor's daughter of his love and why she should stay. He thought the little monkey was asleep with his marmoset!

"Eavesdropper." He peeled the child off his leg and leaped onto the boat as it drifted away from the dock.

"What is *that?*"

"A little boy with big ears!"

Adam had to chuckle when Pepito clamped his hands over his ears, his expression thoroughly bemused. "His ears are almost as big as his mouth."

Finally catching on, the child broke into laughter. "I get it!"

"Now get back up to the church before your aunt has to come looking for you."

"But I have already prayed," Pepito protested. "That is how I *know* you are going to bring me home a new mama."

A new mama? The rascal didn't miss anything! And he was so certain everything was going to be fine. But Adam was a man. It was easy to have childlike faith when one *was* a child.

Adam longed for the reassurance Pepito and Robert had somehow received. The boy was a child, of course, who believed in fairy tales. But how could his friend *know*? Had God spoken to the man?

If he had, Adam wished he'd heard it. The chances of God speaking to him were as good as Adam reaching up and taking a star from that patch of clearing sky above. It looked almost close enough to touch but was as far out of reach as Jenna.

The steamboat slowly hissed away from the docks, nearly drowning out the sound of the church bell. When she struck the main river current, she jerked and then dug in, snatching Adam from his quagmire of torment. Ahead, the moon gave up her cloak of clouds. Suddenly the spotlight mounted on the foredeck paled in comparison. It was as if God were lighting their way.

Dear Jesus, I want to believe!

Adam grasped the rail and dropped to his knees, felled by a powerful force. He couldn't voice his anguish, yet he screamed it to the heavens. He had nothing left to lose and everything to gain.

I deserve nothing, God, but for Jenna's sake…hear me! I humble myself before You as I will humble myself before her, if You but give me the chance. I am half a man, nothing more, without love. I am dead. Give me life again. I beg this in the name of Your Son. Take me if You will, send me where You will, but spare Jenna.

Adam blinked at the stinging in his eyes. Overhead, he saw his hand outstretched toward the stars, as if his soul commanded it to reach up for God's forgiveness and mercy. As his vision cleared, a star broke loose from its blue velvet setting and streaked like heaven's fire across the sky, as if to fall right into his grasp.

Was it an answer? Adam didn't know. What he did know was that he could not bear to believe otherwise.

The serenity of the moonlit river masked its lurking danger. The *Jenna* moved slowly down it. Adam kept lookout from the bow for any sign of Stefan's red speedboat or its inhabitants, as well as floating debris that may have broken loose from the banks with dangerous limbs and roots hidden in them.

He would have preferred to go faster but knew how easy it would be to miss spotting anything that might point to where the boat and its crew were. Hopefully, Stefan pulled into a cove or offshoot of the river for shelter and had the good sense to stay put. Stefan was a city boy, but Adam was counting on the man's experience filming in the wild to make up for the skills civilization tended to dull.

In any case, the radio Robert brought along and installed on the *Jenna* confirmed again, shortly after the boat left the dock, that the group had not yet arrived at Posada Explorador. They had to be somewhere on the river in between Ichitas and Santa Beliza.

Drained emotionally, Adam studied the shoreline with binoculars for any irregularity, coordinating his effort with the spotlight Arturo operated. He'd offered to spell Robert from firing the engine, but the older doctor yielded to the younger's sharper eyes. Besides, keeping the steam up was a busy job, one that did not allow time to wonder and worry.

Ahead lay the widest stretch of the river between Ichitas and Santa Beliza. They'd been crawling along the riverbank for nearly four hours. Nothing. That was what they saw and it was what Adam felt. His anger and contrition were spent. His fear numbed into submission by the same hand that now led them.

If they found the boat, Adam knew now, it would not be by his effort or those of the other men. There was too much to see and too much to miss for the human eye. All Adam's knowledge of the jungle and river, all his skill as a physician and the arrogance man's knowledge manifested were nothing in this overwhelming scheme. It would take a miracle to find Jenna; one Adam could not perform alone, no matter how much he wanted to.

He'd made a muddle of his life. He was tired of being in charge. Tilda's words about the Lord's taking and giving took root and flourished in the humility and insignificance he felt. Yes, Marina broke his heart. Jenna stole it. Had God sent her to mend it?

Adam glanced up at the stars. *Just one more chance, Lord. That's all I ask.*

Another star shot across the sky, arching high upward before changing direction and plunging toward the earth with a fiery tail in its wake. Adam followed it with his gaze, bemused. Stars did not shoot up. They fell.

But flares did!

"Arturo! Over there!"

Adam pointed to the direction from which the flare came. After scanning the water meticulously with the spotlight to see if it was safe to enter, Arturo steered the boat in closer to the shore. Robert came up from the engine area and took over the light so the pilot could concentrate solely on the water. It wouldn't do anyone any good to cripple the ship on debris from the storm.

A second flare streaked up from the bank just beyond the bend ahead of them. This time Adam was able to narrow down the location. Arturo eased the *Jenna* around the curve of the bank. Using the boat pole, Adam pushed a floating tree out of the way and broke up islands of flotsam that might conceal something that could damage the propeller or rudder. It wouldn't do for the rescuers to need rescue.

The jungle grew straight down to the water, with vines connecting the treetops to its shimmering edge. Adam waited for another flare, but none came. Did he hear voices or was that just hopeful thinking?

"Cut the engine!"

Arturo cut the throttle and the piggy-chuck of the vessel dropped to a whisper.

"Over here!"

Adam scanned the bank with the binoculars. Something white waved back and forth, barely visible in the dark overgrowth. He motioned for Arturo to put the spotlight on it. A glimpse of red could now be seen. The white object waved above it. And voices! Adam could hear voices, including a feminine one that sounded as though it came from heaven itself.

"What took you guys so long?" That was *his* Jenna. Adam knelt on one knee, eyes wide open for safety's sake and gave voice to his heart.

Gracias à Dios!

The old puttering steam launch was the prettiest sight Jenna ever laid eyes on, next to the anxious young man crouched on her bow. She knew Adam would come. She didn't know how or when, but she knew it in her heart and soul that he would find her. And this time, God's timing was faster than her own. No one expected anyone to search for them at night. They'd just hoped to weather things out until morning when the river taxis resumed their traffic.

"Is everyone okay?" Adam shouted, stirring the water ahead of the *Jenna* with a pole, searching for hidden dangers.

"We are fine!"

Stefan hopped down from the bow where he'd been flagging their rescuers with Jenna's halter top. It was the only white thing they had. Considering most of her clothes were now pounded into the hole in the bow, it hardly mattered to her...until now. She tucked it back in her little flowered bag.

"Man, you all are a sight for sore eyes." Scott folded

back the canvas canopy so that they could stand. The three of them had been huddled under it for hours, wondering if the wind was going to simply rip it off like it did tree branches all around them.

"You're eye sore yourself."

Jenna wondered if Adam's words were intentional or just another one of his twisted idioms. The way the jungle doc and Scott measured each other from the distance, she was inclined to believe her first impression. Adam definitely needed polish in some areas.

"I hope you know what you're doing, Jen," Scott said under his breath. "He looks ready to pounce."

How could she want to hug someone and shake him at the same time? Adam always had that effect on her. "He's all snarl, no bite."

At that moment, her father peered over the side of his boat at them. "Jenna?"

"I'm fine, Dad! Wet and hungry, but just fine!"

Robert whooped loudly, putting a macaw's cry to shame. "Praise the Lord! Told you we'd find our girl, Adam!"

Jenna locked gazes with Adam DeSanto.

"I knew you'd come." Her eyes grew bright and blurred as her voice with emotion.

"Need a tow?" She couldn't decide which was more devastating—that low Latin rumble in his voice or his rakish wink.

"No, I fear we are damaged," Stefan told him. "Got a hole in the bow, even though we've stuffed it as best we could."

"Yeah, we've taken on quite a bit of water," Scott chimed in. "If we hadn't been able to get the boat up on the bank some and tie her down…"

The wind had whipped them so mercilessly, Jenna hadn't had time to worry about the lightning, which showed just how serious their situation was. Each time the sky flashed, she watched the main tree on the bank where they'd tied the craft. The lines would only reach so far, despite Scott and Stefan getting out and pushing the boat aground as far as they could. The tree teetered and swayed. She prayed the earth would hold on to its roots, that the rushing water would not wash it away— taking the boat with it—or that it wouldn't fall and crush them as well.

But God had not brought her this far for nothing. She quoted her mother's favorite Scripture each time the lightning struck, for indeed they were troubled on every side. Thankfully, the clothing Stefan pounded into the hole in the bow and the bilge pump held out until they were able to secure the boat partially on the bank.

As the steamboat maneuvered inland, it became apparent that there was not enough water for it to get close enough to place a gangway between the two vessels. Adam jumped into the debris littered river without hesitation. It was not over his head but about shoulder depth.

"Oh no, we're gonna have to get our feet wet!"

Jenna laughed at her own joke. Talk about a paradoxical situation! They'd just been sitting in a boat in the water, with a canopy overhead to protect them from the

312

rain. Her laughter earlier was more nervous laughter, but it was either that or cry, and she was *not* going to despair. Now it was just funny—that or she was slaphappy.

"Just don't start singing again," Scott teased as he helped her over the side and onto Adam's shoulders. He could just walk with them out of the water. "Besides, we're ready to be *moved* now."

When they had run out of words of encouragement in the midst of the storm, Jenna started singing the old hymn "I Shall Not Be Moved" with Scott and eventually Stefan joined in on the chorus. Meanwhile, the boat jerked and twisted as though intent on dumping them. Surely God looked down from the heavens and decided these three crazies needed His protection more than even *He* thought.

"Hey, it was either 'I Shall Not Be Moved' or 'Michael, Row the Boat Ashore.'"

Jenna tried to situate herself on Adam's shoulders, but at the last minute, he twisted. Instead of riding piggyback, she slid down into his arms, halting when her face was a breath from his.

"Adam…!"

Before she realized it wasn't an accident, he kissed her. At the contact, time stood still. It was as though it were just the two of them; as though they weren't standing in the Amazon River in the middle of the night; as though they were alone, not being watched by her father, her ex-fiancé, and his late wife's cousin, not to mention Arturo.

All of those thoughts faded, bombarded by his fervent message. He'd been insane, waiting and searching. He couldn't bear the thought of not seeing her again, of her going away, of her in someone else's life. It wasn't said with words. Souls didn't need them to communicate.

The peeping of frogs, the call of the night birds, the noises of the jungle that had frightened her so her first night in Ichitas blended with the primitive beat of her heart in a lullaby of love. She ran her fingers through his wet, dark hair, swaying to the music. Adam sang its glorious words upon her lips as the first Adam must have upon discovering his Eve, words of joy, of gratitude, of longing.

"I doubt you two realize it, but it's a bit chilly out here, amigos."

If Adam heard Stefan, he showed no sign of it.

"Marry me, Jenna! I will go with you anywhere. I will do anything, but I cannot live without you!"

How could he cover her face and neck with hot little kisses and say such sweet things at the same time?

"I cannot live without you. I am but half a man, half a soul!"

Adam pressed his forehead to hers.

Like she *would* run if she could! At that moment, Jenna could spend eternity right here in Adam's embrace.

"You have given me back my soul, Jenna. I have been dead, deaf, and blind, but God sent you with that silly flowered bag and…"

He stopped with a startled look. His embrace tight-
ening, he scanned the spotlighted water, as if realizing
for the first time that they might not be alone in the
water. Then he noticed her father leaning over the rail of
the boat, waiting patiently with a pleased smirk twitching on his mouth.

"Robert, I *am* sorry. I forget myself." Adam turned
toward the boat. "May I have your daughter's hand?"

"You can have *all* of her you can get up here in the
boat," her father teased, winking at Jenna as he extended
his hand to her.

"Ah! But of course."

With a sheepish grin, Adam waded to the steam
launch, Jenna clinging to him like a drenched but ecstatic monkey. She'd never seen the onça in such a bum-
bling stew before. It was absolutely charming!

Somehow Stefan and Scott had crossed over on
their own. Adam hoisted her up into their outstretched
arms as though she were weightless. But then, she felt
like she was. Her feet were on the deck of the *Jenna,* but
she was floating. It was only her father's tight embrace
that held her grounded.

"You didn't despair?"

"Nope."

She didn't even need the lantern Arturo held on her
to glow. She was happy from the inside out, filled with
all the joy of God's precious gift of love.

"May I?"

For a moment, her father looked as though he

thought Adam was about to take him up on his promise to give Jenna up right then and there. The younger doctor stood, water still running off him, waiting like an expectant kitten to seize the prize. Robert clapped Adam on the back, sending a spray of droplets in every direction.

"You've got it bad, son."

"I know." Adam slipped his arm behind Jenna, his gaze only for her. "I don't think I will *ever* get over it."

His lips brushed hers gently; his eyes open, as though she might slip away if he closed them. A myriad of promises and longings swirled in them.

Stefan handed Adam a blanket. "Like I said, I know you are not cold, but the girl has been in the water for a long time, and…well, we cannot have the bride catching pneumonia, can we?"

"Arturo, are we ready?"

Her father took charge, motioning Jenna and Adam toward the side bench. "We can send someone to tow back the speedboat tomorrow, if she'll stay afloat."

She wondered where the silver lining to being caught in the savage storm could be. She knew trials and blessings came in the same package. But to have Adam declare his love for her, his need of her, was more than even a dreamer dared dream.

"Want me to keep watch on the bow?" Scott offered. His enthusiasm betrayed his discomfiture. He'd have to be blind not to know it was more than the call of the jungle making her want to stay behind.

A twinge of guilt caused her to call after him. "Scott…"

Adam was slow to release her, and when he did, he stood statue still, as if it took all his resolve to stand back and let her go.

Scott waved her away. "Hey, I had my chance and blew it."

Jenna wondered if Scott's reaction was out of his ingrained social grace or the suspicion that Adam might toss him over the side. Not that she thought he would go that far, but dark eyes glowering and body tensed, he certainly looked like he was more than willing and capable.

Robert cut through the building tension. "Appreciate all the help we can get, Scott. You take the lookout on the bow with those binoculars. Stefan, I could use some help with the wood, if you don't mind. It's past my bedtime and I'm tuckered."

The last word wasn't in Stefan's considerable English vocabulary. "You are sick?"

"No, he's tired and he wants to give Adam and me some privacy." She gave her dad a grateful look. Had he known how Adam felt? Regardless, he was grinning from ear to ear. She could almost hear him counting grandchildren before they were hatched.

As Adam draped the blanket around Jenna's shoulders, she felt the exploration of his fingers between her shoulder blades and was instantly distracted from her musings. The moment he found the outline of her undergarment, he drew away with a sigh of relief.

"What *are* you doing?" she asked, stepping out of the warm fold of the blanket.

The fierce jungle doc looked like Pepito, caught with his hand in Tilda's cookie jar, or a hapless bull-fighter with nothing between him and an angry bull but a faded blanket.

"I was just wondering where Stefan found a bra to flag us down." Adam's feign of wide-eyed innocence fell apart with the devilish purse of his lips. "You must admit, it was an unusual flag."

"That was a halter top; not what you're thinking. You are so bad!" Jenna gave him one of his own shrugs. "And it came from the *leetle flowered bag,* where else?"

"Ah! I should have known."

Stepping back, Adam held open the blanket for her in an open invitation to temptation itself. She wasn't ordinarily a giggler, but Jenna couldn't help it. She walked into his embrace, her heart cart wheeling off the insides of her chest.

Settling with her on the bench as the boat gathered steam, Adam wrapped and tucked the cover around her like a mother hen nesting its chick. She couldn't have been cold if she'd been in the north Atlantic, not the way he looked at her.

"You have not answered my question, Jenna." He whispered warmly into her ear.

Jenna. Hot flash! No one could say her name like that, especially with that low Latin rumble. The onça could purr too!

Jenna's backbone turned to butter. She managed however to extract her arms from the jungle doc's neat little blanket cocoon. Looping them around his neck, she gave Adam his answer, not with words, but with a kiss as impassioned as his earlier one. He had held nothing back. Neither would she. She met him as Eve her Adam, ready to receive and return his love for eternity.

Her Adam!

Joy welled triumphant, lifting Jenna as she'd never soared before.

Seventeen

———∞∞∞———

Two years later

THE DAMPNESS OF THE MORNING'S SHOWER DISSIPATED WITH the emergence of the noonday sun. It peaked in all its glory, casting no shadow around the village clearing. Jenna stood on the dock, watching as a red speedboat approached. It cut a frothy wake across the river surface.

"How'd he make out?" Jenna shouted above the din of the engine as the vessel eased up to the dock.

A patient came in the night before complaining of stomach pain and high fever. When it became clear that it was appendicitis, Adam decided to take him by boat to Ichitas for surgery.

"Ito will be fine. The doctors were able to catch the appendix *before* it ruptured."

The river breeze plastered her loose dress against a bulging abdomen, nearly nine months ripe with their first child. It felt like at least ten.

321

"Toss me a line." She might not be able to bend over and tie it, but she could hold the boat till Adam did.

"I have it," Adam insisted. Since they discovered she was expecting, he didn't want Jenna to lift anything heavier than a feather.

Her husband lassoed a davit and pulled the boat in. Stefan Murillo not only had the speedboat salvaged but donated it to the clinic. It was their water ambulance; they were capable of making the trip to Ichitas in half the time it had taken before. The photographer, having been hired by a major network after his film on the Orincas, was now shooting a safari type program in Africa.

"So he was saved by the boat, huh?"

Adam hated to do surgery unless there was no alternative. The clinic wasn't designed for it, nor was he trained formally for it. His general practice kept him busy enough.

"No, he was saved by a greater Physician than I *or* the doctors in Ichitas." He grabbed his medical case and held it up with a grin bright as a sunrise. "But, just in the event that God called upon me to perform the surgery, I was prepared, nonetheless."

As her husband jumped from the boat to the dock, Jenna's heart welled to overflowing with thanksgiving. Adam had not only come back to God, but he now taught Sunday school at the village. He claimed it was to get in practice for having his own child, but Jenna knew better. Adam loved kids…and the God who'd blessed them so bountifully.

She gave up a short *Thank you, Lord*, for both his and the patient's safety, considering the unusual circumstances under which they'd left. Ordinarily someone from the clinic would have accompanied him, but her father, Pepito, and Arturo had gone on a fishing trip upriver on the *Jenna*. Since the patient's eldest son ran a river taxi, he went instead, to handle the boat in case of the emergency worsening.

When Adam diagnosed the severity of the mestizo's condition, thanks to the new lab and used-X ray equipment purchased with money from last year's seminar proceeds, he'd been reluctant to leave Jenna. However, she wasn't due for another two weeks, and the clinic's midwife was perfectly capable of handling a normal delivery, so he reluctantly agreed that the patient needed his expertise more.

Besides, he was smothering Jenna to distraction with concern and his natural born curiosity. His affection was one thing, but his game of hourly *twenty questions* was absurd!

"What did you have for breakfast? Did you take your prenatal vitamins? Did you remember sunblock? How much weight have you gained? Wasn't that dress looser last week?" Oh yes, Jenna especially *loved* the questions about her size. Like she wasn't aware there was a change taking place!

"And how are we?"

But he meant well. "Same old, same old. It's kickin'. I'm grinnin'."

Jenna had the chance to find out if the baby was a boy or girl at the hospital in Lima, where Adam insisted on the pregnancy being monitored, but she declined. Her husband, who questioned *everything* the obstetrician told them, was privy to the tests. It was no wonder the poor man was relieved when Jenna insisted the baby be born at Santa Beliza.

Not that she wanted Adam delivering their child. He was to play the father role *only.* Why her husband couldn't have more of the don't-want-to-know-anything-about-women's-matters attitude so prevalent among the men of the area was beyond Jenna. Sometimes she felt like a fascinating toy, one he'd like to take apart to see exactly how she worked. He read everything he could get his hands on about women and babies. As if a book could explain her moods and cravings.

"Don't you think the baby is lower?"

"Adam, if it were any lower, you could hold it."

He shook his head. "No, it is definitely lower."

"If you pull out that measuring tape, I will toss you overboard!"

Jenna wondered if Adam was the only expectant father who carried a tape measure in his pocket to track the daily progress of the baby-to-be. No, for his sake and hers, it was best if Adam played the daddy role only.

Lola's daughter was now a licensed midwife. After a great deal of insistence on Jenna's part, it was agreed that she would deliver their newborn. It was only fitting. The clinic was fortunate enough to be able to hire Anna and pay for part of her education because of the result of a grant Jenna obtained from a stateside foundation.

At the ladder rising from the floating dock to the village bluff, Jenna pressed against her lower spine and arched backward to stretch. She was all belly- and back-ache! Her lower back had been one dull pain since the baby dropped three days ago. Climbing down the steps to the dock aggravated her sciatica. Climbing up would do it no good either, but in this case of low river and high bank, what goes down, must come back up.

Adam stole a quick kiss from the bulge of baby, catching Jenna off guard in her contemplation. It had taken some getting used to his impulsive affections. The cub in the dark, brooding onça, which she only glimpsed before, had been set free by marriage. Sometimes it was embarrassing, but like the big cat, Adam didn't care what anyone thought except her…and God.

"One for baby," he said with a rakish grin.

Love had removed the thorn in his eye. He now saw the glass half full, a blessing rather than a slight. As for his impatience—well, like Jenna and everyone else who tried to live according to Scripture, God was still working on him.

"And one for *mamacita.*"

And she wasn't going to complain. Not when her husband looked at her like that.

"You've only been gone ten hours," she pointed out.

Adam tossed his bag up to one of the natives on the

high bank and took Jenna in his arms. Once a cub, always a cub, she thought, as her husband teased her lips, the tip of her nose, her eyes…

"Ah!"

Adam jumped back as the baby kicked him soundly.

"Jealous little critter, isn't…"

Jenna gave him a warning look.

"…it."

He was going to tell her the baby's sex. Jenna knew it! Adam was so dizzy about the prospect of being a father, she wondered how he'd managed to keep the baby's gender a secret this long. Beneath her husband's cool and collected exterior was a wild, impulsive passion ever ready to escape. Adam was part cat, part boy, and all man.

She scratched his face where a day's growth of beard sprouted. "You need a shave." Although that shadow made him look positively wicked, almost worth the whisker burn.

"We must get to the house first," he whispered, as if he'd read her thoughts. "You go first. I will keep you decent."

Jenna started up the steep steps.

"I got a new Disney video for Pepito and…"

Halfway up, a pain grazed her back and lower belly.

Playfully, Adam shoved his shoulder under her for support and gathered in the billowing cotton of her dress.

"Come on, mamacita. You can do it!" he teased, grunting with far more effort than he was putting out.

"Wait a minute."

Jenna just needed to get her breath. But then, she always needed to catch her breath lately. It was the cost of carrying two people on one set of legs.

"This is what you get for marrying a water buffalo."

Grimacing, Jenna climbed another rung. Two more to go.

"Aw, man, this is the last time I gather at the river till this baby is here!" she declared, winded. Her girth was so tight from the back spasm, her lungs couldn't expand.

"Is everything all right up there?" Adam mumbled against her thigh. He lifted his face, but the folds of Jenna's long skirt blew across it.

Why was he always so impatient? "Yes!"

Her husband spat the whipping material out of his mouth. "You know, Jenna, my experience as a doctor is telling me otherwise."

Jenna would have made some witty reply, but her back demanded her full attention. She rested her knees against the rung of the ladder.

"Jenna? Yoo-hoo."

"Just hold on!"

"No, *you* hold on," Adam protested. "I don't want to deliver my...our baby on a ladder."

"I'll move when I'm ready!"

"Just *try* to move up, darling."

Freeing one hand from the ladder, Adam wadded

her skirt and tucked it under his chin. He yelled in rapid Spanish to the fisherman who'd taken his bag, summoning the man to help Jenna.

"Now, querida, I am going to just push you up the ladder."

Push, her foot! He could *darling* and *dear* her all he wanted, but she didn't dare let loose the bloomin' ladder.

"Whatever you do, Adam, don't push!" If he broke her death grip on the ladder, they'd both go tumbling down to the dock.

"This can't be happening!"

"Ohhh, yes it can. I have seen—" Adam thought better of what he was going to say. "No, you don't want to know what I have seen."

She tried to reach down and pull the back of her skirt between her legs, but putting theory into practice was impossible with a belly the size of a Buddha statue. Adam caught on to what she was doing and helped her.

"Now tuck the bottom of the hem into the front of your belt."

"I don't *have* a belt," Jenna whined as though the contraction squeezed her voice from her windpipe. "Water buffaloes can't wear belts!"

"*Carumba,* just hold your skirt then!"

Adam strained to peer past her where the fisherman leaned over a rail at the top of the steps. Her wise husband had built it there during her sixth month growth spurt just to make it easier for Jenna to get up and down from the dock.

"Take Aurileo's hand."

"With my *third* hand?" One hand held her skirt. Jenna clung to the ladder with the other. By her count that was all she had.

"I have you, Señora DeSanto."

Aurileo locked his fingers around Jenna's wrist, and she let go of the ladder.

"Now!"

Adam heaved Jenna upward the last few feet into Aurileo's arms. The fisherman dragged her away from the edge of the bluff through dirt that was still wet from the morning shower. Jenna dropped to her knees, holding on to her abdomen. It felt as though it were about to pop from the pressure.

"I'm okay."

Contradicting her reassurance, the bottom of her pain dropped out. The vacuum caused by the breaking water took Jenna's breath away. Adam scrambled over to her, the most amazed expression on his face as he frantically assessed the situation.

"Jenna, the baby is coming!"

"You went to school for this?" She didn't need a medical degree or to read a library of books to figure that out! Thankfully, the bind of her abdomen was easing.

"Just stay here!"

Adam ran over to where Pepito had left his wagon.

He had to be kidding. "Oh no. I'm not riding in *that.*"

"You have a better idea?" Her husband was whiter

beneath his swarthy complexion than Jenna felt. She'd never seen the man so pale. Was he afraid?

She forced patience into her voice. "Honey, I can walk. You know this can take hours."

"I don't think so. It was a good egg." They smiled over Pepito's assessment of the situation when Jenna and Adam announced they were going to have a baby.

"The pain has subsided." Jenna straightened and threw up her arms. "Look." And she could breathe again. If she could breathe she could walk.

The skeptical crinkle of her husband's forehead would have been funny if someone else were having the baby. But they weren't. She was.

"Jenna, I *am* the doctor."

And she knew that stubborn little twist of his jaw, the way his brow knitted like a foreboding line drawn in the sand.

"And *I* am the mother. I ought to know if I feel like walking."

Jenna motioned to the women who'd come over from the marketplace to see what the commotion was about.

"I—" she tapped herself on the belly—"am the mama, no?"

With very little idea of what she'd said, they nodded back, smiling.

"Jenna, I will not allow my baby to be born in the street. Now, get in the wagon!"

Adam gained his color back with each angry heave

of his chest. He ripped off his damp shirt and, throwing it on the ground, pointed again at the wagon as if he were some kind of trainer trying to get Fido to jump.

Lifting her head as regally as one could given the circumstances, Jenna snipped, "*Marmosets* ride in that thing."

With a clumsy pivot, she started up the hill toward the medical compound in the distance.

The onça roared behind her. "Someone run ahead and tell Anna the baby is coming."

Jenna paced her breath with her stride, determined to remain calm. After all, she'd read a few books herself. Adam caught up with her and put his arm around where her waist used to be.

"At least let me carry you."

His look was so pathetic, Jenna almost agreed. But she knew how heavy she was and was determined Adam was not going to find out by straining his gizzard to salve his male ego.

"I'm fit as a fiddle! Never felt better. Just help me up the hill."

"I swear…" Adam fell into an angry stride beside with her. "I will not be surprised if this baby has long pointed ears and brays!"

Jenna had to laugh. If anything, their offspring would have a head full of raven black hair and roar to its cublike utmost. She'd adore it anyway. Reaching out, she traced a finger down the bulging taper of Adam's jaw. It softened to her touch.

"I love you, Adam DeSanto."

"Jenna..." Adam gave her a beseeching look. "My mother delivered me while climbing the steps at the hospital in Lima. *Please* hold on to your skirt."

They almost made it to the clinic before the next contraction struck. It cinched Jenna's lower back and abdomen, as though to cut her in half. She grabbed Adam, swaying against him as it bore down upon her. Before she could protest, Adam swept her up into his arms.

"In here!" Anna called out from the door of her office. "I'm all ready."

"So is she," Adam rasped, turning sideways to get Jenna through the opening without banging her head and feet. Sweat beading on his brow, he carried her to the delivery room. The space had been set aside and outfitted for Anna's specific practice.

Gently, he set Jenna on the obstetric table-bed combination.

"Now, chica, just put your feet in the stirrups and—"

"Maybe I should help her into a gown first," Anna interrupted. Her bright eyes twinkled on a round face, very much like her mother's. "Do you think you have time, Jenna?"

"Yes." The pain had dulled again. Jenna could breathe without a struggle. Thank goodness *someone* recognized her ability to realize what was happening in her own body!

And it wasn't Adam. "Don't you think we should check first?"

Jenna snatched her skirt out of her husband's hand. The damp dirt that had collected on its hem shook free on the clean, white sheet.

"Adam, let Anna do her job." *Lord, I'm trying not to hurt him. I know he means well.*

"I *am* the doctor…"

But if I hear that one more time…

"No, you're not. Not this time. You are the *father!* We agreed ahead of time, remember?"

At that moment, Tilda burst into the room, her ample figure jostling on its small frame. Having caught only part of their exchange, the housekeeper stared at Jenna in disbelief.

"He is a father *already?*"

Jenna shook her head. "Tilda, do something with him!"

Not the least intimidated by Adam's stubborn demeanor, his former nurse shoved Adam aside with a reproving look and stepped up to the table herself to give Jenna a hug.

"Pobrecita, what has he done to you, dragged you in the dirt?"

"I wish I had time for a shower."

"No! I think Anna should check you *now!*" Adam gave the midwife a bullish look. It worked on Anna but not Jenna.

"Adam, we are not pulling a *rabbit* out of a hat! Tilda, take him someplace till Anna and I are ready, please!"

"I am *not* leaving until Anna looks under there." He pointed to the mud-caked hem of her skirt.

Jenna lay against the fresh white pillow, staring at the ceiling. Why did she ever think Adam would be a passive bystander?

"For heaven's sake, Anna, go ahead and look!"

"Not you." Tilda turned her former charge's head away so quickly; it was a wonder his neck didn't snap. She was from the old school where a man had no business even being around such things as childbirth, even if he *was* the young doctor she had helped raise. This was a woman's domain.

"I *am* a doctor," Adam turned and spread his hands against the jamb of the door, staring outside. "Not that it matters to anyone *here*. Of all the days for your father to go fishing!"

"As if we needed more men to get in the way." Tilda took up Jenna's hand and patted it. "He means well, niña."

"Five and a half centimeters," Anna announced from the other side of sheet covering Jenna. She couldn't see past her raised knees, but the midwife sounded pleased. "We have plenty of time."

Adam spun around, disappointment spelled out on his face. "Only five and a half?"

Patience was not one of her husband's virtues, and his lack of it was starting to infect Jenna. "Can I at least get into clean clothes now?"

Adam twisted his neck sideways, flexing his jaw, as

if struck by a phantom fist.

"Okay." He lifted his hands in surrender to the three women staring him down. "So the rabbit is not ready to come out of the hat."

Clearly torn between his desire to stay and their silent demand that he leave, he forced an even breath. Not being in charge did not come easy to him.

"The doctor and *father* of this rabbit will wait out here," he conceded haplessly.

He sounded so dejected, Jenna almost reneged. Her heart went out with him. Adam was so...*intense.* Scott Pierson's description hit the proverbial nail on the head. The last letter from Aunt Violet said that the engineer had married an Arabian girl, a children's doctor, no less. Life did have its ironies.

With Anna's help, Jenna bathed as best she could and put on a gown while Tilda changed the bed. Yet Jenna's thoughts drifted to the enigmatic man she loved more than life itself. There was laughter outside. Some of the villagers must have come up to offer him support. Perhaps that would make it easier for Adam to wait and pace like a normal expectant father when it went so much against his nature. Everything her husband did, he did with passion, from the office to the bedroom to...to being a father.

Jenna rubbed her belly, confident in the fact that no baby would ever know more love than this one. God willing, it would never know the emptiness and uncertainty that had once plagued her, not knowing who she really was, who she'd come from.

And its daddy was a born Pied Piper. Pepito, who now lived in the hacienda with them, worshiped the ground Adam walked on. It was a joy to watch them together. Jenna and Adam adopted the boy officially when they returned from their honeymoon in the States. Aunt Violet was already checking on prep schools for them, since the mission school had its limitations.

Once Jenna was back in bed, Anna pulled the sheet up over her swollen belly. "Now you should feel much better, no?"

Jenna nodded, tired.

"You rest while you can, hija." Tilda wadded up the dirty, crinkled cotton dress Jenna had worn and tossed it into a bag. "I will take care of the *doctor*. Perhaps he could call your aunt in Boston."

At long last, the clinic also had a phone. Stefan convinced his uncle in Lima to pull some strings and, as Adam said, voilà! True, the system was antiquated, but it was an improvement. They had come such a long way in the last two years. They'd even started posting regular hours, although patients still came at night or after work, when the situation demanded it.

"No," Jenna decided. "It will just upset Aunt Vi if she has to wait out the labor. Dad called her when Mom went into labor. Waiting by the phone through the nine hours for me to be born was hard on her, and she was younger then."

Although Adam was definitely the one to give the

news when the baby did come. Tia Violetta, as Adam called her aunt, fell completely in love with Jenna's jungle doctor at first sight. Clad in a tailored, custom-made suit, complete with tie and Italian leather shoes, the man had given her no choice. A tall, dark, and handsome picture of charm and grace, he rose above every challenge her aunt tossed in his path.

If he was uncomfortable at the belated reception given by Jenna's aunt and Adam's maternal grandparents, it never showed. The female contingent at the country club turned to mush when he spoke with that velvet Latin baritone of his. When Adam was good, he was very good.

As for their male counterparts, Adam held his own with them as well. A product of education in two cultures, he kept them fascinated with tales of the jungle. In fact, the clinic was one of club's pet projects where Aunt Vi still reigned as queen of fund-raising, even when it involved associating with her brother-in-law. According to Jenna's father, Violet's first visit to Santa Beliza to help plan the wedding was the equivalent to the Berlin Wall coming down.

"Adam?"

"What?" Obviously waiting outside to her husband meant one step beyond the threshold. Adam poked his head around the door.

"Should we radio Dad?"

The corner of his mouth tugged upward. "You mean you don't want to wait for the rabbit?"

"You mean the *mule*, don't you?" Jenna teased back.

He cast his dark eyes down in abject contrition. "I was upset. It couldn't be helped."

"Well, you could kiss me and make up."

"If you will call off your hens."

Jenna crooked her finger at him from the bed.

Granted reprieve, Adam strutted over. The king of the beasts was back. "So you need the doctor now, eh?"

"You put this on, doctor man." Tilda tossed him a shirt. "And wash your hands."

"I know, I know." Winking at Jenna, he stepped over to the sink and scrubbed. When he finished, he slipped on the shirt and held up his arms, as if about to operate.

"The doctor is ready."

"I don't need a doctor. I need my husbaaa…nd! Oh, dear!"

A spasm grabbed the rest of her reply, bringing her upright on the bed. She kicked at the loose stirrups, knocking one off. It fell to the floor with a loud clang.

The flare of excitement that surged in Adam's expression did not infect his manner. He was determined not to get tossed out of the room again.

"I, the father," he said calmly, "am going to sit right here."

He pulled up a chair from its resting place against the wall and straddled it. Jenna didn't miss his worried glance at the fallen stirrup.

"And I am going to hold my lovely wife's hand."

Smiling, he folded Jenna's hand in his. She knew it

was killing him not to put the table back in order. But then, why should she be the only one suffering?

"And I am going to kiss each of her knuckles."

"I need it back!" Jenna snatched her hand away from his lips and grabbed her contracting belly.

"Breathe, mamacita," he consoled, running his hand over her belly, massaging ever so gently. Tilda, who'd gone into the adjoining office with Anna to give the expectant couple a little privacy, reappeared with a damp rag to wipe Jenna's brow. At the foot of the table, Anna repositioned the fallen stirrup and locked it into place. Jenna found it with her foot.

"Here comes another one." Adam reached for Jenna as she started up from her pillow.

She pushed him away. "Turn on the fan! It's hot."

"I got it." Tilda hustled over to where a floor fan sat and turned the switch.

"Just breathe, sweet Jenna," Adam whispered, braving her wavering even temper. "Everything is going to be fine."

Jenna clenched her teeth. The sound of her name on his lips didn't curl her insides the way it usually did. It clenched them with an unbearable force.

"Confound it, I *am* breathing!" she panted. "And don't call me that!"

She didn't feel fine, and she definitely was not feeling *sweet*. A queasy cloud of lightheadedness rose from her belly to her brain, pushed there by the vise closing around her middle from all sides. She wasn't going to scream and get hysterical like women she saw on the movies. She wasn't! She wished she had her mother's sampler to hold on to, because at the moment, the words were scrambled in her pain stricken mind.

"That's good, Jenna! Now can you bear down on the next one?"

"Let the woman do her job," Jenna warned with what little breath she had left.

"Ah!" Adam seized Jenna's face and planted a loud, delighted kiss on her forehead. "How about that, mamacita, she must see the rabbit."

Won't distress or despair…but I might hurt him, Lord!

Another pain swelled to an unbearable proportion. Jenna clawed at Adam, her fingers raking across his belly and locking onto his belt. He was making jokes about rabbits when she was literally coming apart at the seams.

"It's not a rabbit, Adam, it's an elephant!"

"I am certain it feels that way, querida, but…" Adam pried at her fingers, but Jenna would not let go. "Besides, there are no elephants in South America."

"*Must* you be so blasted literal?"

Try as he might, Adam could not break free. If she wasn't so mad and in agony, Jenna would have giggled at the stricken look he gave Tilda.

"I told you this is woman's work!"

"Now get ready…" Anna encouraged.

There was no time to get ready for anything, no rest between the body wracking pain, no time to breathe. A curtain of anguish separated Jenna from what was happening on the other side of the sheet.

Adam stopped trying to pull away from Jenna's desperate grasp and stepped closer. His beautiful, black-fringed eyes mirrored what he saw. Panting, fists clenched, Jenna watched wonder sweep in to assuage anxiety. She *felt* the glorious relief that shattered his frozen features and slackened his clenched jaw. She cried the tears of joy with him.

"Look, it's a girl!" Jenna squeezed Tilda's hand. "I always wanted a baby girl!"

"We're gonna have to put up those ugly pink blinds again." Jenna sniffed, not the least perturbed.

Her father had gotten them out of the attic and cleaned them up but stood ready with a can of blue spray paint, in case she presented him with a grandson. He wouldn't have to paint them after all.

A tiny wail emerged from the other side of the table. Jenna lifted her head, straining to see. It was neither a donkey's bray nor a big cat's growl. It was the most beautiful sound God had ever given her the grace to hear.

Adam took the squirming bundle of red, wrinkled skin from Anna with a look of unadulterated awe. A bystander would think it was the first baby he'd ever seen.

"Look at you," he cooed, attempting to soothe the newborn's healthy distress. "I am your..." His voice cracked. "You know, the one who sings to you."

Her husband had a beautiful voice, deep and resonant. It was like a sedative to Jenna on those restless nights when she couldn't find a comfortable position to lie in because of her baby belly and aching back. He'd lay his head on her tummy and sing lullabies in Spanish and English to his unborn child, but it often lulled Jenna to sleep as well.

He crooned one now. When the baby's sobs turned to little hiccups, his face glowed with delight.

"She knows me!"

Jenna watched the cool, collected jungle doc reduced to a strutting mush of daddy by a baby's burp. Adam had so much to give. Love was the key to unlocking it.

"Adam?"

"What is it, mother of my beautiful baby daughter?" he sang, unable to take his eyes from the infant he cradled against him.

Jenna grew more forceful. After all, she *was* the mother. "Adam!"

"She has the most gorgeous blue eyes…yes, you do."

"I want to see them!"

Adam glanced at her, bemused by the annoyance in her voice. "Ah! But of course, Jenna. I am so sorry. We were just…"

"Adam!"

"And *this* impatient, stubborn creature, niñita, is your mama." Nuzzling the infant's cheek once more, he laid her on Jenna's chest. "You will know your mama because she has the same wet hair and big blue eyes as you! That's right."

Jenna's chin quivered the same as her daughter's. Such a tiny, perfect little body, even if it was red and looked as if she'd not quite grown into her skin yet. *Thank You, God, that she's not as big as my belly suggested!* Touching the infant's long, graceful fingers, Jenna gave way to the joy spilling down her cheeks when the baby girl latched on to her pinkie.

"Look at that handshake. You have your daddy's hands...and all those fingers! One, two, three..."

Adam kissed away the tears on Jenna's cheeks. "I need to check her over. I *am* the baby doctor," he reminded her when she started to protest.

Reluctantly, Jenna withdrew her finger away from her daughter's hand for Adam to do his examination. He chattered worse than Rita over a fist full of peanuts, she thought, as charmed by his cooing and coddling as the newborn. He was a natural with all babies, but with his own, he was magic.

She wanted to hug him, but since that was not possible, she patted his thigh. When the vitals had been taken and recorded, Jenna's included, Adam proceeded to clean the new baby, ignoring Tilda's protest that it, too, was women's work.

"I am a pediatrician, Tilda. This is what I *can* do."

Adam had held back long enough. No longer would he tolerate being an observer only. When he finished, he held his daughter up to the bright light for inspection. She was perfect, even howling and kicking in rebellion.

Love filled Jenna to overflowing when her husband

began to pray, holding the babe as though offering their precious gift up to the One who'd bestowed her.

"Thank You, God, for *two* of them…two angels from Your heaven. I know I am not worthy of either." Adam cleared the blade from his voice. "So I am going to need Your help more than ever now! Father, help me to show them nothing less than the love You have for Your children."

He clutched the squalling baby to him, kissing the top of her head with a breath of "Amen."

His worshipful countenance and awe, however, suddenly shattered with blank astonishment.

"Ah!" He laughed, holding the distraught infant away in a hurry.

Tilda grabbed a stack of paper towels and dropped them on the floor to soak up the mess.

"Baby girl, you are developing a bad habit on your daddy!" he chided as he wrapped her in a clean receiving blanket. The squalling baby girl kicked at the folds, unwrapping herself as fast as Adam could cover her. He sighed in relief when he finally accomplished his task and gathered her up in his arms.

"Mamacita…our little *Eve*, I fear, is determined to raise Cain here in paradise."

"Takes after her daddy."

Jenna took the crying child from her husband. A few minutes ago she was bursting with baby. Now she was bursting with unparalleled happiness. It was more than worth it. Her new daughter was another precious example of trial and blessings delivered in the same package.

"I think we're all agreed that this is not exactly Eden…" she began softly.

The love of her life and father of her child finished with her. "But it's as close as we'll ever get, this side of heaven."

Dear Reader,

I know I should say something really meaningful here about this story and what it means to me. Well, briefly, having suffered from chemical depression, I have felt like the writer of 2 Corinthians 4:8 and clung to it and its truth like gum to the bottom of a chair. But praise God, I was able to retain my sense of humor and laugh at myself too, so I have to share the following.

I was writing a scene where my city heroine is walking alone on her first night in the jungle on a dark path and thinking, in Oz terms, "Lions and tigers and bears, oh my!" I am trying to imagine the sounds she's hearing, including the pounding of her own heart, as she expects a big black jungle cat to jump on her at any moment. The tension is building within both character and writer, when—

My all black pantherlike kitty, Duskin the Dauntless, leaps to the back of my chair with a Siamese howl. (There's an oriental feline in her lineage somewhere.)

I bolt upright, hollering and grasping my chest before my heart blows out of it. Duskin bolts upright and scampers away for dear life, suddenly daunted by "whatever" it was that frightened her mistress.

Dear friends, I fear I was not only troubled and perplexed, but distressed as well. I wasn't, however, in despair. There just wasn't enough time.

Thank you each and every one for your continued

love and support in this new ministry of mine. Because God has surely blessed me through you and the wonderful people at Multnomah, my first Palisades novel *Hi Honey, I'm Home* has gone into its third printing.

Linda Windsor

P. S.: And don't forget to look for my Multnomah historical romance coming out September 2000. *Maire: Tame the Heart,* book one of Gleannmara's brides series, reflects on the spread of the Pentacostal fire in pagan Ireland. When a pagan Irish warrior queen takes a Christian ex-mercenary as hostage and husband in order to thwart an evil druid, her beauty and stubborn temperament "almost" make him lose his religion. But it isn't long before the former soldier's mild example, which at first was seen as a weakness by Maire and her people, becomes their salvation.

You can write to Linda at:
Linda Windsor, c/o Multnomah Publishers, P.O. Box 1720, Sisters, Oregon 97759.

E-mail: Lindwins@aol.com
Stop by online at: http://member.aol.com/lindwins

MAIRE: TAME THE HEART
Book One in the Daughters of Gleannmara Series
By Linda Windsor
ISBN 1-57673-625-3

"The Scots have landed! There's smoke rising over the ridge as we speak!"

Rowan ap Emrys assessed the chaos in and around the villa. Perhaps they could settle the outcome with shrewdness rather than by risking lives.

He turned to his baliff, Dafydd. "Have the men form a line between me and the villa and hold it while I meet the raiders."

Rowan was glad Dafydd did not suspect the palm-wetting fear and dread threatening his cool demeanor at the prospect of taking up his sword again. The Scriptures said to trust in God, but they also said not to tempt Him.

"We will let God decide whether we have to use our swords or not."

Dafydd snorted. "This, from the man who single-handedly turned away a Pictish attack—"

"My sword was my master then, Dafydd."

"And one to be feared, I'll swear by that."

Rowan glanced at the first of the painted warriors amassing on the hill. Merciful Father, give me my sword to save lives, not take them.

If saving his people meant bloodying his sword, then so be it. Thankfully, his words were free of the shared rage and anticipation of conflict infecting the men behind him. "Pray, good fellows. 'Tis a stronger weapon than swords."

Rowan believed this in his heart, but he could not feel the assurance of which he boasted. Indeed, the greatest challenge was not the hordes amassing in the distance, but to practice as he preached: to rely on God to make his plan work.

It was decided. The battle would be decided by a fight to the death between two champions: Rowan ap Emrys and Maire, warrior queen of Gleannmara.

The sun had reached its pinnacle at the start of the contest. Now it dove like a phoenix of fire in the shadowed sea behind the western hills. Darkness was all but upon them, and still Maire had gained little more against her opponent than a few scratches. Time and again, Emrys's God managed to turn her opponent's flesh to air before her quickest thrust.

Not that the forces conjured by Brude's song had not done the same for her. Twice she'd felt the wind of Rowan's sword as it narrowly missed her neck. Her agility and speed were all that saved her. No, it was not the druid's gods Maire doubted, but herself.

She had used all her well-tutored tactics—all but one. Maire gasped for air, her lungs screaming with the effort even as she did so.

"Give it up, little queen. Surrender your sword and return to your home."

"Never!" she managed through clenched teeth. The taste of surrender was too vile to consider.

"I'll not kill you, Maire."

"Then you'll die yourself."

Raising her sword, she lunged at Rowan. His defensive parry felt as though it shattered the bones in her arm.

"There must be a way to settle this without separating your head from that comely body."

Although Emrys offered words of reconciliation, his raised sword belied them. Maire fell back, escaping the deadly, whistling path of his weapon. Thrusting her blade upward as the man charged over her, she felt the engagement of flesh. Twist as he might, he could not avoid the hungry bite of her steel.

A scraping of metal collapsing against metal registered as his full weight dropped upon her. Maire struggled to gather her senses beneath the felled man. Something was wrong. Her sword lay sandwiched between them, instead of protruding from his back. Somehow its blade had been deflected! There was no room to move, much less use the weapon, pinned as she was by his weight.

Was she to die and leave her people to Morlach's dominion after they'd rallied so bravely to her side? At any moment, she'd feel Rowan's fingers about her neck, and, Maeve help her, she had no strength left to resist.

"I'll surrender my sword, little queen, if you give up the notion of taking my head as trophy."

What? Surely, he'd not offered his sword to her in surrender when victory was firmly in his grasp!

"I'll go myself as your hostage to prove my word true. My sword will be yours as long as you fight for what is right under my God's eye." His breath was hot against her ear, as ragged as her own.

"You'll swear loyalty to Gleannmara?" His sword would be an asset, especially if she were to battle Morlach for it—which she'd do or die trying.

"And to its queen, so long as she asks me to do nothing against my God's will."

If his God hated evil, He would see Morlach put in his place. And Maire would need the help of all the gods she could muster.

"As my husband?" Why hadn't she thought of it before? If she married another, Morlach would have no grounds to press her further in the king's eye.

Rowan's surprised laugh shook her from thought. "You ask too much! Why would I take to wife a painted vixen with sword as sharp as her tongue?"

Humiliation boiled in Maire's blood, fortifying her waning strength. She snaked her fingers between their bodies, and the long, thin blade of her stinger came loose.

"We marry, in name only, of course," she added as she pressed the razor sharp blade against Rowan's skin. His wince

351

was barely perceptible, but it was enough.

"May I ask why this sudden proposal?" He grated the words out.

"I need a husband to be rid of a troublesome suitor. You need your head."

"Then I don't see where I have much choice."

"I'd have your word in your God's name," Maire added, somewhat offended by his decidedly reluctant concession. After all, it was *he* who'd admitted aloud she was comely.

"You have my word in the name of God, the Father Almighty, Creator of heaven and earth, that I will take you as my wife."

Maire shook her head. "That I will take you as my husband," she corrected, gaining satisfaction at his deepening scowl.

"However you wish to put it, milady."

"Then give me your sword...carefully." Her fingers closed about the hilt of Rowan's sword. It was still warm from his grasp. A surge of nearly lost triumph welled in her chest as if to explode like heaven's own thunder. Praise her mother's gods, she'd won!

The bards would sing of this in centuries to come, after all. She was just gone eighteen. She'd beaten a seasoned warrior in battle. She found the answer to Morlach's threat and secured the tribute with the same blow.

She held up Rowan's sword to the ecstatic approval of her clansmen. Floating on a cloud of triumph, Maire was unprepared when Rowan suddenly seized her in his arms and kissed her soundly on the lips.

As he released her, only the rising heat of embarrassment thawed her frozen state. Indignation grew to a roar in her veins, but before she could land a retaliatory blow on his smirking face, the Welshman caught her wrist and raised her arm along with his own as if they shared the victory.

"Mother and friends, I give you my bride-to-be! God keep us all."